Murder, She Rode

Also by Holly Menino

Calls Beyond Our Hearing: Unlocking the Secrets of Animal Voices

Darwin's Fox and My Coyote

Forward Motion: Horses, Humans, and the Competitive Enterprise

Pandora: A Raccoon's Journey

Murder, She Rode

Holly Menino

MINOTAUR BOOKS

A Thomas Dunne Book

NEW YORK

This is a work of fiction. All of the characters, organizations, and events portrayed in this novel are either products of the author's imagination or are used fictitiously.

A THOMAS DUNNE BOOK FOR MINOTAUR BOOKS.
An imprint of St. Martin's Publishing Group.

 Printed in the United States of America. For information, address St. Martin's Press, 175 Fifth Avenue, New York, N.Y. 10010.

www.thomasdunnebooks.com
www.minotaurbooks.com

LIBRARY OF CONGRESS CATALOGING-IN-PUBLICATION DATA

Menino, H. M.
Murder, she rode / Holly Menino. — First U.S. edition.
p. cm.
ISBN 978-1-250-01651-5 (hardcover)
ISBN 978-1-250-01652-2 (e-book)
1. Horse trainers—Fiction. 2. Horsemen and horsewomen—Crimes against—Fiction. I. Title.
PS3613.E49M87 2013
813'.6—dc23

2013009707

Minotaur books may be purchased for educational, business, or promotional use. For information on bulk purchases, please contact Macmillan Corporate and Premium Sales Department at 1-800-221-7945 extension 5442 or write specialmarkets@macmillan.com.

First Edition: August 2013

10 9 8 7 6 5 4 3 2 1

For Diane and Kathleen, my original partners in crime

Murder, She Rode

The Test of Brilliant Obedience

1

Accidents happen, and sometimes an accident is just that, a random convergence of time, motion, and unlucky objects. Other accidents beg for explanation.

In October, a week before my gray horse ran in the Brandywine International Three-Day Event, I came upon an accident. A wreck was not unusual in these suburbs south of Philadelphia. There was too much traffic, and the roads that connected the old village centers with the malls were narrow, with no shoulder and hundreds of ungoverned intersections. What was unusual was that I knew the people in the vehicle.

I was on my way back from an expensive celebratory lunch in the city. The sky was bright, the road was dry, and because it was a weekday afternoon, the traffic wasn't heavy. I navigated curves that cut so close around the corners of old stone houses I could see through the four-on-four windows. An armchair. A clock standing across the room with a plant beside it. I was looking into these interiors without really seeing them because I was thinking about how a frailty, a tiny infirmity, could rob you of your place in the world. Last summer I had been a nationally ranked event rider. I took my horses to all the big three-day events on the East Coast. These aren't horse races, where the horses make a mass charge from the starting gate. They're triathlons, and each horse goes alone. Three days, three tests, and I rode them. Dressage, a test of required figures—like ice-skating—a test of brilliant obedience. Speed and Endurance—nobody used the formal title, we just called it the cross-country—a long test done at a flat-out gallop through fields and woods, whatever nature put in the horse's way, along with some big solid obstacles we humans put in his way. I galloped the cross-country tracks, putting the horse to big, solid obstacles. Stadium Jumping, a test of agility after the exhaustion of speed and endurance. I always tried to make this look effortless for the horses. Often this worked. I did okay. Quite okay. I was in the money. Always in the money.

Now I had lost the ride on my own horse. I wouldn't be the one riding the horse in the Brandywine, but I was the one who knew him. I could tell you what he'll eat, how he runs, when he'll take off for the jump. But I was sidelined on account of frailty, nerve damage caused by a fall. This was all the more frustrating because I was almost back to full coordination and strength. But not quite. That's what was on my mind just as I drove up on the accident.

At the crest of a hill not five miles from our farm, I saw at the foot of it the red warning lights flashing on the cop cars and the tow truck and the wreck itself. Just beyond a narrow bridge at the bottom of the hill, a horse van had come to rest on its side at a place where a dirt lane led into a cow pasture. What remained of the cab and the front section of the box behind it was a charred framework. The rest of the vehicle appeared to be intact, although the sheet metal hood over the engine was scorched. The hulk gave off smoke, and on the part of the box where the aluminum wall and the paint survived, I saw broad blue and green stripes. They were familiar, just as familiar as the image of that ruined truck would become.

I pulled off the road just ahead of the little bridge and left the Mercedes. The air was acrid. The odor of burning, rubber, plastic, petroleum, and something else. A makeshift barrier of traffic cones separated the wreck and the official vehicles from the strip of road that remained open. Two state troopers were directing the driver of a tow truck, beckoning as he backed toward the burnt-out van. I stepped up to an orange cone just beside the nearest trooper. He was the younger of the two. Under his flat-brimmed hair, I could see the blond bristles left after his trooper's haircut.

"Where is Joe Terrell?" Then an afterthought, "Sir."

The trooper's face and the flat brim swiveled in my direction. The gaze was the official, impartial, objective one that all troopers seem to have practiced in front of a mirror. He raised his palm to halt the tow truck.

"Yes ma'am?"

"Where is Joe Terrell?" I repeated.

"Who are you?"

"Tink Elledge," I said, and when that didn't seem to move him one way or the other, I amplified this. "Leticia Elledge. I live a few miles from here, and I know Joe. What happened to him?"

"The driver."

"Yes."

"Can't tell you that, ma'am."

"Why not?"

"'Cause I don't know," and maybe this was technically true, because the next thing he said was, "The ambulance left here a half an hour ago."

"Was he alive?"

The trooper shrugged. "Can't say."

Because policy didn't allow him to? Or because he couldn't tell?

Then he seemed to explain. "The girl was in better shape, pretty good, in fact."

"Patty," and I described the girl, who, like Joe Terrell, worked for my friend and rival Win Guthrie. I had known her since she was a kindergartner. "Redhead? Big brown eyes?"

The trooper nodded. "Felt good enough to argue about lying down on the stretcher. Now, ma'am." With a nod he indicated the other trooper and the tow truck driver and turned his attention to them.

"What about Win?"

"Who?" He made a backward sweeping motion with his hand to set the wrecker in motion again, and the tow truck's backup beeper began.

"Win Guthrie. The guy who owns this van. Big tall guy? Probably in riding clothes?"

"Haven't seen him."

"Okay," I breathed. Patty McLaren survived. Maybe Joe didn't, and maybe Win didn't know about any of this yet.

"What about the horses?"

He didn't hear me. The tow truck was aligned now with the skeleton of the cab. "Sir, what about the horses?"

The trooper didn't look in my direction, just shook his head.

"No horses on the van?" But among the burning smells, there was the one I couldn't identify, something that smelled like a hair dryer that had got tangled up with its subject matter. "Why were there two people in the van if they weren't hauling a horse?"

Over his shoulder he said, "There's a horse on there, ma'am. But it burnt up." That was the other smell.

"Okay," I said again, but not to him. It was just a remark of calculation, a ticking off of the damages. I stood there, as close to those damages and the hulk of the van as the traffic cones would permit, and watched the big hook drop from the tow truck. As soon as the connection was solid, the hoist motor engaged. But before it raised the cab something in the body of the van moved. A slow scuffle scraping the wall of the van, a long, barely audible groan, then the thud of a large dense body.

"Stop!" I shouted at the tow truck and its startled operator. "Stop this thing!"

Now I had the attention of the other trooper. He was older, salt-and-pepper bristles left from his trooper's haircut and a paunch that lapped his wide belt. He said, "Yes, ma'am"—as in, *What is it that you want now?* But he reluctantly put up a hand to halt the lift. I dodged past the traffic cones to hop up to the side door of the van, the place where, when the truck is upright, a ramp slides out and the horses are walked up to the stalls inside. It was a Dutch door, and the top half was pinned back against the outside wall. I straddled the corner of this opening in the beached vehicle and looked inside. The horse was a desperate, ugly sight, the kind that wakes you up in the night years later even though you have made your evening round at the barn and know all the horses are fine.

"Ma'am." The younger trooper started toward me. "You'll have to get down from there, ma'am. Out of the way."

"He's alive," I said in despair.

"Not for long. Now you have to get down."

"Bring your gun over here," I countermanded.

"What?"

"You have to shoot him." But the trooper stayed where he was. I was talking to a wall, a familiar wall. It's what divides people who have an understanding of animals from those who think an animal is just an object that moves, who are out of touch with the fact that animals think thoughts and feel feelings.

The trooper said, "Horse is not my property. Now if you don't get down from there we may have to bring charges."

"Maybe your buddy is braver than you," I suggested, looking to his partner. "Are you? Can you get yourself over here with your gun—what are you two waiting for? A memo from the insurance company?"

The two of them glanced at each other, hesitating. The tow truck operator stepped down from the cab of the wrecker, bewildered.

"Look at you. Look at the two of you. Great big officers of the law. Packing your big, bad guns. And too scared to do what is right." I put my hand out to the younger one. "Why don't you lend me that gun?"

The older officer finally broke the standoff. "Ma'am? If you will step away from there and go over to my partner, I will take care of this."

I dropped down from the truck and walked past the line of traffic cones. The blond trooper met me in front of his patrol car with a clipboard and started asking me more specifically who I was, where I lived, where I had just been, and, indirectly, why I felt the overturned van and the agonized horse were my business.

The older trooper conferred briefly with the tow truck operator and then climbed up on the side of the van. He unholstered his pistol, lay down so that his shoulders were over the door opening, and scooted sideways a little to get the right angle. He fired and then after a deliberate interval fired again and pushed himself to a standing position so that he could put the gun away.

He joined us at the patrol car and dictated a note to the trooper with the clipboard. "Three twenty-six, Curatola destroyed horse." My relief was immense. I reached out, put my arms around his paunch and gave him a big squeeze. "Curatola," I said by way of thanks.

His partner pried my arm away from Trooper Curatola. "You can't do that, ma'am."

Can't? Cannot? Or was it shouldn't? Should not? I turned back to my car thinking, What the hell is he going to do about it anyway? The horse had been spared further pain. That much I knew, but I was too upset to think as clearly about what had happened to the two people who had been taken away from the van. I needed to get home to Charlie so he could help me come to terms with what I had seen.

My two tiny terriers met me at the back door with unstoppable enthusiasm. Spit, the wire-haired black and tan with the ears that folded over, skittered sideways, and Polish, the slick-coated black-and-white feist with prick ears, bounced off his hind legs to give me a nose poke in the ribs. In my hurry, I barely acknowledged these friends. I found my large, genial husband in his study, ensconced in his chair with his long-haired cat in his lap—Greenspan making himself comfortable as usual—and without giving Charlie a chance to speak, I blurted out what had happened on the road.

When I came to the ending of the incident and my wrapping my arms around the trooper, Charlie said, "Truly inappropriate," and came instantly upright, digging in his pocket for his cell phone. The cat leaped away from the chair. "We need to find out about Joe. I'll try the hospital."

Charlie was punching numbers into the little phone. He was devoted to the thing, and he, the least handy man I've ever met, would often hold up the cell phone and announce, "Best tool in the world. With this I can fix anything." But the present problem might not yield so easily.

The hospital could give out no information. I used the telephone on the little table in the back hall to try Win Guthrie, but the phone rang repeatedly into empty space.

Charlie and I sat together glumly in the clutter of his study. Autumn sunshine fell through the tall window to shine on the stacks of magazines and newspapers that populated the carpet. The cat crept cautiously back into Charlie's lap, and we considered the many possibilities, none of them reassuring.

"It was gruesome," I said about the bay horse that had to be destroyed, "in the true sense of the word—and the smell. How will I ever shake that odor?"

Charlie only nodded. He said, "This could be terrible for Win."

"You mean if Joe doesn't make it?"

"He was like a father to Win, maybe more."

He went silent, evidently working through thoughts about Joe and Win. The father thing was very big for Charlie. He had adored his own father, who died suddenly when Charlie was fourteen. After a few minutes, he said about his father's early death, "In a way, I was lucky. Mine lived long enough to help launch me but not long enough to disappoint me." Charlie knew, because I had told him, that the senior Guthrie had plotted a cautious, conservative course for his son's life that included prep school and college and certainly would have included law school and a line on his firm's stationery if Win hadn't veered off into a career with horses—at which point Win's dad shunned him. Joe was already on the scene, and he became a durable surrogate, a practical, tough-minded adviser. "Maybe not exactly like a father," Charlie amended his first reaction, "but it will still hurt."

Charlie Reidermann was my third husband, and because I had repeated one of my earlier mistakes, my marriage to him was my fourth. He was tall, as tall as I was, vaguely pear-shaped, and the crown of his head, which before I met him had been covered with tawny-brown hair, was a shiny spot. What had first attracted me to him, and still did, were Charlie's eyes. They held everything, including me, with the warmest gaze blue eyes could ever be capable of. When he looked at me, I liked myself better. Charlie was more immediately huggable than Officer Curatola, certainly, and he was, at least on the surface, laid back. His relaxed, genial composure camouflaged an intense, acute mind and a tight privacy about himself.

The two of us together? So far, so good. With Charlie I seem to have found a kind of comfort I had never known with other men. Maybe because the two of us were quite different. He, for instance, was democrat—with a capital D as well as the lowercase one—the only Democrat or democrat I had become close to, and until I learned how to anticipate him, our first year brought a series of surprises. Soon after he moved in I was astonished to find a thank-you note from the ACLU on his desk. And then there was the fact that Charlie was not what anyone would call a horse person. He didn't try to understand any part of a horse. But he wrote checks for the vet and the farrier without complaint or even comment, and he was unperturbed by the many mornings I left the warmth of our bed two hours before dawn to trailer a horse or two to a horse trial. Now I felt a vague guilt at being here with him in this room where we were so often content. Whatever his fate, Joe certainly didn't have it so good.

We waited, and after a few minutes, he suggested, "Keep trying," as if I might not. I phoned. I left messages.

About the time Charlie would have ordinarily been pouring scotch for me, the telephone on the little table in the back hall rang.

"Tink." It was Win.

"I saw the truck," I said to save him an explanation. "What about Joe?"

Joe Terrell didn't suffer as long as the horse in the overturned van. That was the only positive information in Win's account of Joe Terrell's death: he didn't suffer long. Joe was driving, and Win said Patty was riding in the back to keep the young horse calm, standing so that she could look out the open top of the Dutch door. She must have seen the smoke because she jumped out. The truck crashed down on the driver's side, trapping Joe, and flame took over.

"How terrible! I'm so sorry, Win." I said it although I knew that nothing I said would make any difference and that Win probably wasn't really hearing it anyway. "I am so, so sorry."

"Funeral is Thursday morning, Tink. Tell Charlie, will you?"

I didn't wait for the funeral. I drove out to Win's place the next day. I had made the twenty-mile drive quite often over the years—to look at horses and sometimes to buy them, to deliver horses I sold, to consult with Joe, and for a year or so when I was between husbands, to sleep with Win. During that period the new stables and indoor arena at the head of the drive hadn't been there, just the white clapboard farmhouse and a traditional Pennsylvania bank barn. But today, under a show of brilliant orange maple leaves, the old house, which Win had inherited with the rest of the land, looked just as it had back then, almost vacant. Win had never bothered about curtains, so you could see straight through the rooms on the ground floor and you couldn't help but notice their Spartan furnishings. Charlie thought the place was equivalent to a stable for humans, but I had always thought it was just waiting for someone to inhabit it. Maybe that's why I had tried.

I parked in the turnaround in front of the stable. Win was nowhere in sight, but I found Patty McLaren squatting beside a horse cross-tied in the aisle that ran through the center of the stable. She was wrapping an exercise bandage on the horse's front leg and didn't look up until I put my hand on her shoulder.

"Hi, hon. How's it going?"

She glanced at me quickly, secured the bandage with its Velcro strap, and stood up. She was a shy girl, a bit plumper than the typical no-hips event rider, with large dark eyes and flamboyant red hair that belied her shyness. "It's going, Mrs. Elledge. It's going." The only people who didn't call me Tink were the young people who had suffered under me as a Pony Club instructor on Saturday mornings. This was a volunteer position like being a Boy Scout leader, and in fact, Pony Club is like scouting for horse-crazy kids—the *pony* in the organization's name was the British term for a horse of any size ridden by a child. I took the job because I had no child of my own and knew I probably never would have a child of my own, and I showed up on Saturdays as religiously as if I were going to Mass.

"You had a close call."

She looked away from me to the horse's leg that was next on her agenda. "Not as close as Joe," she said quietly and held her hand up to me so I could feel the tremor. "I'm still shaking."

"True," I said about both of her statements. She may have escaped the burning truck, but she hadn't left it.

"I feel like so—guilty, I guess. I mean, all I lost is my cell phone. I feel like I shouldn't be here. Like I don't deserve to be here."

"We're lucky you are."

"I didn't help him." She bent over to retrieve another tightly rolled bandage and dabbed at the corner of her eye with it. "If he hadn't thought someone needed to babysit the colt, I would have been in the cab with him. But I didn't help him. I couldn't. I saw the smoke coming out from under the truck. I think I got his attention because he slowed down. I thought he was going to pull off, and I just jumped."

"That was the right thing to do, Patty. The only thing to do."

"That's what my dad said. But that's what a dad would say because he wants you to feel better."

"Charlie and I want that too."

"My dad didn't even yell at me for riding in the back of the van," she continued, "and he always does that."

I nodded because this argument was familiar to me. Charlie always took the same position about riding in a truck or trailer with the horses: "Why would any rational person allow herself to be locked inside a giant, rattling tin can with a ton or two of irrational animals?"

"How's Win managing?"

She smiled. "Oh, you know, the way he always seems to manage. Stiff upper lip and 'I know I must be upset, but there's no way around the Brandywine—we've got the owners and all.' "

She had Win down perfectly.

"Is he here?"

"He's over at the old barn with the insurance guys."

The old barn had been Joe Terrell's headquarters, and it held a surprising assortment of tools and machines, many of which he had used on my tack and some on bigger problems, like tractor implements. How many times had I gone to the old barn to ask for Joe's help?

"Oh, right. The truck," and I winced inwardly at the image and stink of its black remains. Then I put the question that had been troubling me since the trooper's gun went off the day before. "What horse was that?"

I immediately regretted the crudeness of this, because the roll of bandage swept at her eyes again. I hated to cry myself, and I hated even more anything that made other people cry, especially if what made them cry was me.

"Quick Fix. He was a full brother to Secret Formula."

The powerful long-legged black mare she named was Win's candidate to contest the Brandywine Three-Day. My gray horse, Exit Laughing, would meet Secret Formula there.

"Win had an offer on him. Joe and I were on our way home from the prepurchase exam."

"Patty, Joe wasn't—" I made the flat-hand-thumb-out tippling gesture.

"Nope." she said firmly. "Not a chance. That scared him too much."

She had finished wrapping the horse's legs and had moved on to saddling. The horse was a bright bay with bold white markings, and he had the inquisitive gleam in his eye that says to me, "lots of heart."

"He looks promising," I said to get on a more cheerful footing. "Is he?"

"I *hope* so," she said tentatively. I knew she would be trying for the Olympics the next time the games rolled around. Toward that end, she had taken a working student position with Win, offering herself as a slave-groom who shoveled manure and groomed and cleaned tack and rode colts in exchange for Win's coaching. It was hard work, but in all possibility, it could eventually pay off with a spot on a team that went to the Olympics.

"He's yours?"

"Well, my dad's." She acknowledged this help with a bit of reverence, and because Patty was at an age when it is easy to dismiss your parents as clueless or to simply forget you have them, I found her love for him quite sweet. In fact, I too owed her father, a gynecologist, a bit of reverence for his counsel earlier in my life. Throughout my marriage to Savage and my two marriages to Elledge, I visited Layton McLaren fairly regularly to try to get pregnant, but by the time I met Charlie I had long since given up. Admitting that there was no pregnancy in my future was the hardest part, and Layton McLaren helped me do that.

"And has the good doctor seen his horse go?"

"Not yet—" she brightened considerably, "but, did I tell you? He's coming out here! It's only a little Podunk horse trials down the road, but he says he's coming."

"I guess it's been a while then?" I tried to remember the last time I'd seen Layton McLaren.

"Yeah, he usually doesn't seem to want to come out this way. You know."

I thought I did, and I let this go because I assumed that what was keeping the doctor out in Chicago was Patty's mother, whom I had never actually met, and the bitterness of their divorce. Although she had lived in the house with Patty and McLaren, she had a fondness for liquor that kept her absent from them. Patty's father had been the one to take his daughter to the stables and to school activities. I turned the chat back to the horse.

"Going pretty well for you?" I asked about the horse. "What does Win think of him?"

She smiled again about Win. "Well, you know, he never gets very excited."

True. There wasn't much that could raise that man's pulse rate anymore. No monster cross-country obstacle, no big-money sale, not the most nubile, fresh young student. Win had turned fifty a year before I had, and we had both aged a lot. But Charlie said no one would ever accuse me of ripening the way Win had, of being hard to excite.

"Getting discouraged?"

Patty shrugged. " 'I've got years, lots of years,' " she quoted Win.

With him, praise wasn't spare change, and I had told Patty that when she asked my advice about going to work for him. He had earned his reputation for honesty, brutal honesty. He often didn't allow himself time to think of a kind way of phrasing what he meant, and more than once I had been withered by his assessments. In the days we were together, I was more obsessively competitive—and hornier—and when we split, Win never actually named the occasion as a breakup. He said, "I can't ride, Tink, if I can't think. And somehow I can't think with you and your horses around." But of course I hadn't mentioned my interlude with Win when Patty and I talked about the working student's job, just the fact that Win's standards were usually unattainable. She said, "I think I can deal with that—I've had you for a teacher, you know—and it could be very important for me." It must have been, because she had kept the job nearly two years now.

I didn't want to interfere with Win's insurance powwow, and Patty was politely waiting to mount until I offered to leave. So I did.

She nodded, stepped up into the stirrup, and swung her leg over the young horse. He moved off in the edgy, tentative way that youngsters do, his black tail and her bright ponytail both swinging slowly, and I could see that just being on the horse was lifting her spirits. As the horse reached the corner of the barn, where they would turn and disappear toward the riding arena, Patty looked back over her shoulder.

"It's easy," she called.

"What?"

"Just like opening a door."

I realized she was quoting me. It was something I said often to children who were trying to steer their ponies with just the reins to show them how the pressure of their legs could take the work out of turning. I remembered her as a pudgy little redhead on a pudgy red pony that had a remarkable talent for walking in a determinedly straight line even with his nose cranked around to his flank. She had her heel dug into the pony. Her face was red. She was the shyest of my students, so I went over to ask what the problem was. She said very quietly, "This is *not* EASY, Mrs. Elledge."

But now it was. She guided the horse around the corner of the barn with a little pressure of her leg and waved good-bye.

"Tell Win I came by, will you? Could you let him know I'm thinking about him?"

2

Joe Terrell had worked in the horse world for more than forty years, and half of those he had spent as Win Guthrie's farm manager. He mowed pastures, hung gates, kept the mows full of hay, looked after the trucks and tractors, fixed what needed fixing, and dispensed advice and remedies for the horses. He was a short, square man with a penetrating squint and a roguish way of shifting the cigar in his mouth when he spoke to you. In the early years of World War II he had served in the cavalry, where he dealt with every kind of horse and mule, and where he was privy to centuries' worth of horsemen's wisdom. So even during his drinking years he could give you a practical solution for the most exotic problem that a horse could present. Many of us were in Joe Terrell's debt, but even so, two days later I was surprised by the size of the crowd that filled the pews and aisles of the parish church and spilled out into the foyer and down the stone steps at the door.

In the knot of people at the front of the sanctuary, I spotted the back of Win Guthrie's head, blond going to gray, chin up, shoulders square. Frankie Golden and I held down a length of empty pew for Charlie. Frankie was my closest friend, if you don't count Charlie. We met during college at the muster for the tennis team, which I turned out for because there wasn't a riding team and because I knew vaguely some of the rules of tennis. Frankie was already a good player, and I had to spend a lot of time sweating in order to catch up enough to be her doubles partner. She was an analytical player and cagey. She wasn't lazy, but she wouldn't move her feet without knowing exactly where she wanted to put them. I rushed to the net, scrambled over the lines. She covered my back. We had stayed in tight formation that way through many years, a number of marriages, and an almost equal number of divorces. I say almost equal because Frankie hadn't remarried since her last breakup—what a joker, what a wild card he'd turned out to be. Frankie had been enduring breast cancer. I won't say *battling* like most people because I don't think it's something you choose to go after. It's something that happens to you. Then you choose a way to try to get through it. In Frankie's case, she chose more chemo and less surgery. The promising report granting her at least a temporary victory against the cancer and allowing her to advance to the final rounds of chemo had been the cause of that giddy lunch the day of Joe's accident. In spite of the radiation and the chemo, she was still a beautiful person. In the temporary absence of her thick auburn hair, she wore a green silk turban, but the rest—the creamy freckled skin, the impressive swell of her breasts under the black blouse, the slow gaze that seemed to but didn't always take the measure of things instantly—was her usual. She glanced at her watch.

"So where was this meeting of Charlie's?"

"I'm not sure."

"I don't suppose you asked what was so important about it that he would make himself late for this service."

"Nope. He'll be here."

Frankie shook her head. In spite of being foolishly swept up by any number of men during the time we had known each other, her approach to marriage when things came to that was entirely practical. She knew how much money there was and where it was, and she had managed to profit from each of her unions. She couldn't believe I wasn't willing to pry into Charlie's business affairs, but I wasn't. It was not that he was selfish, it was that he was careful and about his dealings, intensely private. Charlie would have published graphic details of our sex life before he would have showed me his accounts or where he kept them. It was the one potential sore spot between us. For reasons that I did not yet understand myself and so couldn't explain to her, I didn't want to go there.

Charlie materialized at the end of the pew a moment before the pallbearers started down the aisle. He dropped a quick kiss on Frankie's cheek and quickly settled himself next to me.

"Place is packed," he observed and covered my hand with his own.

All of us crowded into the church had come to hear the words, to hear what might be said to help make sense of a death so sudden and violent, and to comfort us. When the words had been said, Win marched from the sanctuary like an automaton. He was quite tall and usually he moved with a long, languid stride, the kind that puts a big price on a horse because it means he will cover a lot of ground and clear a lot of big fences. But now Win's legs were just carrying him through the rituals. "Terrible for him," Charlie whispered as the rest of us followed Win to the rectangular pit in the cemetery on the wooded slope behind the church. He must have been thinking of his own father because there was a good deal of moisture around his eyes.

If Win's tears ever came, I knew we wouldn't see them, but Patty McLaren's, which had crept down her cheek two days earlier, were abundantly evident now. Patty hung her head, her long red hair sweeping forward over her pale face, which was flushed to a deep pink, and in her fist she clutched a wad of tissue. Her close friend Alejandra Delgado stood at her side. I would spend most of the next week with this young woman because I had recruited her, somewhat reluctantly, to ride Exit Laughing in the Brandywine International. At the moment, Alex Delgado's face was set resolutely, as if she was fending off any emotions that might sneak up on her. It was a sad time, and a speculative gloom penetrated the brilliant autumn sunshine. I looked down at Charlie's shoes. It seemed inexplicable that we should all be standing beside Joe's grave, inexplicable that the smell of burnt hair was still with me.

The dirt was thrown on the casket, and we stood in line to say a few words to Win, the only one left as family to Joe. When the three of us arrived in front of Win, he took little notice of Frankie and me but lingered a moment in his handshake with Charlie.

"I need to ask for your help."

If Charlie was caught off guard, he didn't let on. "Of course, whatever I can do."

"The insurance company," Win said briefly. "I figured you probably have some experience."

Charlie didn't respond directly to this. He said, "I'll come over to your place. What time do you finish up at the barn?"

I walked with Frankie back to her car, and as soon as we were out of earshot, she said, "What was *that* all about?"

"The truck? Maybe the horse. Zipper Lips will never tell us," I assured her about Charlie.

"I'll find out," she promised, and I felt a little sorry for him. Frankie wouldn't quit as easily as I did.

I found our aging red Mercedes diesel at the end of the church's long driveway, the closest place Charlie, one of the last to arrive, could park, and I sat in the passenger seat with the door open waiting for him. Like so many of the horse people who had gathered to say good-bye to Joe, I was yielding to the heartless necessity to leave the dead and return home to keep a horse in the last two days of its training schedule. After that, we would wrap our horses' legs and ship them to the Brandywine. How strange and abrupt both Joe's death and his funeral seemed, a weird interlude that interrupted our lives only too briefly.

Charlie appeared at the top of the drive walking slowly, thoughtfully. When he reached the car, he slid behind the steering wheel and reached over absently to pat my knee. "You okay?" he asked, and we started toward home without talking much. True to form, Charlie wasn't going to mention that snatch of conversation with Win.

"Good of you to give Win a hand," I tried halfheartedly to get him started.

"Umm." He was lost in contemplation. "I've got the time. I'm retired."

Retired only in a manner of speaking. Charlie had owned an investment business and sold it a couple of years before we met. Some days he still took the train into New York to look after the details of his remaining share in the firm or to go to the meeting of one or another of the corporate boards on which he sat. I think he enjoyed all this the way he enjoyed wagering, which was a perpetual amusement for him. But he kept a firewall between any lighthearted risk taking and real-world business. As I said, he guarded information about the decisions he was weighing on any given day and the transactions he actually made. This was something I'd had to accept ever since we began exploring the possibility of living together. "It will not work if you keep asking all these questions, Tink. It makes me extremely anxious—I can't tell you why it does, but it does." I took this to mean he didn't understand *why*—which turned out to be a misconception—and so I was willing to write off this reaction to business questions as an emotional tic.

For my part, I was very open about where my money came from and where it went—I received the interest income from a small trust fund my parents had set up, and until Charlie helped impose discipline on my finances just before he had moved in, I had been rapidly siphoning off money from the settlement of my third divorce. Charlie was very clear about his need for order in the getting and spending. "We can work this out," he assured me. "Give me your spending history, and we'll come up with a budget. Can you live with that?" Yes. I could live with a budget, or try to, because I wanted to live with him, and I gave Charlie an immodestly padded estimate to build into our prenuptial agreement. During the annoying ritual that consummated our prenup, he joked with my lawyer about the limitations of this livelihood—"There is enough to keep each of us in a nursing home, as long as it's the same nursing home and they offer group rates"—but it was *his* lawyer who smiled.

Although I would not understand the anxiety that prompted our deal for some time, by making that bargain we had managed to put his worries to rest for the time being. I won't pretend I wasn't curious about how the money he used to help me out with my horse expenses came to him or, more intensely so, about why Charlie had come to be this way. At times it rankled that he walled off this part of his life from me. But there hadn't been too many of these times, and so far, they hadn't brought any serious arguments. He was the way he was, and I believed he was entirely trustworthy. Being married to him, I told myself, was not much different from being married to a lawyer or psychiatrist who couldn't share the details of his work. Also, there was no getting around the fact that I was pretty good at creating financial messes—because the horses always seemed more important than the money—and this had played, one way or another, into my three divorces. Marriage to Charlie was a return from financial abandon. No more bloodstock bought at auction with canapés and champagne, no more continent-hopping for riding lessons. I was playing by the rules. I'd been through too many men and too much heartache. I didn't want to do that again with the best man who had ever tried to love me. I wanted to keep Charlie comfortable because that kept me comfortable. This strategy ran parallel to what I had learned in eventing: if you want to stay safe, keep your horse safe. So, for the most part, I stopped asking questions.

"What bothers me about Joe," Charlie offered, "is that it doesn't seem like he did anything reckless. All those years of tempting fate, driving under the influence, and then he finally sobers up. He gets off the sauce—and that's when he has an accident."

"What I don't get is how a truck just catches fire like that. Spontaneously."

"Diesel fuel is flammable, Tink," he explained kindly. My ignorance of machines and any of the technology that made them possible always brought out a bit of protectiveness in him. "And a spark from anywhere—"

"So it could have happened to anyone?" I was trying to make sense of it. "It could have happened to me or to you?"

Charlie shrugged. "Except that neither one of us would have been driving that van."

True. But that fact wasn't much comfort. "It doesn't seem right, does it? Just driving away and leaving him there and then taking off for a big three-day?"

"I can't speak for Joe," Charlie said, "but I'll bet he would have approved."

Also true. If it had been me or really anybody but Win, Joe Terrell would have been paying his respects and then wrapping legs and shipping out.

Singers sing, painters paint, and horsemen compete. It is about meaning. To ride a horse, you have to strike a deal with him: If you do, he will do. If he does, you must. Even on an ordinary day the bargain requires your complete commitment, and when it comes to competition, it is compelling—you can't fail to put to the test a horse you have conditioned for it. This bargain is where I've always found my identity.

Right now this identity was a little shaky because I wasn't riding. I wouldn't be the one to pilot Exit Laughing through the Brandywine because I was grounded. I'd had a freak accident that took a baffling toll on me, and Charlie had forbidden me to ride, at least until I could demonstrate I was mended. Much as I resented this ultimatum, I didn't see how I could flout it. He was now the one writing the checks for my horses. Still, it was humiliating, and I had admitted to no one except Frankie—not even Alejandra Delgado, who would take over in the saddle—that the reason I was not riding was that Charlie wouldn't allow me to. Anyone who knew me at all would have found this unbelievable.

My only consolation was that the gray horse Exit Laughing was still *my* horse, and I was still in charge. I was the human who knew everything about him—what he liked to eat, when he was apt to drink, what irritated him, what soothed him, how to make him think my idea was his idea first, how to put him to a fence. I understood him, and I was still calling the shots. So, as soon as Charlie pulled into our drive and I got past the two terriers long enough to change into jeans, I headed down to the barn to start getting Exit Laughing ready for his afternoon work.

If Charlie's study was affably cluttered with his preoccupations and reading, my barn was a highly ordered, obsessively clean reflection of my own preoccupations. From their stalls, the horses looked at each other across a wide aisle—always swept clean of any stray pieces of hay or straw—and each horse's halter and lead hung in neat loops on the stall door. In the tack room several saddles rode their wall racks in a measured procession with the bridles and martingales hanging from hooks above them, unless they had been used the day before, in which case they hung from a cleaning hook. At any moment, under any circumstance, I could instantly put my hands on the required tool or piece of equipment—but not today, however.

On my way through the barn to Exit Laughing's stall, I noticed the door to the tack room was slightly ajar, as if whoever left the room hadn't bothered about the latch. Inside the room, everything appeared to be the same. But it didn't *seem* to be the same. Had something in the room shifted slightly? The tack trunks stood in their customary lineup against the wall. The grooming caddies—one horse, one caddy—were set down in the same arrangement as the horses' stalls. As usual, all of it. But there was one hint of disorder. A drawer in the hulking rolltop desk under the window jutted a half-inch open. I went to the desk. The files for Jockey Club papers and veterinary records were in their usual order and appeared to be untouched. Ditto for the feed and shoeing bills on their spindle. It was only when I unfurled the sheaf of entry forms stowed in one of the pigeonholes that I noticed something unusual: the entry for the Brandywine event and its acknowledgment were intermingled with the papers for competitions long past. The Brandywine was the last of the season, and the entry should have been on top of all the forms. This was baffling. Who could possibly be interested in what was in this desk?

"Hi, Tink."

I glanced up from the entry papers, barely registering the diminutive presence of Alejandra Delgado.

"Ahh . . . Alex." I was aware of how clumsy I sounded. But then this girl always made me feel clumsy. Alex stood only shoulder high next to me, and the black braid that hung down her back was the heaviest thing about her. Next to her I always felt big, rawboned, and—yup, horsy. "When were you last here?"

"Yesterday. Remember?" She picked up a grooming caddy and left the room to bring Exit Laughing out of his stall to the cross ties. "Something wrong, Tink?"

"Nothing on a grand scale." I joined her next to my horse. "But it *seems* like someone has been in the tack room."

"I go in there every day," she pointed out.

"I know. I know."

"Is anything missing?"

"Not that I could tell, but those papers—hell, it's probably nothing. Maybe I'm just reacting to this horrible thing that happened to Joe."

Alex looked over at me doubtfully, trying to figure out if she was actually under suspicion. "Yeah. Everybody's kind of shaken up."

Ours was a careful relationship, very careful. This was because of Stephen, my favorite stepchild. Although Stephen was the product of Elledge's first marriage, I had raised him from the age of two as my own, and he had become mine with all the passion of possession he would have if I had physically delivered him into the world. I called him my favorite stepchild because technically I had two others, girls whom Savage brought into our marriage. But Savage didn't leave them aside as casually as Elledge left Stephen to go sexually adventuring. Savage's daughters were his, and when he left our household, he took them into his next wife's home. I hadn't seen him since then, and as far as his daughters were concerned, I became not much more than an interested outsider. I sent birthday gifts and encouragement, and the girls sent me announcements of their graduations and other important milestones. They were very remote from me, but Stephen wasn't. Although technically he may have been my favorite stepchild, he was even now, as a grown-up and a partner in a successful computing firm, more accurately, my only child. Alex was a petite, dark-haired intruder on the scene, and so far as I knew, Stephen's first real love. I found it difficult to make room for Alex, but I was trying.

After my accident, Win Guthrie had recommended I ask Alex to exercise Exit Laughing while I was sidelined. She was one of his students and Patty's close friend. Her role at my place, however, had quickly begun to diverge from student-friend-exercise girl. I knew she had begun seeing Stephen, and she knew that I knew she was seeing him. But, even though the two of them sometimes arrived at the farm together, she never mentioned him to me outside his presence. I found this a little mystifying, but maybe she didn't want me to try to draw out any information about the two of them from her.

In spite of the uneasiness between us, when my condition hadn't improved enough to ride, much less compete, I asked Alex to take my place and ride Exit Laughing in the Brandywine. This was Frankie's proposal when she heard Charlie had grounded me. "Your entry is paid. You're not going to get that money back. Alex is getting to be a really good rider. Maybe not as good as you, but it will be a fantastic experience for her. Which will make you look good. And," she concluded this supporting rationale, "she's practically part of the family—what? You're jealous?"

"No, I'm not."

"You. Are. Jealous." She emphasized the spaces between the words.

"You know how I hate that," I reminded her. We'd had our own experiences with mothers-in-law, each of whom had injected the green misery of jealousy into our lives.

Charlie supported Frankie's proposal. "You may be jealous," he conceded, "but right now that's not in your best interest. What's in your best interest is to have your horse run in the Brandywine."

How could I disagree?

"And from my point of view it will be a real pleasure," he said. "We'll get to sit together, safe on the sidelines, watching your horse with somebody else taking the risk. Think about it that way."

I did, and imagining myself as a spectator was a dismal prospect. But, as Charlie pointed out, not so dismal as pulling Exit Laughing and staying home with the horse and him. I was backed into a corner. Alex it would be.

This is how it happened that late in the afternoon of Joe Terrell's funeral, I was standing in the field behind my barn watching a pretty little woman school my gray horse over practice fences. In terms of preparation, we were almost down to the wire. Just one more jump schooling and, the next day, a big gallop. I hated standing on the sideline, but even so, watching this horse, this particular horse, Exit Laughing, canter around gave me pleasure. He was all mine. I had bred him, which meant I came up with—I won't say conceived—the idea of the match that produced such a perfect equus. Exit Laughing's mother was Ready Humor, a mare I campaigned to take the big East Coast three-days by storm. His father was No Regrets, a flash stallion whose name may have referred to the price of his services, but about whom it was often said, "If you have a colt by No Regrets and he can't jump, that's *your* fault." But fortunately, as I raised Exit Laughing and showed him his job in life, I never had cause to try to place blame for any lack of ability.

That said, something wasn't going just right with my horse today. As Alex put him to the first set of rails, Exit Laughing launched himself willingly enough but in what seemed like stop-time animation.

"He's too slow off the ground!" I called. I may have been forced out of the saddle, but I never stepped out of the instructor's role.

Coaching was almost involuntary with me, and Alex should have been accustomed to my ongoing commentary. But now, she didn't appear to hear me.

"Ask sooner!" I demanded in a louder voice as she guided the gray down to the next practice fence. "Ask for MORE!"

She circled the horse and, without looking in my direction, sent Exit Laughing back through the fences again. I raised my voice again, trying to get her attention. In fact, I think I was screaming. It was my horse, my farm, my jumps, and damn it, it didn't occur to me to keep quiet. Exit Laughing finished his nonchalant round, and Alex rode him back to me.

She looked directly at me, probably for the first time since we had known each other, and her dark eyes were very wide, as if she couldn't believe what was going to happen. Her voice shook a little.

"Okay, lady," she said. "You think this is so easy, you just plunk your big fat ass down on this horse and ride him yourself." She dropped to the ground and handed me the reins. Then, holding herself taut, she strode out to her car, her heavy black braid swinging with the movement of her little hips in their white breeches.

I returned Exit Laughing to the stable, taking great pains with his care. The fat-ass part wasn't true. Not true at all.

What was true was that the fight wasn't only, or even at bottom, about riding. Why couldn't Stephen have been drawn to Patty instead of her? Why couldn't she have just a touch of her friend Patty's sweetness? Charlie said it wasn't my choice. She would take over Stephen. I had to live with that, somehow. But did I have to put up with her insolence and still let her have the ride? I had given Charlie my word, but surely even he would think this was asking too much.

On my way out, I closed the door to the tack room without giving further thought to why it had been standing open or who had opened it. Alex was still sitting in her little Mazda convertible when I went to the house, probably trying to pull herself together—something I definitely needed to do. I took the servants' stairs. This was habit, not precaution, since there were no servants anymore and there was no one else in the house. A few minutes later I heard Alex's car pull into the drive and stop by the back porch. This was the entrance everybody used. Ahh, I thought, she's going to try to make this up, and I stepped into the bathroom where the window looked down on the drive.

But she didn't knock. She stepped into the enclosed back porch, and the door slammed after her. A moment later, it slammed again, and Alex reappeared lugging a couple of cartons of the feed supplement she and Patty delivered to some of the local stables. She went back and forth, the slamming door punctuating the process of moving the rest of the cartons to the backseat of the little car.

Good, I thought. Get that out from under foot, and don't apologize, little bitch. What do you care about a ride on a world-class event horse? What do you care about that last gallop he's supposed to have?

I cared, I really did care, and I was damned if I would scratch Exit Laughing. I would take Alex's snotty suggestion and ride the horse myself. This was what I told Charlie when he came home from Win's an hour later and found me lying across the bed.

He wasn't surprised, but he said, "Dream on."

"I can walk, Charlie," I protested. "I walk miles now."

He disagreed by shrugging. "You're not really back to normal."

"Close enough. I'm close enough." It was futile. "Listen to me, Charlie—he will miss his last gallop!"

"Sorry, Tink. I just can't allow it."

Who would imagine that a woman fifty years old could bawl with such vigor?

Charlie was unmoved. "Leticia, get smart. Quit while you still have a back, some limbs, and a brain—while you can still enjoy your health."

"I don't give a flying fuck about—"

"That attitude is a luxury some of your friends can't afford."

Plainly a reference to Frankie.

"That's a cheap shot, and you know it, Charlie."

"Well," he pointed out, "dead women can't ride."

"I hate you." But I was touched he wanted me alive, with him. "I really hate you, Charlie."

That didn't appear to worry him. What he was worried about was finding me in the same condition he had found me in two months earlier, which had caused the doctors to ground me. He was still on their side, even now that Alex had decamped and left the best horse I ever raised without a jockey.

"All right," I told him obligingly, "I'll just kill myself."

"You can't," Charlie said. "We may need you for poker tomorrow." He was being impossible, but somehow nobody ever accused him of that the way they did me.

"This is so frustrating! I can't ride. And she can just barely do what's necessary."

"Tink, you and Stephen have both said Alex is unusually talented."

That remark caused me to stop speaking to Charlie. It was gratuitous, I thought, and how low to assign it to Stephen, who was totally, obliviously, infatuated with Alex. Besides, talent is only potential. It doesn't turn into skill until you learn how to use it—and Alex would not take any kind of instruction. I'd be damned if I would speak to him, damned if I would engage in any other positive activity, such as drawing a glass of scotch, on his behalf.

Fortunately, he drew a glass for me and my resolve lasted only through the first scotch, because Alejandra Delgado came back, that very evening in fact. She was contrite. Of course, I thought any girl who wanted to keep her ride on a top-flight horse should be contrite, but still, her apology caused me to realize that maybe her flash of temper was exactly how I would have reacted to a woman like me when I was her age. Maybe it was a sign of how she would approach the cross-country course in a couple of days. She said, "I know you're not trying to put me down, and I bet it's hard for you after all your work with the horse so far—and the money."

"Yeah, the money," I agreed and decided I must make an effort to know this girl better. "This is probably the last good horse I can afford. So we better enjoy it while we can."

What I had told her was true. Exit Laughing would be my last big-time event horse, and as Stephen had pointed out, I couldn't really afford this one. The money was giving out, and apparently, if the doctors were right, I was too. I might never ride the horse again and certainly wouldn't compete him at the international level.

3

When someone dies, the people left behind usually take time to readjust to the exigencies in their own lives. But in the case of Joe Terrell's death, the unalterable demands of a big-time competition had run smack into custom and propriety. Add to Joe's sudden departure the fact that I wouldn't be riding, and the prospect of the Brandywine seemed unreal. Nevertheless, the next day I would be trailering Exit Laughing down to a major three-day event, and all the qualifying riders in the country would be heading with their horses to the same destination.

It felt to me like something was out of whack, and for Win Guthrie, something truly was. Not long after Alex headed home I answered a knock at the back door. Win, in barn clothes loaded with barn dirt. Old friend, old rival. Tough to beat but looking sheepish or maybe just uncomfortable. He stepped carefully on the doormat in the back hall and said, "Tink." He never wasted time on the routines of politeness. "I may need a groom this weekend. Do you know anyone good who would be willing to freelance?"

"Well, *I'm* not riding, and if it weren't for the fact that your black mare will be out there trying to beat Exit—*May?* What do you mean you *may* need a groom?"

"I seem to be missing one," he admitted, raising more questions than the one he was answering.

"Patty? You *seem* to be missing Patty?"

"Yup."

"Are you or are you not? Is she or is she not there?"

"She's not there," he reported, "but her car is."

Always stoic, always hard to read. But was this some kind of panic attack? Joe's death and too much pressure too soon afterward? "Call her on her cell," I suggested reasonably.

"She doesn't have one at the moment. She left hers on the seat of the truck." So it was gone.

"Try Alex," I prompted. "She'll know what's going on."

"I did. No answer."

We talked about whether there was anything in Patty's car to suggest her whereabouts and about the possibility that a friend may have picked her up at Win's place so that the two of them could drive someplace together.

"Possible," he acknowledged. "You have any ideas for somebody else in case she doesn't show up? I'm down to one, a Latino guy I helped get into the country. But he doesn't know the first thing about a horse, and he can't speak English—which will make it pretty tough for him to move as fast as I'll need him to once things get under way."

I gave him a couple of names and was trying to dig up phone numbers when it dawned on me. Win, being Win, was very worried by the prospect of taking three horses to the Brandywine without a groom, but he hadn't yet got around to worrying about Patty.

"Win, when did you last see Patty?"

He thought for a moment and said, "Maybe right after Charlie and I spoke to the insurance adjusters. They wanted to ask her some questions."

"Did that upset her?"

"Not that I could tell."

Charlie had caught the rising intensity of my voice, and he emerged from his study to join us.

"Did she take care of the evening chores before she left?" I demanded.

"No."

"Call the cops," I said.

"What?"

"Call the sheriff," I said with more force and definition, and Charlie nodded at the phone waiting on its table. "She is very responsible and, for someone her age, extraordinarily reliable. You may be stuck with your Latino."

Win surprised me and went obediently to the phone. When he hung up he said, "I need to get home. They're on their way out."

"Please keep me posted."

"I need you and Charlie to keep this quiet, Tink. I very much need to keep this under wraps, at least for the next few days." His clients again, his livelihood with the horses.

"Sure," I agreed. He would need time to locate Patty. Or at least sort things out before questions and advice rained down on him at the Brandywine, where news, gossip, and speculation would travel at light speed.

"No information leaves this house," Charlie assured Win, and coming from him, this promise was as bankable as a Treasury note. "But please let us know what happens."

We watched Win's truck pull out in silence. After a few moments, Charlie spoke. "She might have been upset," he pointed out. "She's very young, and the insurance men were asking some pretty close questions."

"According to Win, though, she didn't seem too distressed."

Then I countered myself. "But *Win*—how would he know whether or not someone was distressed?"

"Maybe they frightened her."

"Maybe. But that still leaves a lot to be explained."

I tried to follow my customary protocol for the night before shipping out: a brandy, a couple of cookies, and to bed by nine with a very dull book. Charlie always followed along amiably and would be snoring contently in the glow of his book light long before I rescued his book and turned off my own light. But tonight this routine didn't seem to be working. After we turned out the book lights my eyes remained stubbornly open, and the silence on the other side of the bed indicated that Charlie too was still awake. We were waiting for thought to come to a standstill and sleep to take over. I didn't know what was going on in Charlie's head, but in mine thoughts about what might be happening or what might not be happening ricocheted noisily. Then, above this mental racket, I became aware of the crunch of gravel as a car pulled into the drive. Spit and Polish scuttled down the stairs, raising frantic alarms. Charlie raised himself on his elbow, and a moment later the back door opened. The yapping stopped. The terriers knew whoever it was who had come in.

"Ma?"

There was only one among my stepchildren, one person in the world, who called me that. Stephen.

Charlie already had on his bathrobe, and a moment later, I joined him at the bottom of the stairs. Even though Stephen avoided wearing anything more formal than the red T-shirt he wore now—it announced "Tear-Ass" with the discreet logo of the modem company where he worked—it was always a very clean T-shirt, and Stephen himself always seemed to have just stepped out of the shower. An elastic secured his long tawny hair into a ponytail at the back of his neck. He crossed the brightly lit hallway toward me, on his way to a hug. Over his shoulder I saw Alex. She stood hesitantly by the door, as if she were surprised to find herself there for the second time that evening.

"I brought you a houseguest," Stephen announced, and there was something careful in his usually merry green eyes. "Too much going on at the apartment."

Some dense part of me could not recognize right away why there should be too much going on at the place Alex shared with Patty, and so I blundered on. "Did Win get hold of you?

"No, the sheriff did," Stephen reported, speaking for Alex. Taking care of her, I noticed. She looked over at Charlie and me in complete bafflement.

"When Patty didn't show up for afternoon chores," I explained, "Win tried to call you. Then we decided he should notify the police."

The whole of Alex's tiny person suddenly drooped. She made her way to the bottom stair and slumped there, shaking her head.

"You don't think that was the right thing to do?" Charlie asked gently.

"It's not the sheriff." She was in despair. "It's my *phone*."

"Your phone," Charlie prompted.

"Patty has my cell phone—you said Win called that number—and she didn't answer."

This was the first real fact indicating that something might actually be wrong. I became aware of the rhythmic tick of the tall clock that stood opposite us, slowly demarcating the parts of the minute. Looking concerned, Stephen ducked into the kitchen and reemerged with a glass of milk and a stack of crackers to set on the stair beside Alex. He stayed there beside her, leaning on the banister. She observed the glass of milk gloomily. "She did not answer."

"Do the police know she has your phone?" Charlie followed up logically.

"No. I was so shocked to see the cops," she told him. "The two of them caught me off guard when they came to the door. Patty usually gets home from the barn later than I do, so there was no reason for me to worry about her. I had no idea that something might be wrong until I opened the door and there they were. I just answered the questions they asked. They said they might need to come back and take a look around. They left, and I called Stephen from the phone in the apartment. But I didn't try Patty because I was too shaken up to make the connection between her having my cell phone and her being missing—until you told me about Win just now."

Charlie looked over at me. I nodded, and he stepped into his study to use his phone. He was right. The sheriff needed to know where Alex was and where her cell phone had gone. As I considered Alex, who was now pulling herself together and politely toying with the milk and crackers, a necessary thought occurred to me. But I waited until Charlie finished his conversation with the sheriff's office.

The tall clock now read a few minutes before eleven. In about twelve hours, we could walk Exit Laughing into the trailer and start for the event grounds. Then the following day we could be watching my horse enter the dressage ring. No matter what had happened to Patty McLaren, some owners' horses would compete. I hated saying it, hated even the thought of what I would propose, but I felt I had to.

"Let's scratch the horse."

I expected this to be greeted with an uncomfortable silence because Alex wouldn't want to agree, wouldn't want to tell me she didn't want to ride, and Charlie would wait to see if I really meant what I had said. But there was no silence. Stephen said, "We knew you would say that, Ma."

The kid always surprised me and had ever since the night he decided to stay with me for good.

"You did?"

"Yes, but I am planning to ride," Alex said, and then, backtracking to acknowledge my prerogative as owner, added, "I mean, I would like to plan to ride."

But I shook my head, and I knew Charlie would back me up. "It's a matter of safety. You're upset, you're afraid. You're too rattled to run a horse at big fences that don't come down."

"No, Tink, I can deal." Alex was more like me or more like the young me than I had realized. Despite the possible tragedy, she wanted to run that course.

"You've ridden plenty of times when you were upset, Ma," Stephen pointed out. "Remember the day after Dad left?"

"Right, and I've made plenty of other mistakes too. But not on behalf of somebody else."

I knew what had to happen and that I had to stand pat. But to my astonishment, Charlie said, "I think the horse should run. I'm sure Alex is upset, but we don't know something bad has happened. We don't know anything. Why assume that the very worst has happened when there could be another explanation—when Patty could turn up tomorrow?"

My authority was breaking up under this pressure, and I tried not to buckle. It was hard. Scratching the horse was the last thing I wanted to do. And maybe Charlie was right. Maybe I didn't have enough to go on to make such a precipitous decision.

Then Alex said, "Win will ride. All three—you know he will."

With no groom.

That did it. How could I let his horses run and withdraw mine?

Charlie grinned and tapped the clock radio. "Better get to bed then."

Alex looked relieved, and when Stephen headed up the back stairs, I realized this was the first time we had seen the two of them together for more than a passing moment. The way he stayed close to her indicated to me that Stephen cared—it was the same way he had shown me love—but I couldn't begin to divine her thoughts about him. Alex followed Charlie and me to the more formal front stairs and the guest room that opened on the upstairs gallery. She paused at the door. "There is one thing."

"Oh?" Charlie and I uttered this almost in unison.

"My family doesn't know any of this—" She stopped.

"Your family."

"My mother and my uncle are coming to watch me ride."

"Your family," I repeated. "They're coming from Mexico just to watch you ride?"

"Well no, not just to watch me ride. My uncle has business in the States, but my mom mainly wants to see where I live."

Right, I thought I saw into this. See who you're hanging out with. Mama wants to get a look at Stephen.

"They don't know Patty, and they don't know about any of this stuff tonight—they will find out, but they won't get here until cross-country day. So there won't be time for my mom to get in the way."

"In the way." I tried to decipher what this meant. What could she do to get in the way? "She's afraid of horses or something?"

"Well, yeah, but she's even more afraid of what can happen to somebody like me. You know, a single woman . . . She will just go off. I mean levitate," she predicted. "She'll try to have me on a plane back to Mexico."

Clearly, this was an outcome that worried Stephen and probably one reason he had put Alex under the safety of our roof. If the Delgado family summoned Alex back to Mexico, he would probably lose any chance he had with her, and—whatever happened to my horse, to Alex, or even to Charlie or me—I did not want Stephen to be hurt.

"I do not say no to my mother," she explained apologetically.

Charlie opened the guest room door for her. "Which is as it should be," he said.

4

On Friday the sunshine found me sitting in a lawn chair beside Charlie, watching the dressage phase of the Brandywine. Against the backdrop of brilliant orange and yellow foliage, the dressage arenas were the picture of decorum. Riders in morning coats and top hats, horses shining like so many Lexuses in a dealer's showroom, trotting precise, polite circles on the manicured greens. The judges and other officials of the Fédération Equestre Internationale were much in evidence, sauntering across the lawns to their posts, men in tweeds and women in hats that had returned from an earlier part of the century. Quite fitting, for a sport that originated in the cavalry. A little something to keep the boys at the fort busy on Sundays.

We were much closer to home than many of the other people on the grounds, only about forty miles, but still far enough for us to need a hotel room during the competition. Behind us a short distance was the trade fair. It was the hub of this three-day event, which took place on a big luxurious chunk of land in the narrow neck of Maryland that buffers the top of the Chesapeake Bay from Philadelphia. The dressage rings and show jumping field lay close to this hub, but the track of the cross-country course spun out for about four miles around it. It wheeled past the stables near the top of its circuit, through the wooded hills, where a steep ravine everyone called the Gulley bisected the grounds, and on around for another couple of miles until it finished where it had started at the bottom of the circuit.

With customary efficiency, Charlie was dozing over his program in the shade of his outback hat—no need to maintain full consciousness until there was something to put his mind to. I was quite restless. I couldn't seem to get the odor of that dying horse out of my nostrils and the questions about Patty out of my thoughts. Added to that was a less urgent misery. I had been reduced to spectatorship. I was meant to be out there in the midst of the riders warming up their horses for the dressage test. I had made a place for myself in three-day eventing, this triathlon for horse and rider, but in a few minutes, my horse would appear there with someone else in the saddle.

This was just the first day of three, and although the sedate scene gave no hint of the speed and guts and agility the horses and riders would have to call on in the next two days, the horses were already looking ahead to that. Experience had taught them that once a three-day gets rolling, the momentum accelerates and takes over. This momentum would capture all of us—everyone riding, braiding a mane, wearing a badge and wielding a clipboard, or even just holding down a lawn chair—and sweep us from the realities that pressured everyday life, sweep us past even the tragedy of the van fire, and for Charlie and me, the silence we were keeping about Patty McLaren. We would be completely taken up with the competition, and I assumed that, unless the news of Patty going missing broke out, that was how it would be until the final test, show jumping, ended on Sunday.

Win Guthrie evidently made the same assumption. On a flat grassy area not far from the dressage rings, he was warming up the tall black mare named Secret Formula, the first of his three entries. He'd won the World Cup on Secret Formula the previous year and had taken several Olympic medals on earlier mounts. He had ridden over so many cross-country courses that there wasn't a fence in the world big enough to scare him. He had become a nerveless competitor. But I didn't know if the emotional turmoil of Joe's death and Patty's absence would get in his way. Usually he rode into the warm-up area with a big hungry grin. Today he wore just a determinedly pleasant expression.

No matter what emotional burdens Win was riding under, Secret Formula was a force to be contended with. She was typical of the kind of horse he succeeded so well with, hot and difficult, especially when she was in season, and now she was attending very carefully to his body's language. She knew her job, and she didn't want too much interference from him. I could read the mare's thoughts: "Just sit there and let me do this. Let me do this."

"If he can keep his focus, she could be hard to beat," I worried out loud. If you want to win, the dressage test is very important. Eventing is scored in penalties that accumulate over the three days. In dressage any move less than perfection earns penalties. They pile up easily, those penalties, and they don't go away. "She could be really tough."

Charlie lifted his head and opened his eyes. "Who?"

"Win's mare. Look at her."

He did. "Your horse could be tough too."

Charlie was lasting the course as my third husband in part because he was conveniently immune to the things, like Win's black mare, that worried me. He opened his program to the back, where he had carefully scored a blank page in his program to create a table. In the far left-hand column he had assigned a number for each horse and carried out four places beyond the decimal—the odds, as calculated from his meticulously maintained diary of stats. This was his pleasure, assigning the luck of the game and then wagering with anyone who wasn't too scared by the presence of officials from the Fédération Equestre Internationale to put up a fiver or a tenner. Betting charmed Charlie's cautious soul, and when there were odds to play, they beguiled him into temporary obsession. But he kept the stakes low, and I'm sure that over the life of these wagers, his losses didn't amount to a half a percent of what I'd lost on stud fees and veterinarians and farriers and divorces.

I looked over the other rider in the warm-up area, Jason Tomlinson, an ascending star in eventing, aboard The Flying Tiger. Jason was a New Zealander, tall, lithe, and fair-haired—a younger edition of the golden boy Win Guthrie had been a couple of decades earlier. But unlike Win, Jason had tact, and he at least tried to cultivate a certain amount of charm. No wonder Patty found all those opportunities to visit his barn.

Although the horse's name had as much to do with his owner's pilot's license as his physical capacities, The Flying Tiger was an apt description of the animal. He was large, long-legged, and yet catlike. Ordinarily, the only rational reaction to a horse that looked as fit and as keen as The Flying Tiger would have been a sinking sensation—I doubted Exit Laughing could better him in dressage. But a thought flashed through my mind, crowding out my competitive impulses. Did Jason know Patty was gone? How could he not know—or how could he at least not ask where she was?

Charlie said, "Jason's horse looks pretty fired up, doesn't he?" and my thoughts zapped back to the competition in the dressage. It was hard to concentrate. I was restless. I had no place in the competition, and in idle moments, questions like the one about Jason and images of Joe's funeral and the charred van flitted through my mind. They plagued me. I couldn't ride, and I couldn't sit still. I wanted back in the game.

Earlier that morning, just as light broke, I wanted to go to the stable to braid the gray horse's mane, and Charlie put up an argument. I could understand his point about Alex needing to manage on her own, but I was constitutionally incapable of waiting around to watch her put on the finishing touches. "I may never ride this horse again, Charlie, but I can still put in his goddamn braids," I said, and I did. We hadn't actually quarreled, but I could see I was making him uneasy.

Now I tried to ease up out of the lawn chair without attracting his notice.

"Tink," Charlie warned. "Better stay here. Let Alex handle this herself."

"I need to be over there with the horses. I feel like Mrs. Got-Rocks sitting in her private box over here."

In response to this reference to jewels Charlie murmured, "The Rocks are gone, baby. All you Got left is Horse—and if you're not going to get involved," he sent a meaningful glance at the old but clean tea towel I had in my hand, "what are you going to do with that?"

I started toward the warm-up area anyway. I've never been good at taking directions, and he gave a big, helpless shrug, lifting his palms to the gods, and returned to his numbers, which at least followed some rules of order.

I joined the grooms gathered on the edge of the grass warm-up area to wait for Exit Laughing to arrive. It was October, and my mood was autumnal. The sunlight may have been brilliant, but it was waning, waning. The years were passing, and enough of them were behind me now so that not only could I not always expect to be at the top of the standings, I couldn't always expect to even be riding. What *could* I expect now? With the fall that had prompted my grounding, death had whisked by me, only to stop at Joe. Waning autumn light. Financial erosion. Physical deterioration. What the hell came next?

Exit Laughing. He strode up the hill to the warm-up area, and my spirits came up with him. My silver horse glimmered like a rising trout. He was not as large as many of the others waiting to compete, and he was lightly built like the racing stock he came from. Even when he was just walking, the way he moved was happy, good-humored. When he stepped up into the trot, it was positively joyful. I was pleased to see that his indicator was on. Exit Laughing had a lop ear, which many people find endearing, sort of like the Easter Bunny. But Exit Laughing wasn't trying to be cute or cuddly. When his ear swung loose, that was a sign he was concentrating. Some people bite their tongues when they are thinking very hard. When this horse got down to business, his ear flopped out.

Watching Alex begin to warm up my horse, I suddenly recognized something I hadn't allowed myself to notice in any of our schooling sessions. She had hands that were magic with reins. That and a huge dose of luck might be enough to get Exit Laughing into the top finishers. She was riding against many tougher, better-seasoned competitors.

Win, a case in point, was motioning to someone on the sidelines, where I was surrounded by a little clutch of grooms. A hefty Latino man had been standing silently on the grass just beyond us. Now he responded, ducking under the crowd-control tape to reach Win and the black mare. This new groom looked up at the very-tall-in-the-saddle Win, and Win pointed down at something below the horse's snakish black head. A long, green string of saliva hung from the bit at the corner of the horse's mouth. This, of course, was what needed to be removed in order for Secret Formula to make a picture-perfect entrance for the judges. The

Latino reached for a back pocket and the rag that should have been there. When that produced nothing, he slapped both back pockets, and then he swiped at the offending drool with an open hand. Win drew up tighter, his mouth clamping. A typical Win kind of set-to was brewing, and I had in my hand a perfectly useful rag. At competitions, these rags are a kind of currency. With use they lose their original color and take on a gray that falls in the range of grays of all the other stable rags. The one in my hand had done this, but since the towel was a gift for my first wedding, it was a little distinctive. It had my initials, new thirty years ago, embroidered on it: LTS, Leticia Trumbull Savage. Savage. All I knew about him now was that he had turned to real estate development on the California coast. Without speaking to or looking at Win, I went over to hand my little towel to his new groom and then ducked away.

I reached the edge of the warm-up area and looked back to see the new man walking alongside Secret Formula toward the dressage arena. The towel swung from his back pocket where he had meant to put his own cloth. I didn't give the towel another thought. Nobody expects to get a rub rag back. But in the end, although I could never have foreseen it, the towel would come back to me.

I turned to my horse and my prospects. Exit Laughing was scheduled a half-hour later, and Alex was working him slowly up to his performance. She was keeping the horse at a distance, and clearly she was avoiding me. I didn't blame her. Right now my nerves would jolt anybody else's into hyperactivity.

So I gave her the distance she seemed to need. Keeping things mellow, as my adored Stephen liked to say.

I made my way back to Charlie and the competition in the arenas. Jason was finishing up on The Flying Tiger. Their test was all grace and delicacy. The figures were dead-on accurate. They were also powerful, extravagant. The red horse could dance.

"Stunning," I advised Charlie glumly. He focused on his table of statistics.

"What's your best guess?" he asked about Jason's score. "I want to pencil in a number here." He probably had a tenner at risk.

"This is like being married to Jimmy the Greek," I complained. "I'd put that somewhere between 27 and 34."

Win Guthrie rode in on the now-presentable Secret Formula and saluted the judges. The black mare evidently found the dressage test an ordeal. Many event horses do, and this is understandable. Asking a hyper-fit animal to perform the intricate patterns of the test movements is like requiring a marathon man to dance *Swan Lake* before being allowed to move up to the starting line. The tests required the horses to turn on their hindquarters, move sideways fluidly, make a smooth transition from a canter to a walk in a stride or two, and hardest of all, halt motionless as the stopwatch ticked. Watching a dressage test is like watching figure skating. To understand which horse and rider wins, you have to know what to look for. But as intricate and controlled and, to many people, as boring as the dressage test is, many a big-time event is won in this first phase.

"Not bad," Charlie declared about Win's ride after looking through his stats on Secret Formula. With Alex's ride approaching, I was growing too nervous to watch any more rides go beautifully.

All the horses and riders were well prepared for the rigor of the dressage arena. The performances were so polished, the blunders so rare, and the flaws so few that the three international authorities serving as judges were having to watch every twitch of every muscle. Their recording secretaries were scribbling furiously. Immediately these notes were quantified and boiled down to penalty scores, and these scores were for Charlie the real object of the sport.

The crowd on the grounds was growing—mostly people like Charlie and me whose lives were tangled up with dreams of great horses. The field across the road was designated for parking, and there ratty little Nissan trucks sat next to Jaguar sedans and Mercedes station wagons. The sun shone on them all. It glittered on the grass and glowed in the brilliant oranges of the fall foliage. It shone down on the enthusiasts, the competitors, the grooms. It warmed the back of my neck.

The rest of me was clammy. My palms were cold and sweaty. Maybe I am a little too competitive. I love competing, and my enjoyment of winning is something physical. But I was more nervous than I'd ever been when I'd been riding a horse into competition. I guess what makes you most nervous is what you know you can't control.

When Alex and Exit Laughing appeared in the arena, I pounded Charlie's knee. I wanted my horse to win even more than I did when I was the jockey. If the gray horse could just escape the dressage with minimum penalties, it wouldn't be hard for him to run and jump for the next two days without accumulating more. If he could just listen to Alex, let that ear lop, he might go to the top. I stopped breathing. Fortunately, this had no effect on the pair performing in the ring or on anyone else for that matter. I was far too agitated to notice anything more than that Exit Laughing got through all the movements and left the arena without any major bobbles.

For the few minutes of the test, Charlie was all eyes. "How'd they do?" he asked, "Bad? Good?"

"Jesus." I was laughing. "It's over!"

"What do you think?"

I tried to sober up. "It had a lot of good points . . . but it didn't really swing . . . and I don't know if the judges saw it the same way."

Charlie knew how to quantify that. With a pencil he roughed

in two digits, a decimal point, and two more digits. Then he pulled the hat over his face and lurched back in his chair for a sunny nap until our scores came up. I said I was going off in search of a hot dog—one of the great things about this sport is that everybody has been up since four A.M. so you can eat a chili dog at nine in the morning and nobody, including Charlie, will give this a second thought. What I really wanted, though, was to catch up with Alex on her way back to the stables.

"Nicely done!" I called out. At the sound of my voice, my gray horse looked around. He was fond of me, and this made me even fonder of him.

Alex's top hat was off, and her dark braid was shaken out. She pressed her cheek briefly against the horse's neck and then vaulted off. "Whew!"

"Charlie and I are going to walk the course as soon as the dressage is over," I invited her. It is customary for everybody—riders, grooms, owners, spectators, in order of significance—to preview the cross-country course the horses will run on the second day.

"Thanks, Tink. I'm going to walk around with Win. Then I thought I'd walk it again by myself."

I was mildly insulted that Win Guthrie's expertise seemed more desirable than mine. But I kept my mouth shut. "Just remember I am available."

Maybe I was learning. Right now I couldn't ride, much less compete. So for the moment, but just for the moment, I would have to leave the riding to somebody else—and today somebody else had proven herself capable enough.

When the dressage judges left their seats in midafternoon, Charlie and I headed for the scoreboard to see how Exit Laughing had fared. Low score wins. You start the dressage—every horse starts—at zero and tries to make it through the three days with the fewest penalty points.

"Forty-three point six," Charlie read the penalties as if I couldn't.

"That hurts."

"You always say that."

"It always hurts," I insisted. "You don't win with 44 penalties in the dressage."

"You have." Charlie would know the exact number of penalties I had survived, and what he implied was true: it was only to the unmounted Tink that perfectly respectable scores of 7s and 8s were not adequate marks, even given the fact that a 10 was a remarkable rarity.

As is the custom after the dressage tests, the spectators and competitors were heading out from the trade fair for the cross-country course. Charlie and I drifted through the concession tents in the direction of the procession, past enormous banners advertising Purina feed, supplements like Vet Essentials and Mighty Fit, Mercedes, Land Rovers, Rolex watches, custom saddles, and insurance. They were a sure indication that we—the old guard—no longer had sufficient resources among us to fund a three-day event. The sport and its following were growing, the standards were rising, and glitz was creeping in. There was open concern about attracting television coverage. Everything was more expensive, and where inheritance left off, corporations had moved in to support our sport. The event was a marketing route to reach our crowd—trade-fair tents, banners on cross-country obstacles, trainer endorsements, and now—most prized by the riders—corporate sponsors.

Charlie was so amiable it took him a while to move beyond encounters with friends and head to the start box for the cross-country course. I stuffed the wrappers and cups I had emptied into a trash container. Charlie marveled at the number of them. I had eaten two chili dogs, french fries, and a sugar waffle.

"Tink—What? Are you pregnant?"

One husband earlier and this light remark would have ignited a firefight. There had been a time in my life, a long time, when any mention of pregnancy would have inflicted instant pain. Each month I brooded over the many wasted estrous cycles I had passed through without even "catching," as the old-time horsemen called it, and I became generally intractable. Approximately three hundred go-rounds of luteal opportunity with two different men, and nothing. I would never have allowed this to happen to a mare whose foal I wanted. I would have had the vets in there tinkering. I was tempted, but somehow I was repelled by the idea of applying the same technology to my own reproductive machinery. I was in conflict with myself.

"I know there are some things I could try," I suggested to Layton McLaren, Patty's father, after several years of disappointment, because I half-hoped he would reassure me there was really nothing wrong with the drugs, the surgery, or even the test tube.

He thought about this, then nodded equivocally and said, "Maybe."

"Maybe what? Maybe I could? Maybe it would work?"

He didn't answer right away. I knew Layton as a trim, sandy-haired man railside at Pony Club meetings. He had a light manner and a good way with kids. But in his office, his white coat gave this man the responsibility to offer a considered judgment. I wasn't the first desperate infertile woman he had counseled, but I was probably one of the more direct.

So he was direct. He said, "Long shot. Right now any of it would be a long shot."

"Why?"

"Luck. I know you're usually pretty lucky, Tink. But you've had two pieces of bad luck. You've been living with a gnarly uterus and—"

"I should have had that surgery!"

He flipped back through my file. "I believe that when I suggested it you weren't married."

"So? I should have had it anyway."

He smiled a little. "We might still be having this conversation today."

"What's the other piece of bad luck?"

"Your age."

An inhospitable womb and precious few eggs. That was that.

Layton tried to soften this. "We all have regrets."

"Yeah." I was wallowing in self-pity, and it wasn't until Layton left Patty's mother and moved out of town that I realized he might have as many regrets as I did.

5

Coming along behind the others inspecting the obstacles on the cross-country course, Charlie and I left the start box and headed for the first fence. The tour of the course was a ritual that began with the riders, who needed a chance to check out the fences they would put their horses to so they could plan their rounds. But over time the course walk had come to include anyone who wanted to see the terrain and the obstacles—anyone except the horses, of course, who were offered no such privilege and who, traveling at top speed over the course must blindly trust their riders and respond split-second by split-second to instructions from these pilots. The procession was also in part social, which often meant information sharing—or leaking. In my time of walking courses I had harvested quite a bit of useful information, about horses, about riders, about deals going down, and romances blooming. This was the reason I was clocking right along, covering the ground at the pace I hoped would allow us to catch up to a group of course walkers a quarter-mile ahead of us.

Charlie, however, was in no hurry and sauntered along slowly enough to preserve the distance between us and the group ahead.

In a low voice he said, "Win is managing to keep the lid on the business about Patty, isn't he?"

"I haven't heard a thing from anyone," I agreed.

"Well," he picked up the pace, "we'll see how long this lasts."

Obstacle Number 1, the Flower Box. A broad, dirt-filled ramp planted solid with a hundred chrysanthemums.

"This isn't going to eliminate anybody," I told him as we passed the massive planter on our way to Number 2, the Hay Bunker, a much-larger-than-life rendition.

"Not you anyway—which makes me enjoy this little hike more than usual."

"Really, Charlie?"

"Really."

"I don't mind a little risk," he said in what seemed to me pure understatement.

"You love risk, Charlie."

"Not foolish risk." Maybe that was accurate. He liked playing with risk, calculating, analyzing it—but only when the price was in small denominations.

"This does feel a little weird. I mean walking the course without planning to ride it. It's been years." I was wondering in a purely matter-of-fact way how long this state of being unmounted would go on. "The last time was when I broke my wrist."

"That was before I met you," Charlie said, and I slipped my hand into his. He liked to put the history we shared ahead of the separate histories we didn't. You may wonder about those stories, about how I came to have three husbands and four weddings. I myself don't find those so interesting as the story of how I came to have a horse that was a good enough jumper, strong and fast enough, to go at a dead run and clear the twenty-some obstacles we were previewing. But that's probably one reason for the four weddings.

Number 3, the Chicken Coop. Number 4, the Pen.

"This sport has changed a lot just during the time we've been together."

True. What had once been an almost private sport of competition among friends had opened up to something more public. More horses. More riders. More accidents. More buying and selling.

"More money," Charlie put in.

"More deaths," I completed the list, at first referring to deadly spills on the course but immediately redirecting to Joe Terrell's death. I didn't say anything about Joe, but I didn't need to.

We passed the next obstacle, a make-believe barn, and came to an uphill run crowned by Number 6, a heavy timber fence. We were catching up to the course walkers gathered around the big timbers, and coming from behind, Hugh Vaughn was catching up to us, bouncing along on good spirits. He put out his hand.

"Good to see you again, Charlie!"

"Again," Charlie repeated pleasantly, offering his own hand but looking disconcerted. He didn't understand Hugh's reference, and he hated coming from behind in a conversation because he didn't remember something.

Hugh was dark and stocky, now verging on the downright round, and his salt-and-pepper curls circled a tan, confident face. He was a positive, happy force. "So. What odds are you offering, Charlie?"

"Still working them out," Charlie said hastily. He didn't want to miss a wagering opportunity, and he had statistics on every horse that ran at the international levels. "I'll get back to you."

"Make those odds short on Hugh's horse," I instructed. Immediately after the big timber fence was a rectangular pit called the Coffin, and I was sizing up the distance between the timbers and the pit. "His horse won't even notice this little divot."

That seemed to please Hugh. He was new to the sport, but he was a quick study and was rapidly coming to prominence in it. He had bought a number of event horses, including The Flying Tiger, whom I thought was possibly a great horse, and he had the good sense to hire Jason Tomlinson to ride those horses. All it took was money, and evidently there was a supply of that. Often he flew his own plane to the events, and the names of all his horses referred to aviation. Hugh was a gynecologist who specialized in female cancers. He was an appealing guy, who always seemed to be in high spirits, and according to Frankie, who was under his care and who had volunteered for his clinical trial of an experimental drug, his sense of humor made some of his more distasteful procedures less humiliating for his patients. The horses, the plane—Charlie said it all had to soak up more money than Hugh could make as a physician. But these days, that wasn't unusual. Family money—and now, increasingly, corporate money—was usually behind top event horses.

He eyed my slacks and running shoes. "You must not be riding."

"I can't," I said. "Charlie won't let—" Then I remembered he was a doctor. "Do you know anything about the nervous system?" Before he could prevent an ad hoc consultation, I launched into a description of the accident and the episode of paralysis.

I had, quite literally, been unnerved. I had taken a young horse out for a hack. It was the bay filly I was bringing along to take Exit Laughing's place when he retired, and she was an amenable sort, eager to please and not silly or spooky. I brought her back from our trot along the edge of a soybean field and was crossing toward the gate when she stepped on a ground nest of bees. They flew up around her. She was momentarily unruffled because they were after me not her. Several buzzed up under my helmet, and with the same reaction that makes you start swatting when you hear a mosquito at your ear, I whipped off the helmet. Then the bees went for the filly's head and the tender area between her hind legs. With the same instinctive reaction I'd had, she took a flying leap sideways. At that point it took very little to shake me loose, and I landed with the back of my head against a fence post not far from the gate.

A few moments later, I opened my eyes to see the filly approaching me cautiously. She must have circled out and lost the bees, and now, bless her heart, she was coming to me to help her make sense of what had just happened and, at the same time, hoping I wasn't the original source of the bees. I told her I wasn't and rolled on hands and knees to get up. Other than some pain at the place where my shoulders met my neck, I didn't seem to be hurt. I had just lost a few moments of awareness, and my left arm and leg felt odd. It must have been adrenaline that put me back up on the filly because I don't remember remounting. We started for home at a walk, and I noticed something odd about the left side of my body. It seemed somehow absent. I could feel my left arm reaching out to the rein, my left leg against the filly's side, and the ball of my foot on the stirrup iron. I could feel my weight settling down through my hip into the saddle. But it was becoming difficult to move any of these parts. Then it was impossible. Unfortunately, this meant that if I tried to dismount, I would come crashing down. I was alone and stranded on the filly's back. Using my working arm I managed to steer her to the house, right up to the back door. But that was as close to the phone as I could get. I let the filly drop her head and graze on the lawn. I was helpless if she should decide to bolt for the barn. But she had it good there, chomping down on succulent grass, and the thought of bolting didn't move her before Charlie pulled in an hour later. By that time, I couldn't see straight. His car was a blur, and so was Charlie. If he wondered what was going on, why the horse was ravaging the lawn, he didn't have a chance to ask before I said, "Hi. I can't get down."

He looked incredulous.

"Too weak to move." I reached across the horse to pat the delinquent arm and leg. "And dizzy. Get me down."

"Tink . . ." he warned. He thought I was putting him on.

"Come on, Charlie, get me down."

But as soon as he stepped up to the horse, it became clear that if he shifted my weight I would crash down on top of him. He went into the inside pocket of his sport coat for his cell phone and called the emergency squad. "Fitting punishment," he said cheerfully when he pocketed the phone again and took hold of the filly.

"For what?" With him there, I was no longer worried, just embarrassed.

"The very definition of purgatory," he said gleefully. "You can ride, but you can never dismount."

"Ha, ha."

But he was still joking around when the ambulance turned into the drive. Maybe he'd been around the eventing crowd too long.

It wasn't pretty, the three emergency squad guys wrestling me off the horse and onto a stretcher. The faces of the EMTs as they drew me off the filly spun slowly, and for a frantic moment, I thought I might vomit on them. It was tricky and awkward and humiliating. Something like working a mattress around a corner in the stairwell. I swore like a drover until the stretcher came to a quiet rest in the ambulance. But when we returned home almost a week later—after continuous monitoring and countless tests read on cryptic screens indicated the pressure inside my skull was subsiding—Charlie wrote a nice check for the squad.

After that came weeks of alternating boredom and hard work. I lay in a hospital bed staring at the parlor ceiling, and once a day my doldrums were interrupted when the physical therapist showed up and began chirping encouragement until I was too tired to try anymore. But I made progress, and now I could walk long enough and well enough that only Charlie and I could tell I wasn't—as the dressage judges like to say—quite level.

I wound up this case history, and Hugh shook his head. "You look pretty strong, pretty coordinated."

I confirmed this by lifting my left foot above my shoulder with my left hand like somebody trying to learn yoga.

"I shouldn't even venture a guess, Tink. When you take a fall like that but can't remember anything about it—I mean, there could be a hundred neurological implications."

I said, "Yeah, and they have to know what it is before they can fix it or make sure that what's working now will keep working."

"Call my office Monday, and I'll give you the name and number of a good neurologist, the very best."

I had already been poked and tapped and wired by two of the same fraternity. But I said, "Thanks, Hugh. Very much. I'll take you up on that," and as we parted company, I did in fact feel genuinely grateful.

"Call the office Monday," he repeated cheerfully, "and Charlie, I'll check back with you. I might to be able to come up with a couple of bucks."

Out there on the course, under the brilliant foliage, Monday seemed a universe away. Charlie wandered along the track the horses would run, contemplating the last page of his program and the new column of scores he had scribed there for the dressage scores.

"The mean?" he asked out loud, "or the median?"

"Last time you said median."

"Forty-three point six." He began a calculation.

"Exit Laughing has run and jumped his way out of his dressage score before," I suggested exactly what Charlie had pointed out a half-hour later. Now that the cross-country course, the so-called Test of Speed and Endurance, was just ahead, our dressage score was beginning to look a little better. "But Alex will need to get him around the course without any time penalties."

"Right. *Time*. But there is some hope here," he said about his data. Statistics or no, hope is the peculiar privilege of the person who writes the checks.

We were midcourse, hand in hand, studying Number 12, the Sunken Road, when suddenly, like a person who has just discovered something he thought was lost, Charlie said. "O'Hare last month. The moving walkway. I didn't recognize him at first."

"Hugh?"

"Yup. Kind of embarrassing, but it was one of those out-of-context things."

Deep into the course the obstacles became more treacherous. A quarter mile into the woods was the imposing landmark around which the course was laid out, the Gulley. It began where a creek poured out over a seventy-foot cliff. The water running over the stone had been carving the descent for thousands of years. As the ravine opened out, the wall on one side of the creek dropped down to meet the slight rise of a meadow, but the other remained a steep slope forty or fifty feet up from the creek. Poised on the brink of this wall was Number 14, the Palisade, a formidable fence with broad pickets. This was the highest point on the course. When you stood next to the Palisade you could look back past many earlier obstacles and see all the way down to the start box.

As we studied the distance from the top of the pickets to the shale ledge where the horse would land and take off again, Charlie said, "It's nice to look at this without having to watch you blast off it on a horse."

"I can always see my spot," I objected. "And I'm adjustable. If we don't get launched to land right, there's always another way to get to the next fence."

Maybe I was bragging a little, but the ability to see a spot has nothing to do with brilliant intelligence. It is just a knack, a kind of physical canniness about timing. Maybe I said it out loud—"I can always see my spot"—just to reassure myself that I still had this poise, because Charlie didn't pretend to understand any of this. The only animal with whom he had any rapport was his cat, Greenspan, who like all cats didn't seem to care whether you understood him or not. But somehow, just looking down the big drop and saying it lifted my enthusiasm.

"My horse can do this. He can do this, Charlie. He could win this thing!" I was conveniently ignoring the fact that even if Exit Laughing succeeded on the cross-country course, the stadium jumps still loomed the day after next. Those fences came apart with the slightest bump from a horse, and every rail sent the penalties up.

"More like the old you." He was looking at something in the gravel at the bottom of the Gulley, and he stooped to pick it up. It was a small round adhesive patch. He examined the bit of flesh-colored litter in his hand and offered it to me.

"Like the ones Frankie wears," I advised him.

"Oh yeah? That's how she's getting the chemo? I never noticed."

"Course not." I pulled down the placket of my polo shirt to show him where she wore the patch and then deposited the thing in my pocket.

Win Guthrie overtook us at the edge of one of two adjacent

man-made ponds collectively called the Water, Number 18. He didn't seem to be hurrying, but his long legs put ground behind him quickly. He was alone, not surrounded by the usual gaggle of younger riders hoping some of his savvy and luck would rub off on them. I skipped along the edge of the water to catch up to him.

"How are you holding up, Win?"

He shook his head but did not slow the methodical, ground-eating stride. "Not good, Tink. This insurance business is just salt in the wound." And it was keeping him agitated. "Why would I want something to happen that would take Joe out with the colt?"

Ahead was a big obstacle formed by a log against a giant boxwood hedge with a huge window cut in it for the horse to pass through. Horseman's Hangover, Number 19.

"You didn't, I'm sure. Nobody thinks you did."

"The insurance people aren't so sure, Tink."

Charlie caught up to us as we paused to size up the monster log. "I thought you and I had come to an understanding with those guys. Wasn't that a done deal?"

"Yeah, on the van. This is insurance on the horse, Charlie. Mortality insurance. It was a real nice young horse."

"Nice enough to cause you to set up an accident for Joe and Patty?" Charlie asked rhetorically. He didn't appear to think this scenario was too likely. Maybe in other horse sports, where it was possible to cheat and steal and even kill horses for significant money. He said, "Event horses aren't worth that much."

"They didn't used to be," Win corrected him. "But the insurance guys know what's happened to prices."

Here, to keep my stock high with Charlie, I should have pointed out that I had spared him any personal experience of these rising prices by breeding my own horses. But suddenly I took notice of the fact that Win was walking the course by himself.

"Where is Alex? I thought you were going to coach her."

"Up ahead somewhere, I guess. All this diddly-squat gave me a late start. What a waste of time." He started to surge ahead but then paused. "A true waste of time—because the insurance guys know what the police have told everybody. The fire probably started with the brakes. The *brakes,* for Christ's sake. Somehow they go from the brakes to me killing a horse that I'm *selling* for a good price—and you know what? They have not said word one about Patty. It's like for them, none of this is happening." He resumed his earlier pace, leaving Charlie and me with this exasperating proposition.

A few minutes later when we met up with a knot of spectators and riders at the last fence, Number 21, Charlie was blowing hard, almost as noisily as the horses would at the end of their run.

"Pretty stiff course," he declared, patting his jacket pockets in search of his program with its back page inscribed with stats. "No room anywhere out there for a mistake."

But there never was. He had watched enough of my cross-country runs to know it was always a balance between precision and chaotic animal experience of rhythm, speed, thrust, and liftoff in which a good rider doesn't interfere. That was somehow what was exhilarating about it, to be able to synch up with the horse, without trying to control what happened in the air over a fence, and fly. So much of it was out of anyone's personal control.

We merged with the procession of riders and grooms that was heading back toward the stables, and just as we came alongside Hugh Vaughn, the doctor stopped. "What's that all about?"

The stables were a series of low shed row buildings with Dutch doors facing each other across the narrow yards of clumpy grass between the buildings. In the opening of the yard that belonged to the shed row where my horse was stabled, a state trooper's car had pulled up. We passed close enough to the car to see two people seated in it.

"Insurance?" Charlie speculated.

But Win wasn't in the car. He had long since returned from the course, and I saw him ducking into one of the stalls assigned to his horses. If Charlie was right, if the cop was here to look into the truck fire, why wasn't Win sitting in the cop car? Who else would be involved?

"Pretty nasty if that's what's going on," I said. "An insurance company barging right into the middle of an event."

"That won't come to anything," Hugh predicted cheerfully, and I remembered then that the horse that had burned was on its way to Jason Tomlinson.

"That wasn't going to be one of your horses, was it, Hugh?"

"God no! I can't afford to buy a horse just when he gets ready for the big time."

"The horse would be Jason's then, I guess."

"Not likely. He needs to have someone else buy another top horse for him. Probably the horse was going to another client, because these young pros don't come by their bucks very easily," Hugh said.

But it seemed to me that Jason was doing just fine for himself. He had several well-heeled clients, including Hugh, and recently he had received a sponsorship from a company that sold a feed supplement called Mighty Fit that was supposed to improve the horse's endurance. With this combined purchasing power, he had been able to ride aggressively up through the world rankings—a lot faster than I had ever been able to move up by developing one horse at a time, paying all the bills. He had three horses at the top levels now, and except for Joe Terrell's accident, would have had four. But I don't want to belittle the kid. He had the riding talent to back up his investors' money.

Charlie and I found Alex standing with Exit Laughing not far away. She was holding the horse for the farrier, and he had one hind leg cocked high and resting on the farrier's knee. A loose shoe. Charlie gave a meaningful pat to the pocket where his checkbook rode. I went over to inspect the newly shod foot, and the farrier, a thin, quirky man who seemed to have a special hinge in his back that the rest of us don't, stayed in his crouch and gave me a look like *You got something to say? This less than perfect?* Then he released the horse's leg, and Charlie got out the checkbook.

The cop car remained where it was parked until Exit Laughing was bedded down and we were ready to return to our hotel. Then someone got out of the passenger side of the patrol car. It was Paul Lamoreaux. He caught our stares and came over to explain.

Lamoreaux was a popular veterinarian who officiated at many of the three-days, and he also looked after my horses at home. "That took a while!"

"Really." I was trying to pretend I wasn't curious.

"Almost an hour's worth of affidavit." Paul was a slight, narrow man, all angles. Even his cropped dark hair made a sharp angle at a widow's peak. He had an impish, teasing manner, and he was a passionate devotee of classical music. Drop the needle, and he could name the tune. But he also had a genius for handling any horse that was injured or frightened, a talent for calming things down.

"Affidavit," I repeated.

"Insurance, Tink, insurance. All of Win's horses are covered, and I'm the one who vets them."

"The prepurchase exam." I came to the idea suddenly. It was a routine condition of sale of any event horse. "You found something?"

"Tink, Tink!" He laughed to fend me off.

"Sorry. I know it's none of my business. But doesn't all this squawk about a horse that died in a trucking accident seem a little unreasonable?"

Paul shrugged. "I've dealt with these guys before. They know how to look after their money."

"Paul," I persisted, "wasn't that the colt everybody said was an even better jumper than Secret Formula? Who was buying him?"

Paul gave a Cheshire cat grin and with his thumb and forefinger pinched together drew an imaginary zipper across his lips. No more information on that subject. Which was as it should be. He wouldn't pass along information about my horses either.

When Exit Laughing had been settled for the evening and we were on our way to the car, Charlie poked his head into the stall we were using as a tack room. "Alex, why don't you come to dinner with us?" He knew Stephen would love that.

"That's really nice of you, Mr. Reidermann." Somehow he got to be Mr. Reidermann while I was always referred to as Tink. "But I have to wait for my family. They won't get here for a couple of hours yet, and, you know, at home everybody always eats late anyway."

It was growing dark by the time we pulled up to the hotel and parked the Mercedes. I kept mentioning the benefits of a new four-wheel-drive SUV. But Charlie said the Mercedes was paid for, and the damned thing continued to thwart my automotive ambitions by remaining trouble-free. The hotel was one of only two within striking range of the Brandywine. It was not the expensive one where many of the owners and officials stayed, but it was new, a chain establishment sprouting just off the interstate.

A message from Stephen greeted us at check-in: Frankie wasn't coming—too sick from the first dose in her new round of chemo—and he was still at work, parsing code for the modem company he had helped found. Probably wouldn't get to the hotel in time to see them before they had turned in for the night.

"He must know the Delgados are coming here. Maybe he's nervous, just thinking of reasons to stay at work."

"Why should he be nervous?"

"Those people are not coming all this way just to watch Alex ride," I explained patiently. "They want to look him over."

This possibility hadn't presented itself to him, but Charlie didn't give it much weight. "He's not stalling," he assured me. "There's enough work in that little shop to keep twice as many young guys doing overtime."

We were on our own for dinner and took our time showering and changing. I wondered how Win would manage the cross-country the next day with only the new green-as-grass groom.

"If Patty is still—" but *alive* would be too brutal, "—anywhere on the East Coast, she should get herself here front and center by dawn tomorrow. I mean she, of all people, should know how much Win has to depend on her."

Charlie and I had talked off and on of the possible scenarios that could explain her absence: a love affair she had to keep secret with, say, a married man. A crisis with her alcoholic mother, whom she was trying to protect from publicity and embarrassment. Intimidation by all the questions raised by the van accident. Now another possibility occurred to me.

"Charlie, you don't think Patty had anything to do with the truck fire, do you?"

"I suppose that's a possibility, but I think it's more likely that she's very young and emotionally rattled right now."

"The insurance company poking into everything. It's so intrusive." I was really warming up. "I mean the Brandywine is a major international competition. Why couldn't the insurance company wait to start hassling everybody until after the weekend? Aren't these the same guys who are promoting their insurance policies down in the trade fair and sponsoring a *fence* on the cross-country course? It's obnoxious. I mean, Win lost a beloved mentor. A valuable prospect. Now his help is missing—and these people are treating him like a thief."

"It's just business, Tink," he said as if I, with horse world myopia, couldn't possibly understand what made the big gears of his world turn. I was irritated by his superior never-argue-about-a-fact tone. We were wandering into contentious territory.

"Charlie, how come business always gets your sympathy?" Was I, an outsider to business, too stupid to have a valid opinion?

I wriggled into my panty hose. He finalized his bow tie. "Who said I was sympathetic?" The conversation was taking on a sharp edge, and Charlie's defenses were coming up. "Anybody in business has to worry about insurance, but insurance itself isn't my line of work." He was talking down to me and straight-arming me at the same time. I was indignant at his lack of respect, his lack of trust. I deserved some of both, which was something Frankie had been trying to tell me for quite a while. Why couldn't I be trusted with the teeniest bit of information? I could see it coming, the fight we hadn't managed to have yet, but really, truth to tell, I was already fighting. "Okay, Charlie, exactly what *is* your line of work?"

"Mergers." He said this quite firmly to shut me the hell up, and this sent me into orange alert. Now I was actually angry. If Charlie was openly determined to put me off, that meant I needed to—I flat out *had*—to know more.

"So is it—what do they call them—hostile takeovers?" Along with anger, the insecurity of three failed marriages was starting to overtake me too.

"I said *mergers*, Tink!" He raised his voice, and this, mild as it seems, was the rudest he had been to me. He had meant to be rude, and my reaction to this was almost animal. Something like fear. Because I had been down this road before, the one that takes you to a place where the man you think you can count on, the man you think cares, turns. Demon insecurity, the evil twin of competitiveness, had me in his clutches. Again. I couldn't speak, not even to ask him to zip my dress. I struggled with it myself and flounced out to the Mercedes. Maybe Frankie had had a point. "How can you be so lax?" she had demanded more than once. "I mean, you can be really, really oblivious."

Maybe I should have pressed him harder early on, asked more questions. Maybe I would have found out where I really stood with him. Now it seemed too late for that. I was really mad and more than a little suspicious.

We drove without talking to the Crab House, a place at a bend in the road near the edge of the bay. The restaurant was a colonial-era house and still retained its domestic layout. The walls were bare plaster with sconces that spread pools of light over the tables and dark floor planks. Off the entrance foyer in what had been a parlor was the bar. People from the three-day event crowded there waiting for a table to become free. I marched in ahead of Charlie, found an empty space along the bar, and ordered myself a scotch. Trying to pin my demon. Too much mottled history with too many men.

Paul Lamoreaux was rounding up a group to share a table. He had Ned Burlingame in tow. Ned was another rider from the old guard, the senior member, in fact. He was taller than any of us and a bony, awkward-looking person who could somehow organize his improbable body and ride brilliantly. A decade ago he had been the world beater Win Guthrie was now and Jason Tomlinson was on his way to being. He was still a good competitor but no longer a top seed. This could hardly matter to him because he had ascended to the role of dean of our sport and could be counted on for hard-hitting but even-handed commentary on the state of play. In short, a good choice for a dinner companion.

As soon as I agreed to join the group, I realized it must include Hugh Vaughn because Heidi Vaughn, Hugh's soft, blond wife, came up behind Charlie to rest her hand in the small of his back. Heidi liked to make herself comfortable with men, just about any man, and she seemed unable to keep her hands to herself. Ordinarily, this wouldn't have incited my jealousy, but ordinarily, I wouldn't have had such an acrid exchange with Charlie. Even when we finally made our way to one of the tables covered in brown paper, her hand remained stuck to his back. He saw me looking at this thoughtless offense. But what could he do? Even I could tell there was no graceful way he could escape it until we all seated ourselves.

Our group dropped into silence when the menus came. I was still rattled from the conflict with Charlie. I hated my long legs and all the angles in my construction. I wanted a heart-shaped butt like Heidi's and plump red lips. I wanted to be just an indolent, smugly kept housewife.

Apparently Charlie was speaking to me. "Tink," he repeated, "I said what are you going to have?"

"Crabs—whatever you want," I said. "And don't forget, I still need to check on the horse."

"Ah, Tink," Ned Burlingame observed, "the moody one." He'd known me ever since I had ridden out of the start box the first time, flapping and kicking on an old Appaloosa. "Tough to sit one out?"

"I know, I know. Don't let me ruin your dinner."

"And don't you let us keep you from looking after that horse," Heidi said sweetly. "Fortunately, that's one chore Hugh is not qualified for. He has to depend on Jason to take care of the stable."

Was she taking a swipe at me? Or was she just blithering, trying to fill the awkward moment that had fallen into the conversation? Evidently Heidi wasn't expecting her remark to have any effect, because she tapped the face of her watch to remind Hugh of something, and he dug into his pocket agreeably for a pillbox.

"Win's not here," Paul noticed.

"Well, he is running three horses tomorrow." I thought this should excuse him, and Paul said, "Right—without his usual help."

"What's happened to her, the little redhead?" Hugh struck innocently into secret territory.

"Kids," Charlie proposed dismissively, as in *what-are-you-gonna-do-about-'em*? "Kid stuff."

"What kind of an excuse is that?" Ned demanded righteously. "Any working student who did that to me wouldn't be back long enough to explain."

But Hugh swallowed a pill and said confidently, "She'll be back, I'm sure, and there is an explanation."

The crabs arrived and were dumped in the center of the table, which was covered with heavy brown paper that would be balled up and thrown away after we had eaten. Following close behind the pudgy waiter was a sleek young man carrying a pair of drinks. His hair was spiky with whatever it is that makes hair look damp but not greasy, and his upper body had been pumped up by hours in the gym. Embroidered above the pocket of his oxford cloth shirt was the logo for the muscle fortifier he was selling.

Charlie eyed the young guy's chest with its label. "Works pretty well on him," he suggested. "Think it does anything for the horses?"

"They come and go," Ned advised. "Over the years, I bet I've tried fifty of them."

"And every one of them ended up in the pile behind the horse," Charlie suggested.

"Should have taken that money and invested it," Ned agreed gloomily.

"Yes," Charlie put in, "in something that doesn't eat while you sleep! But I bet you're still adding something to the feed."

"Supposedly that snake oil Jason uses on Hugh's horse makes the blood take up more oxygen." Ned as much as confessed to using it, and evidently looking for validation, he said to Hugh, "Now you're a medical man. You think there's any scientific basis for using that stuff?"

"I have no idea." Hugh laughed and then said a little defensively, "I don't even know what it's supposed to have in it. But the sponsorships are great for the kids who are up-and-comers, like Jason."

"Probably drinks the stuff himself to keep that check coming in," Paul observed.

I had been silently digging away at the crab centered on the paper in front of me, but at least one fact had to be made known. "It isn't the supplement that makes the difference in the horse. It's the fact that Jason is paying such close attention to the horse and his condition. That's what's keeping the horse fit enough to jump out of his skin."

"Right," said Paul. "Absolutely, Tink."

The steaming heap of crabs and the nutcrackers and picks claimed our attention. We savored the sweet crabmeat dipped in melted butter and the jokes and stories that passed around the table. Charlie had heard them all before. But he enjoyed that about horse people. They liked to tell and retell the same stories about their animals and their exploits and their wheeling and dealing, and at each telling the embellishments changed. With the beers and the slippery eating process, the conversation grew uproarious, and when we left the table, it was piled with the dark hulls and leg pieces of Chesapeake crabs.

But the laughter and high humor stayed at the table. As soon as we reached the car, whatever was wrong between us returned, and silence perched stubbornly between the bucket seats until Charlie parked the Mercedes in the competitors' lot.

"Tink, you're positively stewing—and we've got your horse, Stephen, and Alex to think about. Could I just apologize for being so testy?"

"Yes, you could," I said and kept right on going. "You could just apologize, and that would be that. But you were the rudest, absolutely the rudest, you have ever been to me, and it leaves me in the dark. It makes me wonder whether I know you or not. You know me. You know every little thing about me and the horses. Because I tell you. But with you, there's all this territory that is off-limits—and it makes me uneasy."

"Yes, of course," he said meekly.

"It makes me feel like you turn into somebody who is a stranger, like Elledge did."

He didn't like being compared to Elledge. "I know about the top hat," he snapped to keep me from retelling the story.

I had left for an event and was forty miles away from home when I realized I'd forgotten my top hat for dressage and sped back to the house. But when I rushed upstairs to get the hatbox from the shelf in the closet, there was Elledge, stretched out on the bed with a woman I decidedly did not know and who was laid out so as to give me ample opportunity to size up the competition. I snatched down the hatbox, got back in the truck, drove a hundred miles as fast as I could without shaking the horse off his legs, and cried my guts out on the way.

"Here's your hat, what's your hurry?" He summarized the old gag.

So, okay, I wouldn't tell it, but I wasn't going to let him off the hook either. "Charlie, something, some piece of this is too private to talk about, isn't it?"

This seemed to give him a jolt of pain as electric as the one the dentist sends through you when the drill finds the nerve. But I wasn't going to let up.

"How bad can it be? I mean, was there a second marriage? One I don't know about?"

He rested his head on the steering wheel. He was trying to think.

"Did you have to do time in prison? Lose a child?"—my worst nightmare.

In the dark interior of the car I couldn't see his face, but I sensed there was a major recalibration taking place.

Finally he said, "No, it was money I lost. Only money."

"*You* lost *money*?"

"Quite a bit." The steering wheel was pressing into his forehead. He was loathing himself. "Actually, it was a whole lot."

I was relieved, vastly relieved. "That's nothing, Charlie. Nothing at all."

"She took the money when she left," he said about his first wife, then continued miserably. "I was so shattered I couldn't think clearly enough to defend myself. I must have had some irrational idea that if I gave her the money—what I had made in the world—if I made her comfortable, she would come back. She used the money—she and her lawyer used the money—to buy up all the outstanding shares in the business."

I knew this couldn't have been good. "And so?"

"She took control, Tink. She walked off with the money and the business."

"She was a crook?"

"She wasn't a crook. Everything was done legally."

"You told me she died."

"She did, about a year after the divorce."

"Why was this too terrible to talk about?" But I could see how humiliating this had been. I fumbled over the console for his hand.

"I had to start over."

I probably should have snatched up this opportunity to *start over* and ask exactly how much money recovery amounted to. But I was too concerned about him. I said, "In the horse business everybody is always starting over."

"I meant with you. I am trying to rebuild," he said.

"And I'm not? Two men, three marriages gone—and I'm not? Look, Charlie, I know that with you money isn't just business. Getting the money has something to do with what you think *you're* worth. But that money—that money itself—was nothing, really."

He looked a little alarmed by my attitude. "How can you say that so easily?"

"I don't know. Maybe because I've never had to support myself, never had a job to bring the money in. The only money I ever actually handle comes in and goes out with the horses."

Then, because he had unloaded and I now knew what I should have known all along, he looked weary. "We better check your horse."

The official night watch was ensconced in a trailer beside the gate. The guard poked his head out, and when he recognized us, waved us on. His quarters were lit by a television screen, but except for this gray aura and the evenly spaced security lights that came on as we passed close to them and tripped the motion sensors, the long shed rows were completely dark. We walked down the outside row, setting off momentary pools of light that were extinguished as we passed on, and turned the corner to head toward the stall that housed Exit Laughing. A light came on overhead, and there at the edge of it, half in shadow, stood Win Guthrie and Alex Delgado.

It looked like an embrace, or really the exit from an embrace, their arms dropping to their sides. It must have been a clinch of some sort, but it was hard to say what its purpose was because as soon as it was illuminated, Win turned roughly away from the girl. I backed hastily away from the light pole, but the flash of light had caught all of us in it.

Alex rushed past. She was dressed for dinner in a long skirt and ruffled blouse. She was crying.

"Alex! Are you all right? Can I help?"

She kept moving, head down. "Thanks, Tink. I don't see how."

Whatever that referred to. Charlie and I remained there for a few moments, stock-still to avoid triggering the lights. I felt exposed, as if we had been caught doing something wrong. But Charlie was steady and serious, trying to tease some implication from what we had seen.

Alex's car started, and somewhere at the opposite end of the stables, a pickup. That would be Win.

"Charlie, what the hell is going on?"

Our answer was the little noises of horses at rest, straw rustling, a water bucket bumping in a corner. Exit Laughing blinked when I turned on the light in his stall. He had been standing in a deep horse snooze, and now he stirred himself to lip the water in his bucket. Even in this groggy state, the horse had self-possession. He was keeping himself comfortable, looking after his needs even though he was in a strange place far from his home pasture. This quality is bankable in a horse. I loved him for this poise and for how I had helped him arrive at it.

"Just minding his own business," Charlie observed.

"Unlike us?"

"I never draw inferences from animals." But both of us were, in fact, silently at work on inferences, circumstances and inferences.

Back in the safe mellow light of the motel room, Charlie drew a pack of cards from the briefcase that always traveled with him, business or no, and he sat on the edge of the bed to lay out a game of solitaire on the nightstand. I was pulling on pajamas and imposing scattershot thoughts on him.

"Why are these people, these insurance people, hounding Win, Charlie? And is that why Patty took off so suddenly?" I slid next to him and drew up my knees, watching the cards step methodically from one row to the next. "And what is this with Alex and Win?"

"Aid and comfort?" he suggested. He didn't want to think it was anything else because of Stephen's involvement with Alex. Nonetheless the other idea presented itself.

"Pretty chummy," I grumbled, "and they looked so guilty. Didn't you think they acted guilty?"

He looked at the face of the card he had just turned over. "Let's not go there. He's too old—"

"Too old?" Win was my age, and I certainly hadn't lost the urge.

"Okay, if you want to agonize about what something between Alex and Win would mean for Stephen, let's go there. Maybe Win is good in bed."

"He's not," I said, and he glanced up from the rows of cards. "Now look, Charlie!"

"Yes?" He was beginning to enjoy himself.

"That was a long time—I mean a really long time—ago."

"So maybe he's been getting better."

I doubted this. "He never paid enough attention, you know, to make it personal, Charlie. But that doesn't mean he wouldn't look good to Alex—you know, young and starry-eyed looks up to experience."

He grinned. "Told you not to go there. How about Patty?"

"I am concerned, truly concerned about what has happened."

"*Involvement*, Tink," he prompted about Win and Patty.

"Not with Win. She probably has a thing for Jason Tomlinson—at least I think that's what it is. She goes over there pretty regularly."

"Do you know why?"

"Not really." I hadn't thought very carefully about this, because I assumed it was normal goings-on between young people. Jason was a good-looking rising star, and she was an appealing, big-eyed gonna-be watching his star rise. "I don't like to ask the girls questions, Charlie. Because you know what happens when somebody my age starts asking people their age questions? They shut you out faster than they can turn off their cell phones." Now I had to consider something else I hadn't thought about very carefully. "Charlie. I just remembered that Stephen doesn't like Jason."

"Alex and Patty like Jason, but Stephen doesn't?"

"Right. He may be a little jealous because Jason's a looker and so athletic," I said, "and because he always has such beautiful manners. But Stephen also thinks he's slippery."

"That last part is worth paying attention to," Charlie commented.

"I agree—now. But I didn't before today because Jason is a horseman, and one way or another, we're all a little slippery. We have to be, as a purely practical matter. I, for instance, never tell the whole naked truth about a horse I'm trying to sell."

Charlie's eyebrows went up.

"Come on, Charlie. After all this time with me, you know that every horse—even every great horse—comes with problems. You buy a horse, it's a package that includes problems. When you want to sell a horse, why dwell on the problems when you can talk up all his good points? I thought—and maybe still think—that's what bothers Stephen when he talks about Jason being slippery."

Charlie looked down at the orderly ranks of cards he had created on the nightstand. "Jason," he proposed and sighed.

"Play the ten, Charlie, on the jack," I advised so that he could finish the hand and turn out the light. Then I rolled over and closed my eyes.

I was in a deep, blank sleep when the telephone rang. I fumbled for the receiver to make it stop its noise.

"Ma."

It was Stephen. Charlie rolled over to listen in on our conversation.

"Sorry to wake you up. We got something you need to know."

"No problem, hon. Where are you?"

"Down in the lobby. Alex is here. She's sorry she didn't tell you tonight at the barns, but she needs to talk to you."

"Everything okay?" I inquired idiotically.

"No."

Charlie was out of bed, pulling on the jeans he had laid out for the next day. "Tell them to come up."

Alex was still wearing the long black skirt and ruffled blouse. Whether or not she had been to dinner and with whom were left unexplained. Stephen wore the same clothes he had worn to work, jeans and a black T-shirt with a formula printed across the front, a programmer's joke he had once explained to me at the same time he had explained that he was now as much "management" as "development," which I thought was only fair, given that the modem that was making the company so profitable was his invention.

I would have given him a big hug. But Alex was there, and hadn't I just seen her in Win's arms? Straightaway she said, "I was on my way back to my room to change for dinner. When I got to the car there was a trooper there waiting for me. He said the troopers—the state police—have taken over from the sheriff because Patty's now considered missing. And endangered." She sat down on the sofa near the window.

"Do you have any idea . . ."

"No. The trooper asked me a lot of questions like that, and I had to find Win and tell him the troopers wanted to talk to him too."

Maybe that explained the clutch.

"It's so . . . unreal. I'm sorry I didn't tell you at the stable tonight, but I was just so upset and confused. And Win doesn't want to believe it. He just wants to be pissed."

"Naturally."

Stephen sat on the corner of the bed. "She can't remember the last time she saw Patty."

"That's part of what's so upsetting. It was the first thing the trooper asked me. Why can't I remember that one simple fact?"

"Because," Stephen had analyzed this, "Patty is always around, and her work has her coming and going. Just the way your job and your riding keeps you coming and going. You expect her to go and come back, so you don't pay any attention when she doesn't come back."

"Have they notified Patty's parents?"

"They've talked to her mom . . ."

I had no idea where Patty's mother lived now or under what circumstances.

"And they're trying to reach her dad—they're split, you know—out in Chicago. I wish it were the other way around. Her mom is too out of it to be any help—we need her even less than we need my mom."

Charlie was working on the situation. "What else did the trooper tell you?"

"Not much," she said. "They were going to put out an all-points bulletin. They said a lot of times missing people turn up. They said she could have just been upset, really upset from that accident with the truck, and maybe the insurance investigation scared her into running away."

"Certainly possible," Charlie agreed. I didn't agree—a girl like Patty who has Olympic hopes and the guts to go for that doesn't skip out on her best chance to ride at the international level, and besides, she had friends she could go to. But I didn't say this. I said, "Still think you want to ride tomorrow?"

Alex nodded. "Absolutely."

"So." Charlie came around to the frustrating fact that there was nothing to be done. "We wait to hear from the troopers or, better yet, from Patty."

It was true. There was nothing else to be done. But after Alex and Stephen departed, Charlie and I ignored this truth and lay staring up in the dark looking for what might be coming next. Even if Win and Alex's clutch had been only an innocent reaching out for comfort, bumping into them at that precise moment had fixed my attention on Win and how he might be involved. Was it as simple as he might have been sleeping with Patty and that, though the van accident was none of Win's own doing, it had brought enough guilt down on her and shame toward her father—who, after all, was footing the bills—that she couldn't face either man and ran away? That wouldn't make him guilty of much, though, certainly not enough to make an insurance company, which was concerned about money not morals, suspicious.

What about Win and the van fire? As I had said to Charlie, it had been a long time since I had been close to Win, and maybe my assumptions about him were dated. Maybe I was wrong. I looked back on my own days, and nights, with Win in the old house with no curtains to find something to implicate him. He had been incorruptibly honest then, bruisingly candid. Had something happened to turn those qualities upside down? I mean, how many horse deals can you do without becoming what everybody thinks a horse dealer is? This was something I'd often wondered about myself, and certainly Win had made a whole lot more deals than I had. But right here was where my speculation came to a halt. Even if Win was no longer incorruptible, there was no getting around the fact that he was the one who had made the deal on the young bay horse that died in the van fire. He had effectively sold a horse, a horse that had apparently passed Paul's prepurchase exam, and although no money had actually changed hands, the only thing that stopped the cash from flowing was the horse's death. There was no way Win could have profited from that.

Finally I said, "Somehow Win has managed to get himself into some really deep shit."

"That's not clear," Charlie objected. "None of it is very clear, Tink. It's not clear that Win's truck didn't *accidentally* catch fire and run off the road. But when I went to Win's to meet with the insurance adjusters, that conversation went just like Win described it out on the course today. They were asking questions about the brakes and other mechanical sources of spark, and any evidence that it was something other than an accident burned up with the truck."

"It's all connected to Win," I pointed out unhappily, because I could not erase the memory of that scrap of white truck siding with the gay stripes of Win's colors.

"Statistically, it is entirely possible for two bad things—say, a truck accident and the disappearance of an attractive young woman—to happen in the same person's orbit. Without that person causing it or knowing anything about it."

"But what about this, Charlie? He kept everything running."

"Who?"

"Joe Terrell. He was the one who did the work on all the machines at Win's place. Tractors, mowers, elevators, trucks. Everything tip-top. Win never had to pay a garage to do anything. I mean, what is this talk about brakes? How could Joe have missed something like that?"

The Test of Speed and Endurance

1

Day two of any event is the longest. Cross-country day, the Test of Speed and Endurance. It starts early and spins out with spectacular jumping and phenomenal horse-human coordination, but also mistakes, missteps, bone-breaking falls, and loose horses. So I never would have expected to stay in bed after the alarm went off. But that is what I did, linger in bed, because I wasn't riding. This fact, that I had stayed in bed past dawn on a day when he would compete, was one of the few surprises I had had with Exit Laughing.

There is something about the way in which fate brings a horse to you that has a powerful influence on everything about the way you deal with that horse. This must have to do with hope, the human kind. I've had horses given to me by friends who thought I could work miracles, I've spent entirely too much money for horses who were blood relatives of horses that I coveted, and I've carefully arranged the mating of two animals to produce the best of each of their bodies and talents in the offspring. This last approach is often known to backfire, and I've been responsible for the spawning of some ugly, mean, lazy horses. But not in the case of my gray horse Exit Laughing, whose birth was all tied up with

Charlie and me and who, from the moment he struggled to his feet to nurse, was the ideal combination of his parents.

The mother of Exit Laughing was my chestnut mare, Ready Humor. She was a funny, quirky little filly. She thought people were very amusing, and she thought I had been put on earth to show her where the fun was. She was a trial to break, but once she understood the crazy things I asked her to do, she was all for the running and jumping and even the dressage. A little buck after every fence—"Okay, now where's the next one?"—and steamy brilliance in the dressage movements. I don't need to tell you she won, and kept winning. She was a three-time Horse of the Year and did me the great service of making me look like I knew what I was doing. I retired her before she could start making mistakes and spent months of research to find the right stallion for her. He was a flash bay horse with good big bone and a winning record over the longer distances at the track.

I couldn't really afford this match. But it was made in heaven, and I had just sold two yearlings. The mare-stallion union was consummated about the same time I met Charlie at the land trust dinner. It was during the silent auction, which was always accompanied by cocktails. He was bidding on a painting that I wanted too, but I didn't take much notice of this gentle, well-padded man. In fact, I wasn't taking much notice of any men. Elledge had been gone for five years, and this had given me time to come to the depressing realization that I was not likely to ever be loved for the way I was, for the way I might love in return.

The painting was a primitive, a flat depiction in patches of color with no shading, no lines of perspective, of a house not far from my own. The house was about the same age as mine, the same tall federal style. I hovered around it, and Charlie thought if I was interested in the painting, he should be too. He thought bidding on it would attract my attention. Below his bid, I wrote a higher figure. He had no way to suspect I was sour on men. He wanted to keep playing and immediately upped my bid. It didn't take long for his money to best mine, and then he sat down next to me at dinner. He had nice blue eyes, which I didn't pay any attention to right away, and a direct humorous gaze, which I also ignored. Everybody in the room seemed to know him, and nobody in evening clothes even looked twice at his well-worn sport jacket. Charlie donated the painting to the land trust for its headquarters—I wouldn't have dreamed of giving it away, but this seemed a cheerful indication of who the man was. Before the wine was finished he allowed as how he would like to see the two houses, the house in the painting and mine. This seemed like a reasonable request. But I was a bit of a sore loser, and I put him off. "Sure, sure. Love to have you out, sometime."

Almost a year later, Ready Humor delivered a dark charcoal-colored colt. Of course, I missed the actual birth, which is the way most mares want it. But when I found him he was still slick with amniotic fluid, lying in the straw with his wobbly head up trying to take in the big wide world. Within a couple of minutes, he propped himself up on his long front legs and launched himself upright to nurse. But my happy, game mare didn't seem like herself, and within an hour she was threatening to colic. In case you're inclined to say, *Oh, right, colic*, let me make it clear that what Ready Humor was suffering from was not the kind of temporary distress of a newborn baby. For a horse, colic is a life-threatening stoppage somewhere in its miles of intestines.

I ran to the house to telephone Paul Lamoreaux, but before I opened the back door I could already hear the phone. It was a friend of mine who worked at the bank. "Tink, do you know you've overdrawn your account?" She was kind enough not to say "again."

"How much time do I have?"

"I have four checks—total almost six thousand dollars—that I really can't hold on to."

I could remember only three checks that might have cleaned out the account—the farrier, the hay hauler, the grocery. What the hell was the fourth? I would have to fill the void with money from my modest trust fund.

I hung up, phoned Paul, and arranged to meet him back at the farm in forty minutes.

I made it to the bank in ten minutes and was at one of the convenience counters, scribbling furiously to make out a check from another bank to cover the overdrafts. When I opened my purse to locate my account number, I discovered I didn't have my car keys. At that moment an elevator opened on the main floor, and Charlie got off—how appropriate that I bumped into him in a bank. He was on his way out and smiled as he passed me. Because he looked somehow familiar, I would normally have attempted something like a smile. But the reason I didn't have my keys was that, having scurried luckily into a parking place, I had left the car running. I said, "Shit," left the check and the purse on the counter, and darted for the door. Where I stopped Charlie in his tracks. He let me through. "Sorry," I said, and was I ever when I got to the curb. The car was running and the doors were locked.

"Would you like me to call a wrecker?" Charlie was standing by the curb with my purse and the partially made-out check in his hand. As I said, it was his eyes, the warm regard with which he looks out on everything and everybody, that caught me up. I had a split-second insight that I wasn't managing very well on my own. I had been operating alone for so long I didn't expect help, sympathy, or even friendliness.

"I would love it—and I know you think I'm an idiot."

"Not at all." He was heading back through the bank doors to a phone.

"I have a sick horse," I explained feebly, relieved that he really didn't seem to find me witless. I was in a state, frantic to get back to the barn and at the same time moved by this man's quiet assistance. Charlie called a wrecker and also called Paul Lamoreaux to explain my delay. Then, late that afternoon, after the mare had been delivered to comfort from her bellyache, the phone in the back hall was ringing again.

"Mrs. Elledge? I still have your check."

"Aww, shit. After everything else I screwed up today, how could I do this?"

"You didn't," he said. "I did."

"So nice of you. Really lovely. Maybe I could drive into town now and pick it up," I suggested sweetly. If I could get to the bank's drive-in window by six, I could still cover my six thousand dollars' worth of careless accounting. I didn't realize then that Charlie probably owned some little piece of that bank where my checks would have bounced.

"Give me your account number," he suggested.

"What!"

"You don't need to make another trip to town," he explained. "If you'll give me your account number, I'll deposit the check for you."

"I can't ask you to—"

"Sure you can. Then I'll insist on bringing the deposit receipt out to your place tomorrow. We arranged quite a while ago for me to see your house, remember? And then the two of us can go take a look at the house in the painting."

As soon as Charlie set foot in the front foyer and the terriers were clamoring at his knees, I forgot I was supposed to be showing him around the house. I had a brand-new horse to show him. Spit and Polish were holding him at bay. I could see he didn't have much experience with dogs, and I scooped up Spit in one arm and Polish in the other. "You'd never know they were brothers, would you?"

Charlie looked at the rough and smooth coats doubtfully. The only things the dogs seemed to have in common were a snippy jaw and sharp teeth.

"Dogs do this, you know," I said, and without considering possible details in the house that might have interested him, the formal front parlor and the window lights on the landing in the stairwell, I ushered Charlie out the back door, and we were on our way to where I kept the real valuables. "Same litter," I continued about the terriers. "Different fathers."

"Trick of nature," he said, willing for the moment to suspend disbelief, although there was no need to—it was true about the terriers' mother, a promiscuous bitch.

I showed him into the barn and proudly led him up to the stall where Ready Humor watched over her foal. That was how Charlie became one of the first human beings the little newborn horse laid eyes on. They considered each other thoughtfully, infant horse and full-grown man. Exit Laughing was about thirty hours old, dry even behind the ears, and already named. In a series of three back-to-front movements, the foal bumped himself upright to stand quite surely on long, long legs. The joints in them looked like knots in a string, and Charlie said, "Are they always this homely?" This didn't bother me because it was quite clear to me, even when the colt was just two days old, that he was exceptional.

That was eight years ago. I laid big plans for the gray horse, and while he was developing to fulfill every action item on my agenda, Charlie and I were considering each other—really, it was mostly me considering Charlie because he seemed to somehow have already decided on me—and finally settling in together. This happened surprisingly quickly, given that I had pretty much written off any chance to match up happily. But Charlie knew how to keep someone company, and he kept at it. We did a few of the things that courting couples do, art museums and shows and movies, but mostly he visited the farm and turned up at all the three-day events to take me out to dinner—people in the horse world thought Charlie and I were a done deal long before I did. Charlie himself was fond of saying, "The future belongs to those who show up," and he showed up. He won Stephen over quickly, and I would often come in from the barn to find my stepson, who had been without a father for a decade, in quiet, serious conversation with Charlie.

Skittish as I was, I found that I was also beginning to count on Charlie. I took his advice. I allowed him to help me with my finances, to shuttle what was left of the Elledge settlement into annuities and try to live off the trust fund interest. His good judgment brought a relief from having to live by my wits, and so I didn't think to question him about his own finances. In fact, the first time I posed an innocent question about what seemed to be his work in what seemed to be his retirement was when I had agreed for him—actually, I asked him—to move in. One of the front parlors was to become Charlie's study, and he was standing in one place then moving to another, trying to site the best location for his reading chair and lamp. Spit and Polish were inspecting his shoes. He smiled and said, "Moving my chair here probably means marriage, you understand."

Which brought out his proposal that "we'll need to arrange for the money to live off in the meantime." Which in turn, because I hadn't considered taking money from Charlie, brought a few blithering questions from me, and these prompted Charlie's ban on involving myself in his financial dealings. But I agreed I could live with that, and until last night's spat, had lived nearly contentedly with this restriction because I had been surprised by happiness.

I was more surprised by my life with Charlie than I was by Exit Laughing. The horse didn't surprise me. He did everything I expected he would, worked up through the levels, making the usual horse mistakes and learning from them. He arrived in the international ranks about the time I expected he would, and now he was truly competitive there, in his glory. What I hadn't expected was to have to give up the ride on him and then to have the high point of his eventing career so badly marred by an accident and a missing girl.

I wasn't riding, I had no chores, Exit Laughing didn't start until midafternoon, and the day would leave me with a lot of time on my hands. I dreaded this. I stayed in bed replaying this history of the horse and Charlie and me and at the same time trying to spin out a scenario that would account for Patty McLaren's absence without involving violence.

When Charlie emerged from the shower, water dripping from his paunch down to the towel he was using for a loincloth, I said, "I need to have you let me off at the stables before you go to breakfast." I knew he wouldn't like the idea, I knew it would cause tension, and if I hadn't been fretting about waiting on the sidelines for whatever was going to happen, however the horse was going to run, I would have handled this with more finesse. But as it was, I came straight out with it.

Charlie wasn't much concerned about finesse either. He said, "Nope."

"It's cross-country day."

"Bad idea."

"There are things I always do."

"You aren't necessary," he said.

"What!"

"You'll be redundant."

"Redundant?" Where had he been on all those cross-country

days? But I could see he wasn't about to back down. I would have to fight, and his revelation of the night before and the peace it had won were too valuable to risk. Without actually saying so, I gave in. At least he let me drive.

On to the home fries and eggs, to the Delmarva Diner. The day that would gallop off with every other rider's hopes began with the two of us easing down into the Mercedes's leather seats. Sharp new-day sunshine threw down long shadows from the trees along the road, and Charlie slipped into his own cross-country-day routine, punching buttons on the radio until the weekend summary of the week's stock activity came on. I couldn't figure out why replaying what he already knew about the indexes was so important on a day when eighty or ninety flesh-and-blood horses—each one a complex equation of living probabilities—would burst out of the start box. But evidently cross-country day would be no different than any other weekend day. Charlie tuned in for the numbers. "Flat," he said, "just what you'd expect."

I didn't know enough about stocks and bonds to expect anything, but what came over the radio next was something both of us should have expected and somehow didn't. The news of Patty McLaren's disappearance. It was just a few sentences, but it leveled what had seemed a problem among friends into a stark public fact. She was gone. The police were seeking information, and Charlie wrote down the hotline number.

"It's still early. Maybe they'll get a tip."

At the Delmarva the parking lot was crowded. The diner was a shiny, fake-chrome structure shaped quite vaguely like a railroad car. Inside, there was more shiny metal and puffy aqua upholstery on the booths and chairs, and the first thing you encountered was a tall glass case filled with pies and cakes, all of them trimmed with whipped cream. Almost every available seat was occupied, most of them by people who in one way or another had some connection to an event horse. There were owners, or past versions of them, family or friends of riders and grooms. I'm sure I was the only active rider in the place, and I didn't have much taste for that fact or the home fries that had originally lured Charlie here. Standing by while a waitress who spoke to Charlie as if he were an old friend cleared a table for us, I noticed two people in a booth on the opposite wall. They stood out from the rest of the breakfast crowd, probably because it was a Saturday morning and they were in business clothes. The room was clattering with traffic back and forth to the kitchen, the clink of dishes, and the hum of horse conversation, so I didn't inspect the pair closely.

Big plates of eggs and sausage and pancakes with sides of home fries traveled from the kitchen to their places at the chrome-and-Formica tables. No one with fork in hand was in a hurry, and Charlie watched his plate come down in front of him with contentment. This was an aspect of cross-country day I had never seen. Everyone here was waiting for the action. It made me impatient, edgy. I was out of place. My little dish of yoghurt was too. But Charlie, contemplating something else along with his fried eggs, was oblivious to this.

"There's more information here," he said, "somewhere." I had the same sense of things, and tuning in to the din of the conversations around us, I could hear that word about Patty was getting out. I picked up the sound of Win's name. We weren't the only people in the room speculating. But what was speculation, and what was information?

Charlie's home fries lasted longer than I thought possible. I was ready to go, to be at the stables, and when he finally picked up our tab, he was interrupted on his way to the cash register.

"Charlie? Charles Reidermann?" A short narrow man in a double-breasted suit extended his hand. The accent was Latino of some kind, and the man's fastidiously cut black hair, olive skin, and very dark, almost black, eyes also seemed Latino. He was smiling broadly. Charlie shook his hand automatically, smiling in a bemused way. He recognized this person, but he was struggling to come up with a name. He didn't like any situation that made him seem uncongenial. "Yes, good to see you again."

"Vicente," the man prompted, "Delgado."

"Yes, of course. How are you?"

A tiny dark-haired woman came to stand just behind him. "My sister in-law," Vicente swept her front and center, "Lourdes."

My mind was racing, struggling to catch up to events of the last few moments. These two must be the family Alex had been awaiting. But how did Charlie know them?

Lourdes was a diminutive woman who stood very straight in a narrow skirt of a microscopic plaid and pumps with tiny heels. She too had the black-black eyes, shadowed by lots of mascara. She wore red lipstick and her black hair in a strict twist up the back of her head. A few strands escaped this control at the back of her neck and at the sides of her face, suggesting that she might not be as severe as her skirt and sweater implied. Still, in spite of these wandering tendrils, there was something regal, imperious, about her. Not somebody I would want to mess with. Vicente translated Charlie's introduction of me, and Lourdes repeated, "Tink." I decided she must not speak English.

We were all smiling idiotically, Vicente listening intently as Lourdes quizzed him. Was she asking about Stephen? Or maybe just about my horse, because he would carry Alex?

"Lourdes wants to know about the missing girl," Vicente explained. "Do you know her?"

They had heard the same radio report Charlie and I had, and now I remembered the word Alex had used about her mother's likely reaction. *Levitate.* But was she really capable of whisking her daughter back to Mexico City—before Exit Laughing had a run at the cross-country?

"Yes, we know Patty," I told Vicente carefully, "and she is a friend of Alex's."

"What we don't know," Charlie took over for me because he thought of himself as both forthright and tactful, "is what caused her to leave or if there has been any foul play. We just don't know. That's why I've encouraged Tink to let Alex ride the horse today." Lourdes accepted this quietly from Vicente, nodding briefly.

"Alex loves your horse," Vicente confided. He seemed quite formal but also quite eager to please Charlie. Still, I did not want Alex's family to spend time with her before Exit Laughing launched out of the start box.

"When you come to the place where the horses will run, you should look up Charlie," I told him. "He can tell you all about what's going on—and I assume you will want to change clothes first."

Lourdes's eyebrows shot up at this, indicating for the first time that she understood English. I assumed she hadn't spoken because English was not possible, but now I thought perhaps the reason for it was some customary deference Alex's mother showed Vicente.

"This is not like a horse race," I explained to them. "There is no grandstand. It's all out in the open. You'll need outdoor clothes, like hiking clothes. And boots."

They shook their heads.

"Those nice shoes you have on, Lourdes? They'll make you sink into the ground with every step. Your feet will be killing you. Save those pumps for the dancing tonight."

This brought smiles all around again and directions to a shopping mall that Charlie drew carefully on a napkin. Their shopping expedition would buy us some time and spare them serious discomfort.

"How do you know those people?" I asked as soon as we were back in the Mercedes. It was becoming apparent to me, even in my comfortable horse-focused oblivion, that Charlie, moving circumspectly under my radar, had, in fact, been doing quite a bit of business. Because our heart-to-heart of the night before seemed to open the way for it, I pressed him a little harder than usual.

"Vicente runs the family's business, pharmaceuticals, and I think Lourdes must own a big chunk of it. Last year Vicente made a pitch for funding to the Halefellow board.

"Which you are on. Halefellow?"

"Yup," he agreed. "But I didn't make the connection to Alex. Delgado is a common Spanish name."

"Did they get the money?"

"Nope. Not for the time being anyway."

The cell phone resting on the console between us came to life. Charlie retrieved it, glanced at the little screen, set it to speakerphone, and greeted our caller. "Frankie."

Her voice came into the car louder than real life.

"Is this Patty the redhead?" she demanded. "And do you know any more than the guy on the radio?"

"Probably not," Charlie said.

"Where's the boyfriend?" Frankie instantly presumed an explanation. "Maybe she isn't really missing."

"There is no boyfriend—and what else would you call it?" I came back. "We saw her at the funeral. She went to work the next day, the insurance guys asked her some questions, and no one has seen her since."

"But there's no body." In addition to a passion for prizefights, Frankie had a book-a-day habit that fed on crime novels and bodice-ripper romances, and she prided herself on being able to predict the outcome of any movie.

"Not unless you count Joe Terrell," Charlie pointed out.

"No kidnapping note."

"Not yet."

"Okay, Tink," Frankie conceded. "What do you think is going on?"

"I don't know. I mean, it's easy to assume the worst—she's dead. Or raped and tied up in a deserted warehouse where nobody will ever find her."

"This isn't the right crowd," Frankie objected. "They're too close-knit, and there's no way for anyone to be isolated. The guys who write thrillers know what they're doing. If they want to have someone offed, they get that person alone—and preferably in the dark. When was Patty alone long enough to be brutalized?"

"There's no evidence," Charlie snapped, "of any of your scenarios."

With that, Frankie shifted confidently back into her romance hypothesis. "It's a man. There has got to be a man in there somewhere."

"I hope you don't find that reassuring."

"None of it is reassuring, so I'm on my way down there."

"Do you really feel up to it?" I worried. She liked the cross-country, the speed and the spills, and undoubtedly she was aiming for the party that evening.

"Better than I did last night. I had such a big dose Tuesday."

"Have you managed to get the name of that drug yet?" Charlie demanded. He had a healthy suspicion of the drug trial Frankie participated in. It wasn't that he suspected Hugh Vaughn's procedure, he suspected her slippery grasp of the facts Hugh had presented. As Frankie's self-appointed advocate, Charlie challenged her at any opportunity.

"He told me what the stuff was, Charlie, but I didn't write it down—some oxy-moxy kind of name."

"Look, you are taking some huge risks," Charlie argued with the phone, making his usual points. "You don't know if you're getting a placebo or if you're getting oxy-moxy. This could have serious consequences."

"The main one being that I might live." She laughed. "What time does your horse go?"

2

When we arrived at the grounds, the competitors' lot had not yet filled up, and we found Alex still giving Exit Laughing his bath. Soaking wet, the horse was the color of his skin, a dark pewter. The muscles in his hindquarters and shoulders and the taut tendons in his front legs stood out in high relief. Oh, I really did love this body. He was a running and jumping machine. Nothing about him needed a supplement. Fit for the day, and he might possibly outrun those 43.6 penalties if Alex could ride the course.

Stephen was the groom in name only, as his sole connection to the gray horse was a leather lead strap. My stepson was a brilliant guy, intuitive with machines and anything that came in waves—light, sound, electricity—but his primary qualification for the task at hand was adoration. Charlie clapped him on the back. "Everything in hand? And Alex, how are you holding up?"

"Fine, Mr. Reidermann," she said a little too firmly. She didn't want to be scrutinized. "Absolutely fine." She didn't look away from the hose.

"We met Lourdes and your uncle Vicente at the diner."

Alex became vigilant. "She's not here now, is she?"

"Not yet. She's gone shopping for some more appropriate footgear."

Stephen grinned. "Cool."

He had no competition jitters. He was content just to be in the company of the tiny Latina. I wondered if Alex appreciated the commitment expressed in the simple fact of Stephen's putting himself near her, at the other end of a lead strap where he could be useful. I wondered if she saw what I had seen the night before, the love he expressed this way.

I knew about this kind of love because I had learned it from Stephen, and it had calmed so much of the turmoil in me. Although my preoccupation with the horses kept me from being an obvious candidate for motherhood, I had longed with every cell in my body to be a mother. I longed, and I grieved through my first two marriages to have a child. I imagined this child as a baby. I would hold the warm little body, and it would cling to mine. This happy idea caused rages. It drove the men I lived with away from me. After Elledge left me the first time, I was on my own for three years, moping and sulking, and furious with him not only for leaving me but for removing any conventional opportunity to become pregnant.

Frankie was the patient witness of all this. In spite of her sensuous nature and appearance, Frankie was always the more practical of us and downright rational. In fact, with the exception of Charlie, she was the most rational person I knew.

At that time people drank at lunch, and I was sniffling over a Bloody Mary in a restaurant that had dark wood panels and the kind of waiters who lurked near the table in case you wiggled your finger at one of them or dropped your fork when Frankie gave me the obvious antidote for my grief. "You should adopt."

"They won't accept me."

"Who? An adoption agency? Tink, how can you be so timid?" She was always the one Bloody Mary. I always had two. She was the luxury of auburn hair and ruffled white collar that dipped dangerously toward her navel. I was the blond with the stub of a ponytail, silk slacks, and an aqua sweater I thought respectable enough to get me in the place.

"They'll go after my lifestyle. You know that."

"The divorces," she assumed, since she'd had two of these herself.

"No, the horses, Frankie."

"What?"

"Well, it is an obsession."

"Balderdash. If I were approaching an adoption agency, I would talk about my *commitment*—that's a word social workers will like. Talk to them about commitment."

Frankie knew how to get what she wanted, she saw no reason why she shouldn't have what she wanted, and once she got it, she was satisfied with it, even though on occasion it turned out to be very bad for her. What's more, she saw no reason why I shouldn't have what I wanted. "You have such a good mind," I told her. "You really should go into business."

"Well," she said, "I am an investor." Although Frankie had married for romantic reasons and not with the motive of profit, she had made money from her unions, and she'd managed to make these earnings grow. In spite of one spectacular instance in her relations with men that put her life in danger, she didn't give up on romance. She was still alert to the faintest whiff of attraction. She loved men, but now, paradoxically, she was also financially independent of them.

Commitment was a bright idea that shed hope on everything around me, for about two weeks. Then Elledge was back, with the toddler Stephen in tow.

When he came to live with me, Stephen was the child of another woman and just two years old. At the time, it was unusual for a father to be granted custody of a child. Elledge told me early in our re-run romance that Stephen's mother had an appetite for street drugs, and she had been bouncing from one chic rehab facility to another until he finally gave up on her. Stephen was just starting to talk, and I worried that he didn't know or didn't understand what had happened to his mother and that he might resent me as the interloper who deposed his mama, the witch who magically disappeared her. I watched for this, but Stephen accepted me matter-of-factly, the way he had accepted the women Elledge had paid to look after him during his mother's long absences. When it became clear to him that I wouldn't go home at the end of the day and that he could wake me up for help in the middle of the night, he began to climb up onto my lap with a proprietary air.

"You're pretty important around here," I told him after a yea or so when he could talk more easily. "Especially to me."

"I know," he said.

"Even though I'm not your real mother." It seemed like I'd ha to wait a long time to bring this up.

"I know that." His head was bent over a wing nut he was add ing to his erector set structure, and his tawny mop of hair floppe forward. He wasn't about to be distracted.

"Do you miss your real mom?"

"She has a hole in her arm," he informed me.

After what seemed an all-too-brief period of snuggling and l sitting, he was thrilled when four years later he turned seven a I gave him free run of the garage and the farm shop and all t tools in them. I didn't know any better because that was the w I had been raised. As long as I behaved in a civilized manner a went along to school, I was allowed to pursue whatever I want

to pursue. I was allowed to find out what I was good at—which was horses.

Stephen had a streak of the mad inventor in him, but at the same time he was entirely trustworthy and, even though he was in every other way very much a child, very capable. He showed me the time of my life. When he ate nothing but peanut butter sandwiches and Jell-O, I ate peanut butter and Jell-O. When he graduated to bologna, I graduated to bologna.

He was tinkering in the shop when his daddy's girlfriend pulled into our drive in a derelict Volkswagen with her little boy, smaller and younger than Stephen. He didn't know the woman, but he must have sensed who she was because Elledge and I were beginning to have rows about her and the others like her. She left the car running, the door open, and came looking for me, teetering over the lawn toward the barn in high heels. Nine-year-old Stephen went over to her car and turned off the engine, then stood by. She had gorgeous dark curls and red eyes with streaks of mascara under them. She also had no money and a very sick kid. She couldn't find Elledge. She had to find somebody, had to get help for the kid. I pulled the saddle off the horse I was getting ready to ride, put him back in his stall, and washed my hands at the spigot in the barn. "I'm not very presentable, but let's go."

Stephen watched us crossing the lawn together, and having sized up the situation, now sized up the old car and the kid stretched out full of fever on the backseat. "Better take your car," he advised, because he had no intention of being left behind and no intention of riding to the hospital in a car that seemed like a potential breakdown. He rode in the backseat of my station wagon with the sick child's feet in his lap, and I have been taking his advice ever since.

When Elledge actually left, for the second time and for good,

I was distraught. There was a terrible fight, so terrible that now it hurts me to think about how hard I fought and how hard he fought. It is possible that while he was furiously folding his clothes and Stephen's clothes and grabbing books that I suggested I might kill him. This was an idea with no means of execution because Elledge had already removed his cherished skeet shooting guns to the new woman's place. I went to the barn so that I wouldn't have to actually see him leave. The business of departing seemed to take hours, but then his car turned out of the drive. Elledge and Stephen were gone.

I cried. I screamed. I called Frankie and bawled on the phone. "Hold on, sweetie. You just hold on. I'm on my way over."

"No, Frankie. No. I can't have anybody see me in this shape. I can't have anybody else remember me this way."

It was only seven in the evening, but I went upstairs, closed the bedroom door, put myself to bed, and wept some more. I have never felt so alone, so completely abandoned. Then I heard something on the stairs. I shut up so I could hear better. It was a clumping accompanied by a kind of slithering sound. The doorknob turned, and Stephen let himself in, dragging a sleeping bag to a position parallel to the foot of the bed. I had no idea he was still in the house. He had come in a package deal with Elledge, and I had assumed that when Elledge left, Stephen would go with him. But the little boy put himself near me. "We got a cot?"

His trust was why I resented the fact that Alex seemed oblivious to his devotion. Maybe it was just that she grew shy with him around Charlie and me, maybe it was just the generation barrier. Whatever the reason, she didn't appear to return his adoration. I didn't actually know that she didn't return it. But I suspected she didn't, and I resented even this suspicion. If she did anything to hurt him, I decided, I would cheerfully do physical damage to her charming little body. Or, better yet, take my horse away from her. But in the meantime I had to support her—was this what it is to be a mother-in-law?

Charlie was looking over the chart he had made on the back of his program. "We are standing sixth."

Alex aimed the hose low on the horse's leg. "I know."

"Ten point eight penalties out of first."

"I know." She shut off the water. Charlie was starting to bug her.

"And we have only three points on the horse behind ours."

"I know, Mr. Reidermann," she moaned. "I read the scores."

The public address system rescued Alex by squalling my name through the stable area. "Leticia Elledge. Leticia Elledge. Please come to the secretary's office."

"Damn." The paperwork necessary for these competitions was getting more and more intricate, but I was sure my forms were in order. In fact, Alex, who had a better knack for paperwork, had gone over them with me.

"Tink." The announcer came back more familiarly, more insistent. "We need to see you at the secretary's office."

"Okay, okay." I couldn't believe there was any urgency about this, whatever it was.

Charlie took leave of Alex with a friendly swat of his program. "Just trying to help, kiddo."

We headed across the field behind the stables toward the secretary's office, innocent of what awaited us there. The grass was still wet, and the thin layer of fog that lay over the field and the woods beyond it was penetrated in patches by sunlight. Grooms and riders were finalizing equipment on the horses first in the order of go. Paul Lamoreaux went to his veterinary truck to drive out to his post at the vet box, the holding point for the horses after they galloped home from the cross-country fences. As he pulled out, strains of Mozart from the truck's sound system wafted back to us.

The day was accelerating toward the moment the first horse and rider would gallop away from the start box. The order of go would unfold in three-minute intervals. The entry was big, and horses would run all day. Each horse and rider had his or her moment in the order. It was a ceremony of anticipation, and the horses seemed to share in it. Exit Laughing wouldn't start until midafternoon, but the horses running early in the schedule had begun to leave the stables in intermittent ones and twos, heading out through wisps of fog toward the start box. This was situated on a rise just beyond the level area where the dressage arenas had been set up and where now all that remained of them were the paths worn by horses traveling the patterns of their tests. In the wake of the horses on the way to the start were their grooms and well-wishers. The meadow was alive with keen horses and the colors of the riders' polo shirts. The horses were walking now, but they were wound up and expectant. Their pace would pick up until they reached the cross-country course. Then all you would be able to hear besides the loudspeaker calling the progress of the horses would be the rhythm of galloping. This is the beat that would drive the day.

Charlie and I followed along after the horses, musing appreciatively on these early entries. Although I knew many of the riders and the horses Charlie and I walked among, there were also many I didn't know. Once a sport of cognoscenti, people with money enough and tracts of land large enough to provide a cross-country course, eventing was changing. It had grown now to include more kids, more people who went to jobs on weekdays, and—most telling—more commercial interests. The horses were coming from parts of the country I'd never been to, farms I'd never visited. Now the professionals hired help, and the help was often

Latino—Mexican, Columbian, Guatemalan—men who made it through the border. As I headed across the grounds on foot with Charlie, these newcomers seemed to speed past me into the future. A horse and rider came up from behind, passed us, and left me with a sense of diminishment. I was a bystander, a drab bystander on cross-country day when color entered the competition.

"It's going to be different, Charlie. Very, *very* different." I meant eventing, but he thought I was referring to my life.

"Did you expect to ride forever?" he said gently.

We stepped into the little building where the secretary worked. The walls were hung with full-color posters advertising earlier years of the event, and one of them featured a photo of me taken only two years earlier. I was jumping a big brown mare. The two of us were airborne, heading over a stone wall into the pond beyond it. The horse flew in perfect form, her legs coiled tight against her body, and I, my own legs and form, didn't look bad either. I admired the image sadly. I wanted my place back.

Charlie touched my elbow, and the woman who was the official secretary indicated a place behind the counter at the back of the room where there was a card table and a couple of chairs. "Over there, Tink."

I saw the man's dark gray suit, and then the badge flopped out. Lieutenant Thomas Shaddaux. I read the name carefully, wondering just how he pronounced it, and for one hysterical moment found the trooper's name terribly funny, a cop named Shadow.

But when he announced his name "Lieutenant Shaddaux," he made it rhyme with mattocks.

The lieutenant, a tall guy whose careful Ivy League haircut betrayed too much scalp, had a serious, penetrating gaze that would wipe away anybody's smile. The expression was to make it clear to anyone that he was no dummy. Unfortunately, his shoes

gave him away. Plain, black, and shiny. Clearly the lieutenant had no idea what he might step in here.

"I'd like to talk about Patty McLaren, Mrs. Elledge. Some routine questions." For some reason he felt he had to say this last, and I wondered if it was a lie.

He indicated a couple of chairs.

"What about Charlie? Can he stay?"

Charlie obediently stepped up and extended his hand. "Charles Reidermann. I'm Tink's husband."

The leveling gaze moved to Charlie. "No problem."

I waited for what would come out of his mouth next. But it was what you might expect. How did I know Patty and how long had I known her? What was the relationship between Patty and Joe? What was the relationship between Patty and Win? These were questions he could have asked almost any of the experienced competitors at the event. Why was he posing them to me?

"What about Alejandra Delgado? What is her connection to Guthrie?"

Fortunately, a rider came to the counter with a scheduling problem. This kept the secretary with her back to us and the telephone line busy.

I looked to Charlie. He said, "Win has been Alex's teacher."

"Anything else?"

Charlie shrugged. "We don't know."

Then the lieutenant came up with a peculiar one. "Do you give your horses anything to supplement their feed?"

"I hope you don't expect me to answer that." No one who kept competition horses would have.

"Why else would I have asked?"

I clammed up righteously. I had no intention of telling him anything about the regimes in my stable.

"Tink," Charlie intervened. "He's not going to try to use anything that you tell him."

"He could tell the next rider he calls in here."

"Mrs. Elledge, I am asking for this information to forward an investigation."

"I don't give a rat's ass. I wouldn't tell you if you were the FEI."

The lieutenant mistook the federation's initials for those of our government's national intelligence unit. "It is possible," he pointed out, "that if this turns into a kidnapping or a murder investigation, you will be asked to do just that."

"F-E-I," Charlie interpolated, "Fédération Equestre Internationale."

"Oh." The detective wasn't much impressed, and he glanced at his watch, annoyed at my delay. "Okay, Mrs. Elledge. How about this? If you will let me get on with a few more questions, I'll guarantee confidentiality as to other horse people."

I nodded sullenly.

"What do you know about Vet Essentials?"

"I use some of their stuff—a liniment, one of the ointments, and they have a pretty good poultice."

"How do you get these things?"

"Mail order. I get together with some friends to make a group order."

"And how about a supplement from another outfit, Mighty Fit?"

"Don't use it."

"Why not?"

"Exercise is what I use to keep my horses fit, and I just don't see any substitute for that."

"Mrs. Elledge, in the past six months you have signed six times as the recipient of eight cases of Mighty Fit." The lieutenant fixed on me calmly. He thought he was on to something.

"Yes, I did. But, as I told you, I don't use the stuff."

"Maybe you could explain what you do with it," he suggested.

"The shipments come to me," I could not figure out what the supplement had to do with Patty's disappearance, "because there is not likely to be anyone at the girls' apartment to sign for them."

"The girls?"

"Patty and Alex."

"Mrs. Elledge, what happens to the boxes you sign for?"

"They sit on my back porch," and the next part of my answer was making me nervous, "until somebody picks them up."

"Somebody?"

"Usually Alex. She delivers them to some of the local horse people."

"Why?"

I didn't understand this—why what?

"Why this particular supplement? Why not use a supplement that's generally available in this country?"

Charlie could answer this one. "Because it's *not* generally available—which gives the stuff caché, makes it something you have to be in the know to get—and trainers are always looking for something to make them look like they know more than the next guy."

The lieutenant seemed to accept that, but he persisted. "Why Alex?"

I answered with the obvious. "Her family makes the stuff," and Charlie said, "She's essentially their U.S. distributor."

"Who are her customers?"

I gave him the names of the four stables I knew. But there were others.

"You didn't mention Guthrie."

"Oh right. Alex delivers some there, but Win doesn't use it either. Thinks it's snake oil, just like I do. Alex leaves it at Win's for Patty to take to Jason."

"Tomlinson?"

"I think it's a scheme the girls worked out, you know, so Patty had a legitimate errand to take her over to Jason's."

"And why is that?" The man's seriousness was impenetrable. Infatuation was not in his vocabulary, and so it appeared to be necessary to spell out this novel idea.

"Patty was sweet on—"

"Tink, we don't know that," Charlie interrupted. "We know who picked up the cartons. But we have no real information other than that."

The detective gave Charlie a thoughtful look and checked his notes. "The report on the truck accident that killed Joe Terrell mentions that you were at the scene."

"That's true."

"Have you ever done business with Joe Terrell?"

"Well, sure, I have. Everybody has—I mean, not actually with Joe but with Win. You know, bought horses, sold horses."

"Did you ever pay Joe Terrell," the lieutenant insisted, "to do any work for you, to run any errands?"

"Lieutenant, you have to understand. Joe Terrell worked for Win Guthrie. He wouldn't have taken a dime from any of us. That's the way it was."

"Okay. That'll be all for the moment, Mrs. Elledge. Is there a phone number for you or Mr. Reidermann if I need to reach you?"

Maybe I should have written down the number for Charlie's cell phone, but I wanted to keep the lieutenant at a distance. So I told him the name of our hotel, and he gave me his card. When we left the secretary's building, the October sun was higher and had warmed the frost off the grass in places. Charlie seemed a little agitated, slapping his leg lightly with his program as he walked. I wondered if this indicated he was annoyed with me.

"Charlie, why do I feel like I did something wrong?"

"You did," he said. "That remark about Patty and Jason. You can't pass gossip and intuition to the police."

"I didn't think that was what I was doing," I said lamely, but I had no future in any argument with him on ethics. Like facts, right and wrong were absolutes, and he was right. I could have unwittingly implicated Jason, and this made me uncomfortable and guilty. To bring trouble to Jason was not something I wanted to do. Although I thought he had got where he was awfully fast, I liked him. He was a dedicated keeper of horses, always polite, and for a person his age, considerate.

I didn't agree with Stephen that Jason was slippery. What Stephen thought was slippery I thought came with the territory of making your living from horses. You have to play your cards close to your chest, because the way you make a living is by selling horses, and you can't sell a horse if you talk too much. A horse can make a lie out of every word you say, including *and* and *but*—and that lie will multiply because the horse world is hardwired for gossip.

Charlie and I headed back toward the stables. I replayed our conversation with the detective, trying to tease out some implication.

"Did you get the impression that guy Shaddaux thought I had something to do with Joe's accident?"

"Couldn't tell." Charlie had been wondering about the same thing.

"I got the idea he was trying to connect me to the accident and Patty's disappearance. Did it seem that way to you?"

"Maybe. But maybe it's just one guy's hypothesis. If it's not," Charlie pointed out, "Shaddaux gave us a lot more information than we gave him."

"Right," I said, even though I didn't quite see what he was getting at.

"We know that they think Mighty Fit has something to do with what's going on with Patty. And we can assume they will question everybody who has received a bottle of it."

Jason Tomlinson was starting out from the stables on his first ride of the day, a dark brown animal I didn't recognize. It wasn't at all unusual for a rider, especially a professional, to be entered on more than one horse, and of course, the more horses you can qualify and enter, the more chances you have to win. I didn't have that luxury. All my luck that day would run in just one horse. Jason's brown horse was fresh and surging ahead of its groom, a dark-haired boy in his late teens who was trying to say something to Tomlinson. Jason's fair young face ducked near the horse's neck so that he could hear. There was a kind of electricity between the two young men. It jolted me into an unsettling realization.

"You're right," I told Charlie. He didn't ask about what. He had seen the same evidence I had. Jason had no interest in a young woman, and that was understood by everyone in his generation, all the kids, as I thought of them. They just hadn't bothered to clue us in. "So why was it necessary for Patty to be the one to take the supplement to Jason's place?"

Charlie didn't have an answer. He said, "Maybe it wasn't necessary."

Back at the stables we found cross-country day running like clockwork without any help from me. Exit Laughing was now a very clean horse hanging his gleaming head over the door of his stall. Alex and Stephen were putting away buckets and scrapers, about to go off in search of breakfast.

"Any problem?" Alex asked.

"No, just the usual mix-and-match signatures." I didn't want to turn her mind to anything to do with Patty because the police had already quizzed her, and talking through it all again would just stir her up. Also, I did not yet understand her role or even if she had one. It seemed improbable that Alex had willingly brought harm to Patty, but I was convinced she had information she wasn't sharing, and I had a hunch it was the same with Win.

Charlie brought a deck chair out of the tack stall and settled with his back against the stable wall like a sentry. He would patiently wait out the five hours before Exit Laughing set out on the cross-country course. He was content to just sit and wait, keep company with Stephen and Alex until the first cross-country scores were posted. This is exactly what he always did when I was the one competing. But now it made me impatient.

I ducked into the tack stall, away from direct observation. Alex's purse sat on top of the tack trunk waiting to be hauled off to one of the food tents. She had not fully closed the zipper across the top of the bag, and a couple of keys protruded through the opening. Moving quietly, I pulled the ring of keys out of the purse, pocketed them, and left the zipper gap the same size so that my theft wouldn't be noticed.

"I guess you don't want to walk out to see some of these early horses go," I suggested to Charlie.

"Not yet."

I calculated the amount of time he might allow for me to make it around the four miles of the course, moseying from fence to fence and watching a few horses attempt each one. It would take about the same time as I would need to check out both places, Win's and Patty's. I gave myself a little extra. "Why don't I meet you back here in two hours?"

I didn't see any point in trying to coax him to come along with me. If he knew where I was going, he would try to stop me, say it was none of my business. Whoever's business it was, the business of Patty McLaren seemed pretty urgent—and of course, if Charlie hadn't grounded me, I wouldn't have had this time on my hands.

3

The apartment Alex shared with Patty was about twenty-five miles from the event grounds on a triangle between Win's place and mine, in Chester Mills, one of the many small towns connected by sprawl to the outskirts of Philadelphia. Win's place would come up first. I drove the Mercedes slowly through a couple of lines of parked cars in the competitors' lot, trying to appear unhurried to anyone who might see me leaving the grounds. Just Tink, out for ice, maybe, and beer for the lull while the cross-country rides finished up. But I was in a hurry and calculated my route to avoid any malls, which would draw Saturday traffic. Thirty minutes to Win's, then ten minutes to the girls' apartment, and thirty-five minutes back to the event. That would leave me a little bit of time to look around both places.

Turning in Win's long drive, I slowed the car again and drove past the tall house, past the building called the old barn, and then parked by the stables because I didn't want anyone to see my car outside Win's house. I would have been more uncomfortable about going into Win's house without him knowing about it if my confidence in him hadn't been shaken. Charlie's very reasoned questions about Win and Patty and my almost automatic questions about why the shipment of a valuable horse had been interrupted by its death made me very much aware that over the years the incorruptible Win may have changed. Still, I knew that revisiting his house could bring my own past toppling down on me.

It seemed odd that the place Win's horses stayed was deserted. But there was no one there, and the horses left home from the event had been turned out into the paddocks that backed up to the stable and arena, where there was plenty of grass to keep them busy. Whoever had moved the horses outdoors was nowhere in sight. That was good. Before I went on to the house, I made a cursory inspection of the stables, where the only evidence of Patty I found was in the tack room—a saddle too small to accommodate Win's long legs. I walked quickly along the drive, pausing only a moment or two to poke my head into the door of the old barn, the place Joe Terrell had called "my office." It looked exactly as it had when Joe was working there, an expanse of wide, aged floorboards, two long, heavy workbenches outfitted with a couple of vises and a tidy array of tools, and drums of lubricants stowed along the wall. There was no point in examining any of this close up, because I didn't know enough about the tools or how Joe used them to recognize if anything was awry.

Win's old house was a different case entirely. I knew it well, too well, and knew what I was looking for there. It made me feel bad that I needed to be looking for it, because under ordinary circumstances, I wouldn't have bothered to investigate who was sleeping with Win. I would have hoped that whoever that was made him happy. I headed for the glassed-in porch at the back of the house. Win never locked the house, and no one ever came in the front door. Right away, as soon as I stepped inside, I found something. The porch was an afterthought attached to the back wall of the house to shelter the back door and then enclosed. It was unheated and used as a mudroom. On the floor along the house wall there were plastic trays where boots in various states of repair and with various loads of mud tumbled together, and above them harness pegs served as coat hooks. The boots and jackets filled the porch with the odors of horses, and almost all of them looked to be Win's size—except for a bright blue jacket hanging on the peg nearest the back door. It belonged, unmistakably, to a woman. Evidently Win wasn't living there alone. Maybe another woman was succeeding where I had failed, and in a way I hoped that was the case. Nobody needs to be lonely. I sighed and let myself into the house.

Other than the blue jacket on the harness peg, the only thing about the house that surprised me on my brisk tour of it was how remarkably unchanged it was. In rooms this sparsely furnished even a small alteration, say a shift in the position of a chair or the addition of a wastebasket, would have been immediately obvious. But in the kitchen, the toaster with its customary load of crumbs held the same position on the counter where every morning Win and I, numbly awake in the dawn, nearly collided, and in the upstairs bedrooms, only Win's bed was made up. Sheets and blankets but no bedspread. Except for the absence of dust, which when I had stayed there had sifted out of the air to film every surface, Win's house was exactly the same as it had been more than sixteen years before. I felt guilty for showing myself around his house when he wasn't there and even more guilty about the fact that I was relieved I no longer stayed there. I hadn't trusted Win enough to be happy with him, and I wasn't sure I trusted him now.

The upstairs probably wouldn't yield any more information, and I didn't want to waste time confirming that. But if another woman were, in fact, living here, there should be some trace of her. Maybe she left some things in the house's only bathroom, maybe lotion or mascara or birth control pills. When country people modernized their houses in the 1930s, they often consolidated their plumbing efforts, and the door to the bathroom was just off the kitchen. On my way through the hall leading from the stairs to the kitchen, I was startled by the sound, quite loud and near, of a toilet flushing. I came to a dead stop. The bathroom door opened. The young woman who emerged was quite short, and the man's T-shirt she wore revealed the plump roll of her body above her waist. She had a wide soft face and thick dark hair cut in uneven lengths. She considered me briefly. My heart was knocking, but she didn't seem at all surprised to find herself with me, a stranger. She said, "Hi, Tink. I give you a scare?"

"A little," I admitted, further rattled by the fact that she seemed to know who I was.

"Nobody ever knocks here," she observed. "You movin' back in here or you just lookin' for Win?"

"Looking for Win." I agreed because that seemed closest to the truth. Who in hell *was* this?

"He's gone with the horses this weekend." The girl's bright blue eyes landed on me with a knowing gaze. There was something too familiar in this. But I couldn't tell whether it was sinister or not.

"Oh right," I said carefully, even though she had me truly off balance. She had seen me, and she knew my name. My pulse sped on. "I should have figured that."

"It's the only time I come, when he's off with the horses someplace. I can get in here and beat back the dust without walking around him." She grinned, showing a black molar among her upper teeth. "That way, when he gets home the place looks good—good as it can. It's my job like the other jobs Win gets me. But you know, no curtains, no cushions, no spreads on the beds, nothin' on the walls. Home sweet home—and I can't make much of a difference." She laughed and started into the kitchen, evidently headed for the back door along with me. Before she opened the door, she turned to me pertly. "You know where that girl has got to, Tink?"

I was flabbergasted, speechless.

"Didn't think so," the young woman agreed with herself. "I sure don't, and that's what I told the police."

"The police," I repeated numbly.

"They was just here, a little while before you come to the house. I wished you had been here by then, because it made me nervous, you know? But I kept tellin' 'em I didn't know anything because that was all I had to say. You think I did right, Tink?"

"Absolutely," I said. "Absolutely." Because that was all I had to say.

Once on the back porch, she took the blue jacket off its harness peg, and I saw the flash of something precious, a gem or glass, on her hand as she zipped it—an odd counterpoint to her T-shirt. "This morning I had to put them horses out in their little fields too, 'cause Win don't have the horse help he needs, and he says he knows I can still manage 'em—and they were good," she advised. "None of them gave me any trouble."

I registered this because it meant that there was no one else at Win's place to have seen me there, and if I was lucky, maybe this strange girl wouldn't remember to say anything to Win about it. When she closed the porch door behind us, I realized she didn't have a car. "My car is up by the stables," I offered even though I knew I couldn't spare the time. "Can I give you a lift?"

"Naw. Thanks, Tink." She waved me off good-naturedly. "Take me longer to walk up there than to get home." She ducked through the backyard, cut across the corner of the hayfield next to it, and disappeared in the blue jacket. Something about seeing the girl walk across the short stretch of that hayfield, that particular field, almost triggered a memory. But I was too unsettled from my encounter with her—too stirred up by trespassing on Win's place, so familiar and yet now so alien—to summon up whatever memory might have been lingering in some recess of my mind.

I had spent more time than I had planned at Win's, had a weird chance meeting with someone I didn't know but who knew me, and turned up nothing. I hustled back to the Mercedes, and when I drove out, with no one there to see me leave, didn't bother to try to hide the fact that I was in a hurry.

The main street of Chester Mills was smugly upscale, the storefronts freshly renovated, and the coffee shops offered espresso. Alex had a job in the city doing market research for a big ad agency, and the girls' apartment was a convenient way station between her work and her hours with the horses. It was above a posh dress shop, a bright loft with a sanded wood floor. A wide curving stair with a dark ornate banister led from the foyer up to the apartment door, and on my way up, I sorted speculatively through the keys on Alex's ring. I decided on one but had no time to try it before the door opened on its own. I was face to face with the detective in the dark suit, the person I'd given a hard time in the event secretary's office. It was a jolt, as if I had bumped into an electric fence, the second jolt that morning. I hadn't been caught at anything the way I had been caught snooping through Win's house, but I felt like I had. My presence on the stairs was perfectly legitimate, and if Thomas Shaddaux thought there was anything questionable about his presence in the apartment, he didn't betray this.

"Hello." I meant for this to seem pleasant, but probably my irritation at finding him in my way was all too evident.

"On a mission?" He didn't mean for this to sound pleasant,

just authoritative. But couldn't I have been asking him the same question?

"Gloves," I lied. "What about you—" and I noticed a checkbook in his hand.

"I have a warrant," he explained.

"But Alex might need that," I protested about the checkbook. I would have protested anything he wanted to remove from the apartment. But he in his gleaming shoes was at least one step ahead of me. "I will inform Ms. Delgado of anything of hers that I actually remove from here. This isn't hers."

He hadn't finished in the apartment. He had come to the door because he had heard me on the stairs. I had to get past him. Over his shoulder I could see the desk where her computer sat. The computer was on, and one of the desk drawers was open. I saw my spot.

"I have to get back quickly." I tapped the big dial of my sports watch. "Okay if I just come in and get the gloves?"

He stepped aside to let me into the room. Obviously I was supposed to know where the gloves would be. I remembered the jacket Alex wore when she came to exercise the horse, and I passed the computer on my way to the closet door. What was on the screen was a list of e-mails. Beside the machine on the desk were some horse magazines and—I registered this—a bride's magazine. I couldn't help myself. I reached for the magazine and leafed through it quickly until I became aware that Shaddaux was regarding me quizzically.

"She is, I guess you would call it dating, my stepson," I explained. "I had no idea whether she was serious, but I guess this means she must be, don't you think?"

"Or maybe," he suggested, "she's just thinking about a wedding, any wedding."

The open desk drawers held the usual clutter but no records or writings of any sort. He had in his hand the best information to be had from the apartment. I put the magazine down, located the jacket in the closet, and in one of the pockets found a pair of gloves. They weren't of the quality used in competition, but I didn't expect the detective to notice this. I held the pair up as verification. "See you."

He nodded. "Maybe."

He no longer considered me a source of useful fact. I gave the apartment one last look-see and wondered how the scene would affect Layton McLaren when he saw it.

"Sooner or later," I suggested, "Patty's dad will get here."

He didn't comment one way or the other but responded with an odd, uncomfortable look.

"So," I concluded brightly, "see you. Don't forget to lock up when you leave."

I returned to the stables to find the scene much as it had been when I made off with the keys, except that with horses returning from the cross-country course as well as leaving for the start, equine traffic had doubled—and this increase in activity made it suddenly evident how oddly quiet the shed row opposite ours was. Win Guthrie's stables usually drew as many well-heeled fans and friends as the FEI would allow. Not today. Win's solitary Latino groom moved from the horses to the tack and feed stalls without dodging the usual onlookers. Just doing the business of competition. Patty's disappearance was a public question now, and people wanted to distance themselves, as the politicians say, from Win.

Charlie was sitting exactly where I had left him and had progressed through the newspaper to the financial section.

Beside him in another lawn chair was Frankie Golden, fiddling with a switch on her video camera. Charlie looked up, barely registering my presence before his eyes dropped back to the paper. But Frankie appraised me curiously.

"Where have you been, sweetie?"

Fortunately there was no way to answer because I was smothered in her lacy green mohair sweater and the lemony scent of Chanel. Her camera bag thumped gently against my side. Wreathed in green silk to cover the chemo damage, her creamy face was ornamented by a heavy sprinkling of freckles. Her body swelled gently under the sweater. She was a ripe, humorous person. I always said she was the most beautiful person I knew, and she always said, "Just keep sayin' it, sweetie."

I had said it often over the past year during the ordeals of her cancer treatment, and who looking at her now could know there was anything in the world threatening her?

"Oh, good," I said about the object of her attention in her lap. "You brought the video."

"And what other excuse do I have for coming here—the lost girl, maybe?"

Stephen and Alex had Exit Laughing out of his stall. The horse stood patiently with one foot lifted so that steel studs could be screwed into his horseshoes, and while Frankie bent close to watch this operation, I ducked into our makeshift tack room. Alex's purse had been returned to the top of the tack trunk. I slipped the keys back through the opening in the zipper and noticed a small blue notebook there. It was dog-eared from much handling.

Without reflecting on what I was doing, I pilfered her purse a second time and leafed hurriedly through the little notebook. This was what—or part of what—Shaddaux and I were looking for. I saw enough to verify that. Alex had recorded each shipment of Mighty Fit, listing each case according to its lot number and its destination, and her accounting for the cases appeared to add up to the total shipment. She delivered to most of the farms and left three cartons at Win's for Patty to deliver. I put the notebook back in the purse. I didn't like what this implied about Alex, and following it through to its logical conclusion, I recoiled from the pain it would cause Stephen.

It was almost two, an hour and a half before Exit Laughing would start into the cross-country test. When I emerged from the tack stall, Alex was twisting in the studs on the last shoe. Either this girl had absolutely nothing to hide or she was a very cool hand. If she was hiding something—knowledge, connections, or perhaps her own involvement in Patty's disappearance—whatever she was hiding would devastate Stephen. Somehow I had to get her to explain the notebook and its contents to me.

"Frankie," I announced, "I'm heading out to the start."

She shouldered her camera bag.

"Charlie?"

He barely stirred.

"I would like you to come with us." I made this as pointed as I dared. He folded the newspaper.

"Okay."

4

The cross-country was running full throttle now, and occasionally we had to pause for horses coming and going to the start. The stylish impression Frankie made with the heathery green mohair and rusty corduroy held only down to the point at which her heavy socks and hiking boots took over. She walked along looking over Charlie's shoulder at the scores written on the last page of his program.

"That dressage, Tink!" she exclaimed cheerfully. "Alex is going to have to run and jump like hell to leave that score behind."

My mind was still churning over the numbers I'd seen in Alex's notebook. I said, "You won't be surprised to find out I took a little sightseeing tour."

Neither of them was.

I told them about what went on at Win's place and at the girls' apartment, and Frankie said, "You sure you don't know that girl at Win's?" Frankie pressed.

I wasn't, but I said, "How could I have forgotten someone that strange? Besides," I countered, "she won't see Win to tell him I came into the house until Monday, at the very soonest. But

Shaddaux—he'll figure out why I was at the girls' apartment. Hopefully, that will be later rather than sooner."

Charlie and Frankie accepted that at face value, and I came finally to the notebook in Alex's purse. "I feel like I've seen something I shouldn't have seen."

"You have," Charlie said. "But the notebook might not be important. All it indicates is that Alex was a kind of bookkeeper."

"Which could," Frankie pointed out, "implicate Alex if the detective is really on to something with the supplement deliveries."

"We can't do anything that might upset Alex until Exit Laughing runs," I said hastily. "But what about Stephen? Shouldn't he know that Alex might be involved? I mean, how can we let him be blindsided?"

Charlie took a moment to consider this. "How can we do anything else?"

"I know. If I try to clue him in and Alex is innocent, then I look like a jealous bitch."

"If she *is* involved, you still look like a jealous bitch," Frankie pointed out, "because either way you're putting him in a position where he has to keep a secret from Alex."

"Right. So now what? I need to get Alex to show me the notebook but act like I don't know it exists."

"You need to get her to show it to Shaddaux. This isn't your investigation." But Charlie's reminder was as much for himself as for me because he was as compelled to find out what was going on as I was.

"No." I considered this only fleetingly. "Of course not, but I—"

"Just tell her what happened this morning at the secretary's office, ask her what she knows that could help the police. She will bring out the notebook—if not, we'll go to Shaddaux."

"Charlie," I could not relinquish the need to work this out for myself, "all the farms where Alex made deliveries got more or less the same size shipment, if you factor in the number of horses at each farm. But the cartons that went to Win's place for Patty to deliver to Jason? It was three times as much per horse as what the other stables got. Win doesn't use it. So Patty delivers all three cartons to Jason. But I'll bet Jason can't use it up in triple doses. So what does he do with the rest of the shipment?"

Neither of them responded, but whatever was running through Charlie's mind made him pick up speed—not something he does readily. We crested the hill that overlooked the start box and the busier scene in the nearby vet box. The start box wasn't a box at all. It was a small open-ended corral fenced by sturdy uprights and a single top plank along each of its three sides. The horses launched out of the open side for the twenty-some obstacles on the course. The vet box wasn't a box either, just a holding area cordoned off with crowd-control tape that was used for the veterinary examination of the hot and blowing horses after they galloped home from the big obstacles in the cross-country test. A horse who came away from that effort exhausted or who just didn't recover from it quickly enough would get a long, hard look from Paul Lamoreaux and his crew. The vets might ask the rider to retire the horse from the competition. Fitness reigned.

The start box was empty for the moment, and we moved down the hill closer to the vet box to watch the activity there. The grooms pulled saddles off hot horses, perspiring riders hunched over bottled water, the veterinary crew milled about with stethoscopes and clipboards, and a couple of austere tweed presences emitting authority oversaw all this. We could hear a horse galloping down to a fence somewhere behind us. Charlie had been trying to put it all together. He said, "The truck fire wasn't an accident, and it had nothing to do with Joe Terrell."

Another horse passed closer, pounding rhythmically.

"Somebody was after Patty?"

"Seems that way," Charlie said, "because that supplement never passed through Joe's hands."

Frankie lifted the videocam and was scanning the scene in the vet box. She said, "Who's that?"

It was Lourdes, waving from behind the rope on the opposite side of the vet box. Vicente was at her side. They now wore jeans and boots. Her jeans were designer, and on top she wore a bright orange boiled wool jacket. Except for the creases in Vicente's new jeans jacket, the two of them looked like they belonged there.

Although Frankie could be relied on to catch good video and she knew how to hold a horse and when to remind you to take the studs out of the horse's shoes after the cross-country, her idea of a three-day event was a party, a party mixed in somehow with sport. Now she saw her spot, and without waiting for Charlie and me, she set off for the Mexican delegation, greeted them exuberantly, and struck up a conversation. Charlie and I followed along smartly.

"Frankie speaks Spanish?" he asked.

"Second husband," I explained. "He was in the State Department, and she went to parties all over South America with him. You remember. He was the nut I told you about. When they recalled him to the States, his load shifted"—I tapped my temple—"he went way off. Spanish and some big bruises were what she got out of that deal. But it could come in handy," I said, looking significantly at the elegant little woman with Frankie.

"The Spanish, not the bruises," Charlie said. He thought I was always trying to run too much by too fast.

When we joined the visitors, the two of us made warm noises in English. There were four horses in various stages of recovery stalking the grass in the vet box. Ned Burlingame's horse was headed by one of his students, a teenage boy receiving instruction from the vet team, and a tall girl from the West Coast worked at cross-purposes with her mother trying to get cold water on a hyper-fit chestnut everybody was talking about—a great expense of water and not much on the chestnut.

Jason Tomlinson's dark brown horse came off the course, and his young groom met them and got busy. Really busy. The brown horse would need plenty of cooling out. His neck was wet with the clear, clean sweat of a fit horse, and this darkened his flank. In the meantime, outside the vet box, not far from the start box, Hugh was holding The Flying Tiger, who had yet to start. Jason held the brown horse's head while his groom pulled off the saddle, ducked under the crowd control tape and out of the vet box, and transferred the saddle to The Flying Tiger. Then he returned to the brown horse to take over. It was a Chinese fire drill. Hanging from the boy's belt was something familiar, a grayed-out towel with the initials LTS in frayed embroidery. My tea towel was making the usual rounds among the grooms. Evidently Win's groom had handed it off to somebody, but why would Jason or his groom need a favor from Win?

I stole a glance at Lourdes's feet. The heavy-treaded nylon lace-ups had that brand-new sneaker look. "Much better," I assured her. "Now you'll still be able to walk at dinnertime and maybe even dance afterward." She smiled bashfully, her mascara-laden lashes fluttering at the mention of the homely shoes. Homely was not something she was accustomed to. I could imagine the stack of designer luggage rolling ahead of her at the airport. A few yards off, Charlie had joined her brother-in-law to explain the proceedings in the vet box. There was something about Vicente that made me uneasy. He was so watchful, and he attempted English only to talk to Charlie, as if I weren't capable of speech or thought. Also, there was the way he hovered near Lourdes. Wasn't he her *brother-in-law*, for Christ's sake?

Jason had left his groom in the vet box to finish with the brown horse and was mounting Hugh's horse when Win Guthrie rode into the holding area on Secret Formula. The black mare was blowing but decidedly not winded. Win swung off, and the Latino fumbled with the girth to loosen it and struggled to get a cooler blanket over the mare. Probably the first time the man had tried to do this.

I turned my attention to Barbara Beecher, a longtime but friendly rival who had just come off the course on a gawky-looking buckskin horse. A perfect mount for Ichabod Crane, he sauntered into the vet box without drawing a long breath. Win's attention was also caught by this unlikely looking animal. He was sizing up the buckskin when his substitute groom lifted the cooler covering Secret Formula to try to remove the saddle.

That effort unleashed a bizarre event. The black mare sprang up as if from sharp pain and fell, crashing over on her side. The astonished groom stood with his hands raised as if he were trying to catch a pass, and Win, seeing the saddle as the cause of the problem, dove for it, pushing the groom aside. "Stay at her head, Ruben!" he snapped.

Within moments the vets and officials had circled the prostrate horse. I couldn't see what they did or even if they did anything. But I kept watching, and after a minute or two the horse was up on all fours again. She shook herself vigorously, and Win barked an order at the Latino, who led the mare in a tentative circle to see if she could stay on her feet. As the big man turned, I noticed a red line running from the corner of his mouth down toward his jowl. It was a cut fresh enough to smear. Probably didn't know enough yet to keep his head away from the horse's head. You can really get clobbered if you're in the way when a horse jerks its head up. I felt sorry for him and his bewilderment. That was all that crossed my mind.

As the groom retreated with Secret Formula, Win was arguing with one of the vets, a young woman with dark bobbed hair. She was holding something in the palm of her hand. Paul Lamoreaux, who had been at the other end of the vet box and too far from Win's mare to get a close view of the incident, stood by listening and looking uncomfortable.

Dr. Helena Morgenstern, the senior FEI official at the competition, the technical delegate, interrupted the confrontation. She was a tall, svelte woman. As usual, she wore black—black blazer, black slacks—to set off the dramatic white streaks in her dark hair. Off-duty Helena was a fount of hilarious gossip. But she was on duty now, and her hair was pulled back into a severe chignon. Her humor was confined to a superior smile. She held out her hand and confiscated what the vet handed to her. Then she spoke briefly to Win. He tried to protest, but Dr. Morgenstern dismissed him. He walked away, shaking his head angrily, about to follow the mare and her groom back over the rise to the stables.

All of this was appalling—the horse's collapse, Win's apparent disqualification—and it was followed immediately by another equally appalling occurrence. Charlie, Charles Reidermann, who as my husband should have known better, ducked under the restraining tape, and strode over to confer briefly with Win. He left Win with an expression of blank amazement and then presented himself to Dr. Morgenstern. Dr. Helena Morgenstern, the technical delegate.

"What does he think he's doing?" I demanded of Frankie and Lourdes. But Frankie was no longer beside me, and I was speaking only to Lourdes. As soon as the black mare had thrown herself on the ground, Frankie had hopped up on the tailgate of Paul Lamoreaux's truck to train the videocam on the activity in the holding area.

"Charlie! Don't!" I squalled. "Get out of there!" He was speaking calmly to Dr. Morgenstern. Her head was lowered attentively, and her eyes were wide. She was incredulous, I discovered as soon as I reached the two of them. I could tell because her uppity smile failed momentarily. Charlie was still talking.

"So, you may choose to disqualify Mr. Guthrie and this particular entry, the black horse. But—given my interests as a representative of the company that owns Mr. Guthrie's two later entries—I want you to understand that you cannot bar Mr. Guthrie from riding those horses today."

Helena Morgenstern's jaw followed the direction of her wide gaze, and a defiant grin appeared. She was recovering herself. "The disposition of those entries, Mr. Reidermann," she feigned jocularity, "is at my discretion."

"Yes, of course," he agreed. "But only until your decision is challenged by litigation." Another horse burst out of the start box, galloping for the first fence.

"This is preposterous," she exclaimed, laughing softly.

"I know," I agreed and tugged at the sleeve of Charlie's jacket. "Come on, Charlie."

He shook me off, and Dr. Morgenstern finally responded. "Are you threatening me, Mr. Reidermann?"

"Absolutely not. I am just advising you of my company's course of action should you decide to proceed so unfairly."

"Then, Mr. Reidermann, would it be correct to call this simply a formal inquiry?"

"If that's what it needs to be," he said agreeably.

"You are aware that your protest must be accompanied by a fee of one hundred dollars?" Dr. Morgenstern bobbed her sleek head in the direction of a burly, red-faced man in a tweed driving cap. "You'll pay Mr. Samuels, the head of our Ground Jury."

Charlie reached into the pocket of his trousers for the roll of bills that always insulated his car keys there, peeled off two fifties, and strode over to the man in the cap before returning to Dr. Morgenstern.

Her mouth was still closed in a tight line. She wanted the last word, and speaking not to Charlie but to those close enough to catch her slightly raised voice, she said, "Some people would protest the Second Coming."

I too resented the speed with which he paid up. Would he have done that for a horse of mine?

Dr. Morgenstern said, "I will give my decision directly to Mr. Guthrie."

"Yes." Charlie never dropped his politeness. "And please do so at least one hour in advance of his next start time."

I slunk from the vet box behind him. I couldn't understand what I had just seen and heard. My mind simply would not yield to what apparently were the facts. Charlie crossed the grassy lot with as firm a stride as I ever saw him take. He was heading to where Win was standing, horseless now because his new groom had led Secret Formula away. The tall man looked quite vulnerable without a horse.

"They will give you a decision in writing," Charlie said gently. "An hour before your next start time. However, if I were you, I would go ahead and get the next horse ready to ride."

How could it be that Charlie could be the owner and the sponsor of not one but two horses Win Guthrie was competing? His disloyalty hit me broadside. He who had just agreed we were done with secrets. It unnerved me. I folded my arms to hide the shaking of my hands. For some reason, I was still walking beside Charlie.

When she saw us coming, Frankie passed the videocam down to Lourdes and jumped down from the truck's tailgate. "Did you see that?" she demanded.

"Oh yeah," I said, "the whole goddamned thing."

"It was just like mine!"

What was she talking about? I was too rattled to wonder what had actually happened when Secret Formula came into the vet box.

"Just like mine," and Frankie put her hand on her breast as if she were about to recite the Pledge of Allegiance. Lourdes gazed at Frankie in wonderment.

"They took something off the horse," Charlie explained, ignoring the fact that he had something more important to explain to me.

"It was a patch," Frankie declared. Charlie reached for the videocam and squinted into the viewer to watch the playback. After a moment he said, "Yup," and passed the camera to me as if his connections to Win and his thrashing horse were to be expected.

I tried to get a grip on myself and keep Frankie's replay steady. By standing on the tailgate, Frankie had managed to shoot over all the shoulders in the knot of people who had blocked our view of the incident. Here was Win filling the frame as he dove at the mare to unbuckle the girth, stripped away the saddle, and then peeled something away from the cupped place where the back of the horse's front leg met its chest. He looked numbly at the thing resting in his palm. Dr. Morgenstern extended her hand like a mother insisting that a child spit out his gum, and there it was in her palm, a round, flesh-colored Band-Aid like the ones Frankie wore.

Now Lourdes, caught up in the excitement, wanted to see, and Vicente was hurrying toward us for an explanation. I fingered the lookalike patch still crumpled in the pocket of my khakis, the one Charlie and I had found when we walked the course the day before.

"Why would anyone give a horse the stuff I'm taking?" Frankie wondered.

"The patch is just a delivery system," Charlie pointed out calmly, as if we should all have expected what he had just revealed about himself, as if his disloyalty were not shocking. "We don't know what 'stuff' it was delivering."

The videocam passed from Lourdes to Vicente, who watched the discovery of the patch and gave Charlie a troubled look. Mild-mannered Charlie. Standing there as if nothing about him should surprise anyone. It was not to be believed.

Frankie reached out to touch my elbow, which was still locked against my chest. "Are you all right?"

I knew my face was red. At the moment, Charlie's betrayal was trumping everything else—the patch still in my pocket, the one in Helena Morgenstern's pocket—and for a few instants it even trumped my concerns about Patty and Alex. I turned away, as if I were heading out on the course, but Frankie and Lourdes followed.

I tried to pretend there was some purpose to my turning away from the men and tapped my watch, trying to indicate that I was about to part company with the two of them. Lourdes followed along after me without comment. But I could tell from the concern in her gaze that she noticed the tears leaking from my eyes. I didn't want that to happen. I didn't want to bawl, but as we walked away from the vet and start boxes and followed the track toward the early part of the course, drops of liquid seemed to be rolling down my face.

"What's going on?" Frankie demanded when she caught up to us.

"Charlie never told me about those other horses—please tell Lourdes I'm sorry, and I know how foolish this must seem—I had no idea."

"What other horses?"

"He owns two of the horses that Win is riding."

"Not the one that just collapsed?"

"No, a chestnut mare Win's running next and a bay gelding . . . he never said a goddamn word."

Frankie recognized the transgression in this, but after a moment she tried to reveal its bright aspect. "Look, Tink. It's not like it's another woman."

Cold consolation. But now Lourdes, bless her imperial Latin heart, was patting my arm with a Kleenex, trying to comfort me, trying to help me pull myself back together. Which was something I really had to do, the sooner the better. I had a horse, a very good, possibly great horse, starting the test in a half hour. I couldn't undermine Exit Laughing and Alex, not to mention Stephen, by showing up at the start blubbering. I patted Lourdes's back and mopped my face with her Kleenex.

"There is an explanation," Frankie said flatly. "I'm sure there is a very good and probably a very obvious explanation. Let me talk to Charlie."

"Don't you dare." I was trying to control my sniffling. "I'm going to be talking to my lawyer."

Lourdes's head came up watchfully. Maybe she actually understood quite a bit of English.

We passed Number 1 decked with its bright flowers and stopped a hundred yards behind it, slightly uphill from the vet box and the start.

"*Elegante,*" Lourdes said, and I thought she meant all the yellow mums. But she meant the plain bay horse lifting into the air over the ramp full of flowers. The horse and rider thundered past within a few yards of us. Lourdes didn't step back. She wasn't intimidated, she was fascinated.

"*Elegante.*" Lourdes looked away from the horse to me. "You are generous then toward Alejandra—is it because you are too old to ride so fast?"

I couldn't hold such an honest question against her. "I had an episode," I began to explain, slowly so that she could follow, and Frankie said, "Okay if I just tell her what happened?"

In Spanish her explanation seemed to take a long time. I couldn't tell which parts she was leaving in and which she was cutting from the account.

Lourdes nodded thoughtfully. I appreciated her concern and found myself liking this woman in spite of the touch of imperiousness in her manner. I had been afraid that she might get in my way, foul things up for Exit Laughing. But she gave no sign of that. She was a good sport and polite enough not to mention it if she found me a little crazy.

Frankie shifted the camera bag strap on her shoulder. "This isn't the best place for me to shoot. Lourdes and I will be at the Water. Where will you be?"

I stopped to think about this. Exit Laughing would travel the four miles of the course and jump the twenty-one fences in about eight minutes, and there would be no way for me to watch him at more than a couple of series of obstacles.

"I want to see the Palisade and as soon as he clears that, I'll hustle down to the Water."

"Number 14 all the way to 18? You are going to have to burn your buns to do both," Frankie advised. "But I'll have video of the splashdown if you don't make it in time." The two of them left me and turned east toward the two ponds that made up the water complex.

There were still forty minutes before Exit Laughing's start, and it seemed early for Stephen to be leaving the stables. But here he came from the opposite direction, heading toward the vet box, where he would meet Alex and Exit Laughing when they came off the course. He wore an assortment of tack and was carrying a couple of buckets. A lead strap in his hand was slapping against his leg in time with his stride, a hint of agitation.

"Ma. Something bothering you?"

"Charlie. I am furious with Charlie."

He didn't respond to this. He said, "You and Charlie know something."

It wasn't a question, so I didn't try to answer it. But Stephen could read me more accurately than anybody.

"You find out what happened to Patty?" he suggested.

"No. I don't think anyone knows." I was relieved to be able to be truthful, but I was dreading the questions that might come next because I could not lie to him.

His next interrogation, however, didn't come in the form of a question. "There's something creepy about him."

"About who, Stephen?"

"That guy Vicente," he explained as if that were obvious, as if there was only one other man on the grounds. "I mean the way he just hangs. Know what I mean? And is all over Alex's mom."

"Like a bodyguard," I agreed.

"He can speak English," Stephen pointed out, "but only to Charlie—and Jason. He went over to check out Jason's horses this morning. He thinks the rest of us are deaf mutes."

"Jason. How would he know Jason?"

He shrugged. "That Latino guy who works for Win was there with them. Little chitchat and Vicente was back looking for Lourdes. But she is clueless."

"About what, Stephen?" I had found Lourdes quite observant.

"Him. Vicente. That dude wants to have everything under control. Know what I mean?"

"Not really. What does Alex think about him?"

"Just says, 'He's my uncle,'" Stephen answered. "She's just as clueless."

So Vicente was suspect. Lourdes and Alex weren't.

"I doubt he has anything to do with what's going on with Patty," I pointed out.

He looked at me a little sideways. "Do you *know* that?"

He was fishing. I said nothing because I was wondering if he knew about the little notebook Alex kept.

He seemed to take my silence at face value. "Okay, Ma. You can't talk," he said and didn't seem to hold that against me. But I couldn't stand being so guarded with him.

"You're right," I said. "I can't talk. I don't want to say something that might come between you and Alex. I don't want you to be hurt."

"By what?" he demanded. "Alex? Ma, I know I don't know what I'm doing. I'll be the first one to say that. I'm going to make mistakes, because I don't understand girls—women. I don't understand what making love means to them or even to me. But how else am I going to be with somebody if I just don't just try it and make my mistakes?"

I was touched that he would still tell me his thoughts, and I didn't see what was coming next.

"Look at you, Ma."

"My mistakes?"

"Yeah, and all to do with love and making it and whatever. You have cried a lot."

"I know." It wasn't criticism, so there was no point in trying to defend myself.

"And Frankie," he said, honing his point. "As cool a person as she is and still screwing around. Probably she's going to keep sleeping with all these men until she stops making mistakes—and if *she's* still making them, still getting hurt, what makes you think I should get by without getting hurt?"

"You're grown up," I concluded. "More grown up than I am. But I can't tell you anything right now. Later."

He skipped into a jog, ponytail and lead strap flapping, and delivered a parting remark over his shoulder. He was twenty yards off before I took in what he said: "Charlie was right to do what he did, Ma."

"Shit," I said miserably. Obviously, if he knew about Charlie's confrontation with the technical delegate, everybody at the event knew about it, and soon the horse world at large would hear of it.

Still troubled, I headed out alone to the high midpoint of the course, where the Palisade poised at a tipsy angle at the edge of the Gulley. Maybe it was more than Charlie's defection. Maybe the terrible thrashing spasm that knocked Win's mare to the ground. Maybe there was something surrounding this competition that was larger and more dangerous than any of the fences on the course. Maybe something with violent potential that I couldn't put a shape to.

Win Guthrie, riding a red chestnut mare named IthinkIcan, galloped up to the stockade pickets hiding the big drop. She was one of the horses owned in some mysterious way by Charlie. The mare launched, dropped down into the creek bed, leapt over the fence on the opposite side of the draw, and ran on. She and Win were having quite a good go when—if Charlie hadn't spoken up for Win—she might have been left back in her stall to munch on hay. It didn't add up. Why had Charlie done that? Why had Win been involved in something as dirty as drugging? He had changed—all of us change over the years—but had he changed that much? Win was never what anyone would call idealistic, never a romantic about horses. He had been practical and unrelentingly honest. Had he become cynical enough to undermine a partner who had worked so hard, given him so much, and was a wonderful horse? The episode in the vet box belied everything I thought I knew about Win. But maybe it was possible. After all, hadn't I had two husbands turn into men I no longer recognized?

Coming next was another chestnut horse, this one piloted by the girl from the West Coast. The horse ran up to and catapulted over the stockade pickets, but scrambled on the drop and dodged the next fence on the uphill violently enough to leave the girl at the edge of the field on the other side of the ravine while he circled back in the direction of the start box. The girl didn't get up, just rolled over on her back, and within moments whistles sounded all over the cross-country course. All new action on course ceased. While Win and Ithinkican cleared the last four fences, the officials held back the horses waiting to start, and an ambulance pulled up across the ravine. The EMTs brought out a backboard and stretcher.

In his confusion, the loose horse had turned back toward the scene of his crime and was galloping up my side of the ravine toward me, reins and stirrups flapping. At the sight of me walking down the hill toward him, the whites of the chestnut's eyes flashed. He slid to a halt and spun on his hindquarters to retrace his path. Then, seeing a man trotting purposefully up from behind, the horse spun again and came to a quivering standstill.

It was Win's stand-in groom, Ruben, running up on the chestnut. If left alone, the horse might have figured out he was lost and dropped his head to graze, at which point I could have easily caught him. But the trembling animal was being charged from behind, alarmed by loud orders in Spanish, and he bolted. I was in the dead center of his path. If you have ever heard that old saw that a horse will do anything to avoid running over a human, don't act on it. Any horse that is worried or scared enough will gladly trample you. Which is why I scrambled to get out of the chestnut's flight path. But he caught me with his shoulder, and I spun off into the ground.

For a moment I lay on my back, stunned and rattled and taking inventory of my arms and legs, my head, and my back.

"*Lo siento!*" Ruben's large, square face peered down at me anxiously. The deep scratch near his jaw had been wiped clean and even at this close range was hardly noticeable. "*Lo siento?*"

He was afraid. I wasn't. I knew I was all right. But this man, who needed his job to be able to stay in the U.S., couldn't afford to be involved in my accident. And he was. I hauled myself off the ground to avoid being the object of his wide eyes.

"Never. Never," I was trying not to shout, "run up like that on a loose horse!" He stared, uncomprehending. I turned away from him to catch up to the chestnut, but his rider, risen from her stretcher like the phoenix itself, limped up out of the Gulley and reached her horse before I could.

"Just knocked the wind out of me," she explained as she untangled the reins. This is what most event riders will tell you after emerging from a few minutes of unconsciousness.

"Yeah, me too." I needed to get back to my post at the Palisade to watch Exit Laughing take that fence.

But Win's new man had taken my spot there and, along with it, the best view of the fence. He was watching me, and for some reason I didn't feel I could simply go up to stand next to him. So I took a parallel vantage point from the other side of the fence on the edge of the Gulley. Ruben's study of me, or rather my feet, continued. It was something beyond curiosity. He stuck there, stubborn as a tick on a terrier. Every time I attempted to meet his gaze, he responded with a big, mechanical smile. Did he think I had caused Win's problems? I was uncomfortable, but I was also damned if I would abandon my post until I had seen how Exit Laughing would take this fence. Our meet 'em–greet 'em with a fake smile continued until it suddenly dawned on me that this man was not where he should be.

"Win's horse has already gone through," I said. "He needs you at the vet box. Is someone else managing that?"

Big smile, but he didn't move off. Maybe the problem was his English. He didn't understand that Win would be expecting him. I didn't look away. He stared, I stood, and I wondered if he felt threatened by me. That would be his problem. I kept my place until Hugh Vaughn materialized next to me.

"Yours is next up," he reported. Then noticing the grass stains on the back of my shirt, said, "What happened to you?"

"Loose horse."

He nodded and, with no apparent cause, glanced over at the Latino.

Down at the start of the course I could see Stephen and Exit Laughing with Alex perched up on him lightly. My gray horse sauntered along at Stephen's shoulder toward the start box. With only one horse going, we had no need for a hired groom. That was the way it used to be for everybody. You'd get a friend or somebody in the family to help out. Exit Laughing knew that soon he would be going much faster. He knew he would be allowed to gallop, but he, savvy animal, seemed to be conserving himself. His head was low, the reins swung loose along his neck, and he carried Alex as if she were weightless.

This is the way every horse should start. Relaxed, with everything about him speaking of power. Power to spare, power in reserve. "Looks like he's taking a nap, doesn't he?" I said admiringly, and Hugh beamed agreeably.

A minute later the start. The announcer called the progress of Alex and Exit Laughing. They put the fences in the first part of the course behind them quickly, flying Number 8, then 9, 10 too rapidly for the announcer to catch up to the action. Now Exit Laughing surged up the hill toward the Palisade. His petite pilot set him up for the stockade. He lifted off. Her braid swung. His landing gear came down deftly, catching up the momentum, propelling him down to the stream at the bottom, up the other side of the ravine, over the fence, and out. This matter-of-fact performance dispelled any possibility of danger at the fence.

"Textbook," Hugh commented. "Just the way it was meant to be jumped."

Alex was giving him a good ride. Leaving Hugh with Win's groom, I hurried on past the other spectators, traveling the course, then taking a shortcut through a narrow strip of woods, hoping to make it to the Water before my horse did.

I broke into a jog to keep up with Exit Laughing's progress and then a run. But I got to the second pond and its log fences only in time to see gray hindquarters flashing over the last log and up the hill toward the finish.

"*Maravillosa! Maravillosa!*" Lourdes was popping up and down, alternately clapping her hands and clasping herself in excitement. She grabbed me around the neck in a fierce little hug and pounded her diamond-studded fist into my shoulder. "*Maravillosa!*"

Frankie switched off the video camera and interpreted Lourdes's continuing explanations. "She can't believe her Alejandra is such a wonderful rider. Such a wonderful rider."

Lourdes was still chattering. Frankie listened.

"She wants to see more fences, and she wants to come to the next event."

Mother's blood-thirst. I had seen it before when Stephen was on the high school varsity wrestling team. With mothers in the audience, it became a gladiator sport. The sweetest, most dedicated maternal spirits in the gym would squall savage encouragement—"That's it, hon. Get his shoulder down! Go for his neck!" Now Lourdes forgot any possible injuries that Alex might incur. She had a taste of the fences, and she could see the win.

The remaining fences on the course would come up too fast for us to see Exit Laughing clear them. We would have to hustle even to see him come off the course and into the vet box. We hurried back in that direction and listened for the announcer's call of the action at the fences.

There was a hand on my arm. Charlie had been watching the horses from the far side of the Water complex, and he had come up from behind to catch me by the elbow. He was trying to slow me down. "Tink, could I have a word?"

"Just one?" I didn't slow my pace. "I'd like to throw the whole goddamned slang dictionary at you."

"No doubt you could. Now slow down. I need to talk this over with you. In private."

"You, sir—Sir Flasher of Fifties!" I stormed on a few strides ahead of the three of them.

"You and Lourdes go on ahead, please," Charlie instructed Frankie. "I need to chat with Tink about this inquiry business."

"Yes, get that straightened out, Charlie." Frankie was practical as usual. Drawing me out of my snit would let everybody relax a little. "There's no point in having bad feelings over a couple of horses."

So I was trapped into having this out with Charlie. We watched the two women heading up the first of the hills between us and the vet box.

"I owe you an explanation, Tink," he said to my back. "And I'm sorry you don't trust me even enough to allow me to make one."

It irritated me that Charlie was such a gentleman, but he caught up and walked beside me as if there were no trouble between us. This was a way he had of keeping the lid on things, a trick I'll bet he picked up in one of his big-deal meetings. He had figured out that if you put yourself very close to someone who is about to blow up, that smothers the spark.

"Tink, you are too quick-tempered," Charlie said. "Haven't we been together long enough for you to give me the benefit of the doubt? Have I ever been untrustworthy?" If he was trying to shame me, he was succeeding. "I do not own those horses Win competes."

"Then why did you say you did?"

"I do not own them personally, and I do not personally pay Win anything to support them."

"Did you *lie* to the technical delegate?"

"I am on the board of directors of Halefellow Corporation."

"I know that."

"Bear with me now. Halefellow is the holding company that owns the Zircon Group."

"Which owns and sponsors those horses for Win. Why didn't you just say so, Charlie? Would it be too *dangerous* for you to let me know anything about where your money comes from?"

"An error of course." He used the eventing term for straying from the pattern of a dressage movement. "A simple error of course. And I'm sorry. I tried to say that last night, and I'm still sorry."

I said nothing.

"But I didn't *know* Zircon was sponsoring those horses until I read it in the program when we arrived. Then when I realized the horses were going to be eliminated from the running unfairly, I felt I had to interfere. Do you think I was right?"

I had to think about that. "I guess so, Charlie. But Dr. Morgenstern thought you were out of your goddamn gourd."

"I knew that she would back down," he said, "and Win would ride the other two."

"But maybe he doesn't deserve to ride." The patch on Secret Formula was not easily explained. I couldn't reconcile it with what I thought I knew about Win Guthrie—but then I was beginning to wonder what it was possible to know about any man. "I mean, what kind of drug was he giving that mare?"

"He wasn't."

"You think somebody else put that patch on her?"

Charlie thought this was too obvious to answer.

"Why? Just to put Win out of the running?" Then I answered myself. "That would be too easy. Just a little too simple."

"Yes, I think it would."

Too simple with no practical means of execution. The pace of cross-country day and the riders' and grooms' constant attentions to the horses would make it difficult for someone other than Win or his fumbling groom to administer a patch to that hidden place behind the horse's elbow.

As if he hadn't taken me by surprise enough for one day, Charlie reached for my hand. "There is something important I need to ask you for."

I found this alarming. I mean, there we were, stopped on the cross-country course in this awkward teenager pose. But I said, "Okay. Try me."

"Your trust—I'm serious, Tink. I'm finding this flap between us quite stressful."

My armor was sliding off, great plates of it falling around my feet. Charlie has such great eyes, and this is what snared me in the first place, his gaze. It had great warmth, and it was very accepting of anyone it fell on and their flaws and foolishness. Now I was in his gaze again, and to my embarrassment, he still had my hand. I felt sorry for what I had put him through, but I did feel he had set himself up for some of it.

"You keep secrets," I pointed out. "I don't. There's nothing you don't know about me. It's all right there, right up front."

He laughed. "True. True. I wanted to protect you."

"From what? The fact that all your business buddies tell their wives what's going on?"

"From yourself. I thought you would go through the money."

That stung. "What money? I've done my best to live within our means."

"You're a bad financial risk. You don't have a clue about money. I thought if you knew what we have, you'd go right through it."

"Or budge into your business and take it over?" Even though his assessment of my financial prowess was completely accurate, I would never have interfered with his dealings, much less tried to take control over any piece of it.

He nodded regretfully to acknowledge this reference to his first wife. "But," he put in quickly, "you have many great qualities that make up for that. You're very entertaining. Generous and affectionate . . ."

"So, Charlie," I rebutted. "*You* didn't trust *me*."

"I can fix that, but I can only fix it if you will continue to let me manage the finances."

"Manage," I said. "Manage away. But I would like to hear a little more about all those meetings and who you see there." I wasn't interested in handling the accounts, and as I so often explained to Frankie, keeping Charlie comfortable was more important.

"Deal." He put his arm around me, letting his hand rest in the small of my back.

"Deal," I said, which was really no concession at all, and we set off for the vet box again, listening for the announcer to call Exit Laughing's progress over the last fence.

When it came it carried the news that Exit Laughing had made it around the course without any jumping penalties.

Charlie was alight with the possibilities in the numbers. "You hear that? The horse went around clean!" He smashed his program with his careful columns of numbers affectionately against my shoulder. "What about the horse's time? Were you keeping a watch on her?"

I was, and while it was not likely to agree exactly with the official clock, it showed Exit Laughing to be very close to the time allowed. Every second over the time limit would add to Exit Laughing's penalties.

The path we took back along the cross-country course to the vet box was well traveled. Ned Burlingame was taking the same line as we were. He passed us, hustling right along to meet a student and horse in the start box. But then he paused and dipped down to pick up something from the grass.

"Know anything about these?" He handed Charlie the cell phone he had found and hurried on. He was a New England tightwad and wouldn't have bought into what he considered the cell phone fad.

"We can drop it off at the secretary's office," I suggested, but Charlie had already started playing with it—anything holding numbers was a fascination to him. "Should be able to find out whose this is," he muttered about the phone, which was as current as they come. Its metallic red case framed a dark rectangle of screen, which lit up when he found the on button, and he walked along watching the tiny screen instead of where he was going, pushing buttons on the keypad and getting beeps of various pitches in response. We crested the hill that overlooked the vet box and the start, and Charlie stopped.

"Recognize this number?" He held the phone up so I could see the digits.

"It's Alex's number. Where are you in that gizmo? What part of the menu? Let me see."

Charlie turned sideways to block my effort to take the phone but obligingly opened the speed-dial list. There she was, Patty McLaren, in the midst of a series of unknown names. Charlie continued scrolling, stopping at the name Guthrie, then at two numbers in Mexico.

"It's Alex's. This has got to be Alex's phone. And Patty had it on her!"

He nodded and stared thoughtfully back toward the stables, past the flat area where the dressage rings had been set up. "So what's this doing way out here?"

Patty had disappeared from Win's place. The phone lay on the ground twenty miles away. It was confounding.

"Any messages?"

"Nope."

"Look through Recent Calls."

He tapped some buttons and gazed at the little screen for a few moments longer and then shook his head. No names or numbers he recognized as hot links here. Nothing familiar. He closed the phone and put it in his pocket.

"We'll have to hand it over to Shaddaux," I said with a certain amount of resignation.

"Not until we've had a chance to talk with Alex."

"This isn't our investigation," I reminded him teasingly.

"No, it isn't." Charlie was heading toward the vet box, walking in that careful, backward list he used to go downhill. "But it wouldn't be very smart to hand over information before we know what it means for Alex—or us, for that matter—would it?"

Frankie and Lourdes had rounded up Vicente and were watching Alex and Stephen and my gray horse finish up in the vet box. Vicente stood with his hands in his pockets the way so many men stand at the track, looking over the entries going out to the post and sizing up their own chances. Lourdes was chattering excitedly to Vicente, and when he had a moment to turn to me with congratulations, he grinned and made a pantomime of striking his forehead in disbelief. Still not conversing with me, but not only had he seen the win, he had seen what a horse can do.

It was a heady moment, and when the vet crew had released

Exit Laughing our giddy entourage followed the horse back to the stable. Charlie and I were the only ones weighed down by the awareness of the cell phone in his pocket. Alex's family was jubilant. I could see there was no longer any danger they would ever prevent her from riding. The only danger was that they would want to be in attendance every time Exit Laughing left the start box.

As we turned the corner at the end of the shed row, Charlie touched my elbow, and I looked up just in time to see Thomas Shaddaux walking away from my horse and from Stephen and Alex, who had just started to cool the horse out. Stephen resumed walking with Exit Laughing but Alex remained motionless, staring after the cop. Her mother and uncle descended on her joyfully. She appeared bewildered, but she smiled and gave each of them a dutiful kiss. Charlie hung back watchfully. I think he was waiting to see if Alex would offer any information. But I couldn't do this. Congratulations were in order.

Alex was too distracted to listen. She glanced over at Vicente, who was pounding Stephen on the back. "You and Charlie, Tink. Can you—?" She bobbed her head toward the tack stall.

Frankie figured out that she wanted to see us privately, and she took the video camera over to distract Alex's family with footage of the ride. Alex and I receded into the tack stall where Charlie had intuitively staked out a position.

"It's Mighty Fit," she breathed, doubting it even as she said it.

"I—" I was going to say "I know," but Charlie's glare silenced me.

"A detective stopped me before I could even get off the horse. He took a little notebook I kept in my purse."

"Umm-*umm*," Charlie sympathized. "What was in it?"

"It's where I kept track of Mighty Fit shipments, who got what. And he told me they searched my apartment."

"I know." I was finally able to say it. Alex was representing herself honestly, why shouldn't Charlie and I come clean? I told her about my visit to the girls' apartment. "The detective who just questioned you inadvertently tipped off Charlie and me this morning."

"They think it's my family, don't they? That my family has something to do with Patty?"

"We don't know," Charlie said. "That might be a logical next step, but they could be considering others."

This was real news to me. "Why would that be logical, Charlie?"

"The Delgado family owns the company that makes the supplement, among other things."

"What other stuff?" Alex had a child's obliviousness about where the bread and butter came from. "How do you know that?"

"I was involved in a couple of meetings with Vicente. It's not a small company anymore, Alex."

This last fact seemed to make Alex miserable. She sat down on a tack trunk. "I took on that little job for them," she said helplessly. "I delivered those shipments."

"I received many of them," I pointed out. "And Patty always helped with these shipments, didn't she?"

"This is really scary. Really scary. Should I tell them? Try to get them to leave the country?"

"That would make you and them look guilty as sin," I pointed out.

"I am really scared," she said finally, but she was in fact calming down enough to think more strategically. "I have to explain this to Stephen somehow. I mean, what is he going to think of Vicente, of my mother? Of me?"

So she was, as Stephen had said, clueless. By delivering the Mighty Fit she had only been doing family business, nothing more. This was the second very positive event of the day, the first being a clean, fast cross-country round. I put my arm around her shoulder, and giving advice I never could have given myself, I said, "We need to stay cool. Figure out what we know for a fact, what we don't know."

Charlie listed gently backward to be able to look out the door of the tack stall and see the rest of our group. Except for Stephen, who was meandering lazily with my gray horse, they were still gathered around the video camera. They hadn't missed us yet, but within minutes they would start looking around. I had to get to the point.

"Alex, I noticed in your notebook that Patty always took three times as much Mighty Fit as you delivered to any of the other stables. Why was that?"

She looked nonplussed. "Well. There was Jason's place and Win's place."

"Win has never used supplements of any kind—and, you know, Joe always joked that the only supplement he himself ever used—the booze—nearly killed him."

Alex took this in carefully and shook her head. "Then I don't know. I don't know why she would take so much."

"Another thing. You recorded the lot numbers of each carton—"

"What is your cell phone number?" Charlie interrupted hastily. He handed her his own phone, what he called his tool-that-can-fix-anything, and instructed, "Dial it, please."

The phone in his pocket rang. She looked at the gadget he brought out of his pocket as if it were radioactive.

"Could I see?" Alex took the phone and began punching buttons. "Where did you find this?"

"Ned Burlingame picked it up about halfway between here and the start box. He didn't know the first thing about how to use it, so he handed it off to Charlie," I explained.

"Any messages?"

"Nope."

We watched over her shoulder as she worked expertly into the phone's programming and beeped down a list of phone numbers.

"Recent Calls," Charlie explained, and Alex began to recite the owners of the numbers she recognized. "Her dad—"

"The Chicago number?"

"Yup. Me. Win. Her mom. Don't know. Don't know. Her dad."

"Isn't that a lot of calls for someone her age to be making to her father?"

"Numero uno," Alex said briefly. "He is numero uno."

"Old Messages," I prompted because Charlie and I had listened to these. "Maybe there is an old message stored in voice mail."

She pounced on the idea, putting in the number hurriedly and waiting for a connection somewhere.

"Him! Dr. McLaren. Says don't send any more Mighty Fit." She stared at the little screen in bewilderment. "Why would he want any in the first place? The only horse he owns now was right here with Patty. What was in those three cartons?"

I cut off her question because I remembered the date stamp before the message. "He left that message right after Joe was killed."

She looked down at the phone like it was something distasteful and thrust it back to Charlie. There wasn't time to harvest all the information her phone was going to yield, but I had more questions for Alex.

"Alex. As soon as you and Stephen have settled the horse, meet us at our hotel."

"My family," Alex worried. The delegation from Mexico was staying at the other hotel, the expensive one.

"Let's not involve them, get them upset—just yet," Charlie said. "They're not in any danger, assuming they don't know any more than we do."

Frankie was replaying the videotape to keep her new friends

occupied, but now Lourdes and Vicente were waiting expectantly for Alex to emerge from the tack stall. We pulled Frankie away from them and promised to call and make arrangements to regroup for dinner.

"What is going on?" Frankie said quietly.

"We found the phone Patty was carrying."

Frankie examined the cell phone. "Anything on it?"

"Local calls, mostly to Win and Alex, a call to her mom, and several from her dad in Chicago—a doctor." I explained about the shipment of supplement made by the Delgados' company.

"This doctor keeps horses?" Frankie's question brought silence.

"Did you actually hear the message?" Frankie navigated through the menus and tucked the phone under her silk turban to her ear. "Not emotional," she reported, "Certainly not desperate. This guy isn't worried."

"Even so." Charlie saw that Frankie was entertaining the thought of keeping the phone or at least delaying its delivery. "We need to have a chat with the detective."

The three of us returned to our hotel and waited in the lobby for Stephen and Alex to follow us in from the event grounds. But before they arrived Thomas Shaddaux materialized as a large presence in the revolving door. At the sound of the door swishing open, Charlie, expecting the young people, turned to collide with Shaddaux's lapels. "Sorry," the two of them said in unison, and Shaddaux took a step back to straighten his suit jacket.

"This is convenient," he said.

"Very," Charlie came back instantly.

Shaddaux eyed Frankie cautiously. "I was coming to pay you and Mrs. Elledge—"

"I have something you need," Charlie interrupted, "and we were on our way up to our room to phone you about that."

Alex and Stephen appeared outside the glass doors, and after waiting outside for a moment to size up our little gathering with the cop, they joined us cautiously just as Charlie presented Alex's cell phone to Shaddaux.

"Alex owns this phone, but Patty was carrying it," he explained. "It was found in the field between the stables and vet box. Maybe fell out of somebody's pocket or purse."

Shaddaux appraised the item in his hand. "Found by you?"

"By Ned Burlingame, who gave it to me. He never bothered to learn how to work one of these things."

Shaddaux glanced over quickly to Frankie, then Alex and Stephen, trying to calculate what they knew about the phone. "But you know how to work this," he said to Charlie, "and I imagine you did just that."

"Sorry about the fingerprints," Charlie said. "There's an old message from Dr. McLaren still on the server."

"Not likely to have been planted," the lieutenant observed as he turned on the phone. He studied the message information and then listened thoughtfully. "Have you tried to phone Dr. McLaren?"

Charlie shook his head, and Shaddaux considered the five of us carefully, at length. No one spoke. He was weighing something, and when he broke the silence, he justified this by saying, "You'll see it on the news tonight anyway—Dr. McLaren is dead."

This brought another round of a different kind of silence, a stunned silence. Then I began stammering.

"Where?" I should have known better than to question Shaddaux. "I mean, how did—"

"Shh!" Frankie demanded so that Shaddaux could continue, and he obliged.

"A car fire," he told us. "On an interstate near Chicago. Activated by a cell phone—maybe this one right here." Evidently he wouldn't investigate that possibility just then. He pocketed the captured cell phone and said, "Thanks," which really meant, *So long.* He would have left the lobby with any further information, except that Alex stepped in front of him.

"Sir."

He waited.

"I need to speak to you about my family." Her voice was quavering. "Since you asked me a lot of questions about Mighty Fit, you may know that my family owns that company that makes it."

Shaddaux didn't indicate what he knew or what he didn't know, which I found infuriating. He was hoarding information, blessing those of us involved with only a sprinkling of fact, just as much as necessary to flush out more fact.

Stephen spoke up, louder, more insistent. "Her family is here at the competition."

Our pitched conversation in the lobby bothered Shaddaux. He looked around, and making a little sweeping motion with his hand to gather us together, led us a few yards down a hallway and into an empty function room.

Stephen held back until the double doors were closed behind us. "Alex is very worried that her family is in danger."

"And she wouldn't be very smart if she weren't," Charlie said to point out that the five of us had shared information, which I recited in outline.

"Joe Terrell. Patty McLaren. Dr. McLaren."

"Who is next?" Alex's words rushed out in sibilance. She was trying to keep her voice down. "And why aren't you doing anything about it? What about my family?"

"What about you?" Shaddaux came back calmly.

"I have nothing to do with what's happening."

"Really?" Shaddaux said neutrally. "Do they?"

"No!"

"Then why should they need protection?" His question seemed genuine, and he did seem concerned.

"Because whoever it is who killed Joe and Patty and Dr. McLaren could be closing in. And my family has the most money at stake. They have the deepest pocket."

"Ms. McLaren is still a missing person," he corrected her before he went on to consider the rest of her argument. It was clear he didn't know whether to trust Alex. "We know of nothing to implicate anyone in the family," he said carefully.

"You had nothing to implicate Patty or Dr. McLaren," Stephen pointed out. "Your ignorance didn't help them."

"Ask them to leave the country," Alex urged. "Or if you police can't do that, let me ask them."

Shaddaux certainly didn't like this last proposal. He shook his head and considered the pleat in his trousers, the shiny tips of his shoes, at length. "Ms. Delgado," he said finally, "would it put your mind at ease if we were to assign someone to keep an eye on your family while they're here in the area?"

"Yes," she said immediately.

A police guard for her family might have resolved the dilemma as far as Alex was concerned but not so far as I could see.

"Wait a minute, what about Alex? For Christ's sake, the way these guys were operating, isn't she the obvious one to protect? Wasn't she making the goddamn deliveries?"

"Right." Shaddaux snapped to. "Right, Mrs. Elledge." He should have seen this himself.

"Use my room for whomever you assign," Stephen offered, thereby informing me that he and Alex had not been sharing a bed, at least not while Alex's family was in town. I didn't know what the arrangements would have been otherwise, but I would have choked before I asked.

"We won't get in your way," Shaddaux assured Alex, who was

too surprised by the thought that she herself might be a target to worry about exactly how protection would take place.

"No suits," Stephen declared emphatically. This brought laughter from Shaddaux, the first evidence of any kind that he had a bone of humor in him. He left us with a bit of advice. "Stick together when you can. Makes it easier for us."

We trooped obediently into the elevator, in a group as per instructions, and as we watched the floor numbers light up, Charlie announced a decision. "Party."

Not being a competitor and not being able to free my mind of the murder investigations, I had completely forgotten about the competitors' party. It was a tradition on the night of the running of the cross-country, a kind of blowing off steam after surviving the perils of the course. It was de rigueur at any three-day, the only difference from event to event was the lavishness of the food and drink.

"We're going?" I wondered.

"Absolutely," Charlie said. "All of us."

"Good plan," Frankie commended Charlie when the elevator stopped at her floor. "Keep things normal and have some fun." She beckoned for me to get off with her.

She swiped the plastic key card in the lock, let the two of us into her room, and went directly to a bottle of makeup remover on the bathroom counter and just as directly to what she had on her mind. "There is a body. You sensed that. I know that now, and in spite of what Shaddaux says about 'missing person,' the only thing missing about Patty McLaren is her corpse—and I don't like the way this story is going, Tink."

I didn't have a chance to say "Is that my fault?" before Frankie resumed.

"You are involved." She was smiling brightly, which is something she did when what she said might be hard to take. "You are too involved." She returned her attention to the mirror, smiling at her image there. I didn't say anything.

"Someone is going to get hurt. You know that, don't you? Don't tell me you can't see it coming."

Too much crime fiction, I thought. But I hadn't said anything yet.

"Scares me shitless. I don't want it to be you, I don't want it to be Charlie, and I don't want it to be Stephen or Alex. I want this murder mystery to play out with all of us still in it."

"Okay," I said meekly. I was touched that she wanted to look out for me, that she thought she could.

"Just okay?" she demanded. "Fine. So don't take my advice."

"Frankie, I'm not . . . Charlie and I aren't—"

"Why do you think it is," she pressed further, "that I am even here to dish all this good sense?"

Because she had listened to me a decade earlier when I dished to her, because there was symmetry in our friendship.

"The gun in the wine rack?" I suggested. She nodded.

It was about ten years ago when Frankie had phoned me to beg off a tennis match, and I knew from her voice, from the way her inflection kept lifting, that she was lying the moment she made her excuse. "It's my period again, Tink. After all this time, and I'm just too miserable and mean to be around. Don't cancel the tennis, though. Angie will fill in for me."

I cancelled the match and drove to her place. It was a nice big house built in the twenties with a mansard roof, boxwoods crowding the edge of the yard, and a little concrete cherub balancing on his toe in the garden pool at the side of the house. The peonies were in bloom. Cupid in the posies, I thought grimly.

I let myself in the kitchen door and stepped into the hall by her pantry. "Frankie? No need to hide. I know you have marks on you."

After a few moments I heard her on the stair. "I'm not blind, and I don't have any other friends who wear makeup on their arms."

When she emerged in the kitchen I saw that it was her face this time. A bright red-blue blotch covered the freckles on her cheekbone. I closed her into my arms. "The thug. The fucking thug."

She didn't say anything.

"You've got to get out of here." But I felt her stiffen.

"I know it's your house, but you don't need to stay in it right now. You can win this some other way."

Frankie led me into the pantry.

"This isn't like you. You are a brave girl, Frankie, a lot braver than I am."

At first I didn't see the handgun for all the dark woodwork. I didn't expect to see a gun because it was not something—except for the ones worn by the embassy security guys—that could ever be found near her. The gun was lodged casually on top of the built-in wine rack, left there by her husband. It was a kind of threat, I suppose.

"This is going."

She still hadn't said a word.

"I don't care if it is his," I argued, carrying on the conversation alone. "What's he done to make you feel this way? I mean, this is going, lovey. Believe me, it and he are going."

I had lifted and fired a shotgun often enough to shoot skeet and once even used a rifle to put life and pain out of my beloved Sky Horse, who had cleared so many fences handily only to end up trapped and broken by the one around his pasture. But this was the first time I had closed my fingers around a revolver butt. I raised my hand and looked down the sight. "This is going first because Ted doesn't happen to be here."

But then he did happen to be there. His convertible pulled

past the kitchen door. He walked as confidently as if his entrance was about to be announced at a party, a reception, like it had been in his State Department days. I met big, blond, baby-faced Ted before he could get his hand on the doorknob. I was holding his gun in two hands. He looked innocently confused. "What?"

"You can't come back here."

I don't think he was frightened of the gun itself, just the way the nose of it was wandering. Frankie's bruises, his bland nonchalance, and my frightening willingness to fire the revolver had me riled up.

"You don't know how to use that," he said calmly. "The safety's on."

"Right." In my nervousness I had overlooked the catch. I fixed it and said, "If you think I can't use this, ask Elledge about my skeet shooting."

Whatever he believed, he knew he was too close to risk catching a wild shot.

"Okay, okay. I left my credit card case upstairs. That's why I came back. Can I just go up and—"

"No." Then I called out to Frankie. "Get him his toothbrush and one credit card. Be sure it's one that doesn't have your name on the account."

When Frankie handed it to me, I threw the card past his head and watched him turn and grovel for it.

Frankie hadn't believed there was anything truly dangerous about him. The first mark had just been something that happened, something she might have even caused to happen, she said. Just one isolated incident. But then there was another isolated incident. And on and on. But she couldn't recognize the pattern until I made her see it.

Maybe now I wasn't recognizing something dangerous.

"Right now," Frankie continued her lecture, "I can predict the way all this is going to end for us, maybe not for Alex's family but for us. We'll all be driving home Sunday evening. So don't do anything more, Tink, that might change the way this story goes. Just stay back behind the crowd-control tape and behave yourselves. You and Charlie. No more snooping around." She had reapplied the eyeliner and mascara. She dusted her nose with a little brush, and when she had the makeup right, she turned the beatific smile back on me. "So? Go to the party. Just like always. Have some fun."

5

It was good advice, and I probably intended to follow it. But in the time it took to close the door to Frankie's room behind me and walk to the elevator, I had put things together. Vicente, who was making and shipping the supplement. And Jason, lucky Jason with a corporate sponsorship. Of course. The two of them knew each other.

Then, when the elevator door opened, Stephen and Alex were inside, and I joined them. I had intended to head up, but the two of them were going down. He was on his way to the registration desk to arrange for another room, and she was on her way back to her family at the expensive hotel.

"Are they expecting you at any particular time?" I wondered.

"No. Why?"

There it was, plain as day, my spot. It was too tempting. Without even thinking about Frankie's parting instructions, I went for it. "We have an hour and a half before dinner," I said. Although the elevator door opened to the lobby, Alex and Stephen paused inside, not comprehending, until I motioned for them to follow.

"We have time for Alex and me to take a ride out to Jason's place."

Now Stephen saw my point. "See how much of the stuff is there?"

"We should take your car, Alex. After all, you could have a legitimate errand there. And Stephen, could you call Charlie and tell him I've gone with Alex? Don't lie, just don't say where we've gone. Let him make his own assumptions."

Stephen seemed to go along with this but he said, "Don't be long. Because then I will have to lie, and you don't want that. I'm lousy at it."

I'm sure this wasn't the first time Alex had entertained doubts about me, prospective mother-in-law, owner of the horse, or whatever I was to her. She didn't say anything, but she drove the little Mazda convertible looking ahead with serious purpose. Occasionally, her hand flicked back automatically to straighten her dark braid. She was pretty and little, and in her presence I was always aware of my own height, the heft of me, and the real size of my hands. In a half hour we turned the last corner before the short drive to Jason's barn, and she said, "What is the worst thing we could find here?"

"I don't know."

Jason's barn was a vast new building unattended by a house. It was not a home place. It was a business and a sign of the professionalism that was creeping into our sport. The metal siding was a conservative dark green, and there were new shrubs, like mall plantings, to soften the hulking outline of the barn. There was an apartment upstairs for Jason's avid young groom. But he was at the event, and there were no cars in the drive. Whoever was looking after the horses had gone home for the day. A benefit to us now.

"Better pull around behind the barn," I suggested. Back there the little convertible wouldn't attract attention from the road.

The back door was unlocked. It was rare that anyone locked a main barn entrance. There were too many people and horses who needed to come and go—this was why it had been so easy to deliver Mighty Fit. Alex led me up the broad aisle between the stalls to the tack room at the front of the building. "I bet this is where Patty usually left it." She tried the door. It was locked. But it had a safety-glass window, and in the dimness on the other side of the small panes, we could see a wall where the hooks and racks were mostly empty. The bridles and saddles had gone with Jason to the Brandywine.

Alex glanced over her shoulder guiltily, then pressed her face closer to the window and cupped her hands around it. "There are two on the floor," she reported. "Two cases just sitting there."

"Damn!" Then I remembered that hay bales were held together by a pair of wires. Once they were cut and the bale open, the wires were thrown away. I went to Jason's feed room, where the trash can yielded a number of lengths of used baling wire neatly bound up for a trip to the dump. I pulled one free. Alex looked worriedly toward the front door. "Patty McLaren—wherever you are—look at what you have got me into!"

I jimmied the wire in the door lock. "When we get this open, we don't turn on the light." A light in the window could be seen from the road. "If you have a flashlight in your car, that would be really handy."

By the time the tack room door swung open, Alex had returned with a flashlight. The beam played over a cardboard carton with a familiar shape. It hadn't been opened, but a hoof knife from one of the grooming caddies severed the strapping tape. What the open box flaps revealed were orderly rows of white, eighteen-ounce bottles capped with dark red plastic screw tops and held in position by cardboard dividers. Mighty Fit.

"This doesn't tell us anything we don't already know," Alex said.

"No," I agreed and drew out one of the bottles to take a closer look. I turned it under the flashlight beam.

"What's that?" Alex stopped my hand.

I didn't see it until she put her finger on it. It was a red dot on the back label centered under the manufacturer's name. The red was nearly the same red as the screw top on the bottle. Alex pulled out another bottle of Mighty Fit and located a red dot in exactly the same place on the label.

"What about that one?" I nodded at the next carton. The bottles in it were marked with the same red dot.

"That's not part of the label," she pointed out the obvious. "It was made with a felt-tip marker."

Overhead there was a thud like a soft footfall. The two of us froze. The other foot never came down. The first sound of activity overhead was followed by a light pattering.

"Cat," Alex decided, but we didn't actually breathe easier until the creature introduced itself, fawning against my leg.

While the gloom in the tack room deepened, we determined that every bottle in the case carried the red mark.

"What about the lot number on this carton?"

"The double nines?" She stared unhappily at the box. "Right! I always left three cases for her at Win's. I was supposed to make sure Patty delivered the lot numbers with double nines. She said those were specially for Jason, and it seems like there were always a couple of cases like that, but I can't be absolutely sure. Damn, I wish that trooper hadn't taken my notebook!"

"But Jason wouldn't use up two cases every month. Were both of these cases intended for Chicago? Would Patty have shipped them if Layton hadn't left that message?"

After a moment of puzzlement, Alex said, "Jason feeds this

stuff to the horses. Let's see if we can find a bottle from a case he uses."

A shelf in the feed room obliged with a half-full case of Mighty Fit. One of the bottles stood beside the box, and a plastic coffee measure lay next to it. That bottle was obviously in use. There was no mark on it or on the other unused bottles in the carton.

"Pour some out," I suggested.

What came out of the mouth of the bottle was a viscous dark pink fluid. I went back to the tack room to fetch one of the marked bottles. The liquid that flowed out from it was clear and thin.

"God." Alex stared. "How depressing."

I recapped both bottles and handed them to Alex. "For Shaddaux. Why don't you take these back to the car? I'll try to clean up after us."

She turned obediently toward the back door, and I shone the flashlight around the feed room and then into the tack room, wondering how to erase the evidence of our visit. It would be hard to disguise the fact that the carton of Mighty Fit had been opened and a bottle removed, but easy enough to put our makeshift tools back in their original places and slow the discovery of our pillaging. Unfortunately, I didn't even have a chance to begin. A diffuse light struck the front of the barn and was channeled into the dark by the glass panes on the door. A split second later the crunch of gravel and the clatter of a diesel engine signaled the pickup truck out front.

I turned and ran, switching off the flashlight in the first steps. Alex, who had almost reached the back door, heard me coming and looked back into the now illuminated building. At the slamming of the truck's door, the two of us dodged into an empty stall near the back door. A light came on in the stairwell at the front of the metal building, and then we could hear feet in the apartment overhead. The apartment lights shone down from upstairs and lit the window at the back of the stall. Water ran, a refrigerator door closed, and then music came on. I went to the window. The shadows of two people were cast down from the apartment to the paddock below.

"Jason and Roger," Alex whispered. "Let's go before they stop moving around."

Our exit in the dark wasn't noiseless, but the sounds in the apartment masked any we made leaving—until I settled the Mighty Fit bottles between my feet and Alex started the convertible. I admired her timing and the fact that we rolled around the barn to the driveway without the benefit of headlights and then picked up speed to get to the main road. She put on the headlights.

"Nicely done!"

"At least they didn't see us—and maybe they didn't even hear us. Did you get anything put away?"

"No. It will be pretty clear that someone went through that carton."

"Fingerprints."

"If," I pointed out, "they report a problem."

"If they don't report a problem," Alex reasoned, "they're involved. They know something about that carton." She drove without speaking for a few moments. Then she said, "Someone in the company, my family's company, was tampering with each of those bottles, hand-marking each one that was special for some reason. Doesn't that make you sick?"

"No. But then it's not my family, my family's money."

"I should have asked some questions. But no, here I was happily schlepping those cartons for them—whoever they are. Happily, quite happily."

"Yup," I said sympathetically. "Ignorance is bliss, but nothing that came to you was suspicious on its face. Did Patty give you any sign she knew what she was doing?"

"Not that I remember—" She paused, and for a couple of minutes the only sound was the deep whirring of tires on pavement. Then Alex spoke abruptly. "She knew. Patty had to know the bottles she shipped to her dad weren't full of Mighty Fit. But she never said anything to me because she knew her dad wanted it kept quiet—yeah, that's probably what it was, she was keeping it quiet. Anything he asked her to do, she would do. She idolized him."

"Layton? Then why would he put her in danger?"

"Maybe he didn't think he was. Maybe he didn't see it coming her way—maybe he didn't realize the game he was playing was hardball."

I pressed the button on the edge of my sports watch to light the dial. "Charlie must be getting suspicious by now. Can you drive any faster?"

"Sure." With no sign of agitation, she nudged the accelerator, and the roadster rocketed along, sweeping around the corners and through the curves. She drove fast enough to deposit me and the bottles of Mighty Fit at the hotel a few minutes shy of an hour and a half. No sign of nerves at all. Something like me. In fact, maybe she was a lot like me, and maybe that was one reason Stephen had liked her and I hadn't.

"Hope you can steer like that tomorrow!" But this light remark glanced off her.

She said, "I hope Charlie doesn't get mad at you for this."

"Charlie? Charlie doesn't get mad," I kidded her. "Just even."

But when I strode through the door of our room with the supplement bottles and my important new information, I found the amiable Charles Reidermann in a cold fury and quite ready to get even.

"Where have you been?"

I was stunned. I'd never seen him in such a state. But I could tell he knew the answer to his own question. Stephen had not been able to dissemble, and the time Alex and I had been gone seemed long to both of them.

"I was about to call Shaddaux."

"I'm glad you didn't do that."

"What a boneheaded stunt! Couldn't you find a legal way to get yourself hurt?"

"Sorry I scared you."

"Scared me?"

"Yes, and I am sorry. Want to know what we found?"

"No!" he snapped as his eyes fell on the Mighty Fit bottles.

"Charlie, it makes everything—"

"I am not interested," he said righteously. "What I want is for you to think about consequences for once. Think about the worst possible—" But he continued to eye the bottles and was recovering himself. "What are you doing with those?"

"Marked. Some of the bottles are marked by hand. This one," I set it on the hotel dresser like it is regular old Mighty Fit, "has no mark. And this one," I set the marked bottle down in opposition to the first, the way they do in cheapo TV ads for detergent, "is full of something else."

Charlie considered this somberly. "Secret sauce," he suggested, and fell silent for a few moments. "Nice information. But I wish you hadn't gone after it."

So I was forgiven in a grudging sort of way. But I had scared him, and because I had brought out a side of Charlie I didn't want to see, he had scared me. I didn't want to see it again.

We were changing for the party when the phone on the nightstand rang.

Charlie listened for a moment and said, "Yes, sir. Certainly."

When he put the phone down, he said. "Shaddaux. You might want to make yourself presentable."

My stomach dropped the way it does when a plane descends suddenly, and I thrashed through the hotel room closet for my dark gray dress slacks, the frilly pink blouse that Charlie always said he liked, and the trim darker pink wool jacket that went with it. In the two minutes it took to reapply clothing, Shaddaux was at the door. His shirt was fresh, and he was newly shaven. I was fumbling for my gray flats.

"Mrs. Elledge," he said. Since it seemed to be a statement of fact, I didn't respond.

"Jason Tomlinson has reported a break-in at his barn. Nothing taken, and other than the lock on the tack room door, the only thing disturbed was a carton of Mighty Fit. Would you and Mr. Reidermann know anything about this?"

"I would—not Charlie," I said quickly.

"That convertible only seats two," he agreed. After he learned of the burglary, he had seen Alex's car pull up to the hotel. Now he fixed on my Brand A–Brand B demonstration with the supplement bottles. I seized up very tight, the way I do when the horse grows tense and frustrated in the dressage ring and I know he's going to explode.

"From Jason's place. We were about to call you," I said.

"To save me the trouble of driving over here to arrest you and Alex?"

"No, to tell you—" I started, then realized, "—she's not here."

"Yes, she is." Shaddaux had also been keeping an eye on the traffic to and from all of our rooms, and in a way, I was glad to learn this, that after our bungled foray, she hadn't dropped me off and driven away to join her family. She had come back to the comfort of Stephen's arms.

"Maybe there will be a wedding after all," I suggested, brightly referring to the bride's magazine Shaddaux and I had seen in Alex's apartment.

Ignoring this, Shaddaux ducked into the bathroom and returned with a towel. "You were about to phone," he prompted, and he used the towel to appropriate the two prize bottles without actually touching them.

"One is full of Mighty Fit. The other has something else in it," I reported.

"We're checking all the bottles you left behind." Evidently he had sent someone to Jason's place to retrieve them. "Now, Mrs. Elledge, do you want Alex Delgado to ride this horse of yours tomorrow?"

What an inane question. I didn't bother to answer it, but noticed Charlie, who had been silent throughout this interview, wearing a watchful little smile.

"Your safety is being assured by our people," he said. "If you want the girl to ride tomorrow, you will stay with your group and follow the directions our people give you." By using the plural he made it seem that the whole division was looking after us. "Otherwise—and I want to make this very clear—otherwise I will bring the two of you in and charge you."

"Okay."

He had me where he wanted me, and Charlie was now smiling quite broadly.

"Our operations are ongoing," he explained as he left. "We can't have you interfering in them."

Charlie waited until the sound of Shaddaux's footsteps faded out. "He can't have you interfering, but he also can't remove you and Alex from the event without showing his hand."

He was quick, Charlie was. He was way ahead of me.

"And Alex is in no danger," he continued. "We—and she—know

too much. The cops don't want our Mexican friends to get spooked and leave the country."

"Why didn't you tell Shaddaux that Vicente had approached your company—what was it you said, some kind of capital?"

"Venture capital," he agreed. "Because it doesn't seem relevant. Halefellow never made an offer, never even invited them back. Seems like a red herring."

6

We squeezed together at one of the larger tables under the party tent set up at the edge of the trade fair, downed—speaking here for myself—scotch and then white wine, and then confronted lobsters and clams and sweet corn. Stephen cracked open the lobster that was staring down Lourdes and broke it down into manageable parts. He was an engineer, after all. Frankie saw how neatly the prey was laid out on Lourdes's plate and said, "Do me, please."

There was a band, live enough to issue occasional squawks from their amplifiers. As desserts were being finished off—the wispy Vicente substituting a second lobster for the lime pie—the musicians shifted to dance tunes. People began to push back from the tables and roam. If they didn't dance—to my enormous frustration, many of our better athletes like Ned and Win didn't dance—they wandered in sociable slow time among the other competitors and owners. Jason Tomlinson and Roger, the young guy who was his groom, had arrived in time for lobster. They weren't dancing, but they might as well have been. They stood, drinks in hand, a careful distance from each other. There was a bruise on the teenage kid's well-defined jaw. I hadn't noticed it that morning, but it's not unusual for anyone in this crowd to come away from cross-country day with an injury, a cervical collar, a cast. I barely registered the mark on him and certainly didn't pause to speculate on what had caused it. Jason greeted Charlie and me cordially as we passed on our way to the dance floor. This seemed to confirm that he hadn't seen Alex's little convertible, and if he suspected me of anything, much less of breaking into his tack room, he certainly didn't show it. I felt relieved and a little guilty, because I was beginning to think that maybe Stephen was right, maybe Jason was slippery. Or maybe he was worse than just slippery.

Dancing with Charlie was delightful, satisfying as always. I used to find it sad that on first meeting so many men told me they loved horses, they loved to dance, and then proved themselves early to be liars on both counts. Charlie hadn't lied about either, although what he loved about horses was the probabilities they generated.

I was in line for another glass of wine from the bar when I saw Win approaching with two plastic glasses. Only a few people gathered near the bar greeted him. He was being politely shunned. Guilty until proven innocent, I guess.

Ignoring the fact that he was persona non grata, Win handed me one of the glasses, his way of saying thanks. It made me feel a little guilty for the suspicions I had been harboring about him. He said quietly, "I wish you had told me about Charlie and the horse." This was more like the Win I had known for so long, undemonstrative and brave.

"I wish I had known, for Christ's sake—you think I would have put up with Charlie owning such a competitive horse? In fact, I don't think Charlie realized his situation until he read the program. He really pores over those programs, you know. Keeps all those numbers in his copy."

"Can't make book without stats." Charlie came into the conversation agreeably.

"Saved my ass, Charlie—" Would Win have said this if he had anything to do with the patch? If he didn't, what was his involvement? "—the piece of it that could be saved, anyway."

"What about your mare?"

"Seems fine."

"Do you know what it was?"

"On the patch? Probably some kind of speed, but we'll know when the analysis comes back."

"You'll be suspended," I concluded.

"For sure." Then, being as incorrigibly practical as he was, he said, "That mare is already so hot and so fit she wants to jump out of her own skin. Only somebody who didn't know the first thing about a horse would try to hype her up."

"You could have been killed."

"Hunh? Me? It's a pretty dicey proposition, trying to get me thrown," Win pointed out with his usual innocent, unstoppable self-confidence "But maybe that wasn't the point."

If that wasn't the point, what was? Win looked out calmly on the gathering of horse people, the so-called friends and self-acknowledged rivals. Was this the old Win, the one who had tried to love me so many years ago? There was something in his expression and the way he was bearing up that, even more than my snooping mission at his house that day, took me back to those days when I had tortured him with my competitiveness and insecurity. I saw clearly how difficult I had been for him and how callous and oblivious I had been about that. I saw clearly that it had been necessary for him to simultaneously fend me off and try to get his arms around me. With crystalline recall, I saw myself stomping out through the back porch, again and again.

Then I saw, also with startling clarity, the young woman in

the bright blue jacket. She was nine or ten years old, Hallie Vanderkay. Poor Hallie, the neighbor girl, kicked in the head. Before the accident, Win yelled at her at least once a week to go home, and I pointed to the field beside the house and shouted that his farm was not her playground. Threatened that if she went into the field beside the house to play with the weanlings that were turned out there, we would go to her parents. But she knew we wouldn't, and she didn't stop until she caught both of a youngster's hind feet with the side of her head. She suffered some brain damage, and Win used family money to pay for her tuition at a special school. She would be just about twenty now, but Win hadn't forgotten her. Suddenly I had a fuzzy recollection of Win phoning Charlie to ask if we needed a cleaning person. We probably did. But Charlie was adamant about withholding and Social Security, and so nothing came of it. That cleaning person would have been Hallie, and encountering her as she was looking after his house was reassurance that Win still stood by her, that he hadn't changed. He was still the old Win, and he wouldn't change. Somebody wanted to turn the police's attention to him.

Paul Lamoreaux had arrived late and was looking for a place to settle with his plate of lobster. Then he saw Win. Paying no attention to the distance other people were putting between themselves and Win, he stepped right up.

"Results on the patch are back," he announced. Win remained silent, so Charlie said, *"And?"*

"Nada." Paul grinned. "Nothing on that Band-Aid but horse sweat."

I had two reactions, almost in the same moment. "So you're off the hook, Win—but something happened to that mare. Somebody did something to her."

"Could have been an embolism," Paul pointed out. "Or a plain old heart attack."

"That would be a relief, wouldn't it?"

Win shrugged helplessly. "There's still the blood work to come back."

Win and Paul would just have to wait out the findings of the lab and the deliberations of the police and the FEI.

I said, "What about the other stuff, Win?"

He didn't know what I meant.

"Mighty Fit."

"Don't use it."

"I know you don't, but did the cops ask you about it?"

"Yeah. I told them I didn't use it."

"Can't figure out why they thought it was so important," Paul put in. "Win had a few cases of it sitting around, waiting to be picked up or whatever, and we were kind of speculating about what might be in it. We had a bet on. So I pulled a bottle and sent some of it to a spectrometry lab to have it tested."

"Win!" I grabbed his wrist so hard the wine slopped out of his glass. In that instant it had become clear to me what had happened to his mare and why there was nothing on the patch. "Bute." Pronounced *byoot*, as in *she's a beaut*.

"What?" Win looked askance at the suggestion.

But Paul locked on the idea. "Phenylbutazone—but it would take a needle. And the needle would have had to be in the vet box or somewhere very close to it."

"The liquid," Win was catching on. Bute in tablet form was ubiquitous in the horse world because it was a painkiller. Horses gobbled it up at about the same rate people gobbled up aspirin, but it was illegal to use it to help a sore horse compete. "The injectable liquid."

"Intravenous rather than intramuscular." Paul gave him the method. "Could cause a horse to thrash around like that, but more than likely kill it. I've seen it happen. I had a vet student with me once—"

"I remember that time," I interrupted. "It was my horse."

"The student got in wrong with the needle, into a vein. Really bad scene."

"That bute will show up in the blood work," I said impatiently, "and somebody put that patch on your mare to make sure she would be tested."

"Maybe that's all they wanted," Win continued my line of reasoning. "A little bute to show up."

"But the needle," Paul repeated emphatically, "would have had to be used right there in the vet box because it only takes a few seconds for the horse to react—and somebody had to put it directly into the vein."

My gaze turned to Jason and then to Roger, an experienced groom who would probably do anything to please his boss. Jason had been warming up a horse for the start when Secret Formula had come into the vet box, but Roger was right there. And he undoubtedly knew how to use a needle. Was Jason slippery enough to frame Win? And was it just to put Win out of the competition or out of business for good?

I wanted to ask Paul more about the lab procedures, how long they would take and what kind of information came with the results. And if there had been a red mark on the bottle that went to the lab. But I couldn't delve any deeper because I noticed Vicente a few yards off, staring at us and then, when I caught him eavesdropping, smiling. It was, as Stephen had pointed out, weird how he hung at the edge of the crowd, always trying to be part of it and yet always observing. I wondered how loyal he really was to Lourdes, and this made me aware that I did not trust this man any more than Stephen did. I lifted my drink toward him and concentrated on it until Vicente directed his curiosity back across the dance floor to Jason and Roger. He started in their direction. This three-day had gotten so completely out of whack.

I turned sideways to speak to Charlie. "What's his deal? What's he doing here?"

"I think the deal was that Alex's dad merged his company with his brother's, with Vicente's. Vicente got paid in shares, and then he started buying up more."

"Looks to me like he wants to take over more than company stock." But maybe the real reason he hovered around Lourdes was her company stock.

Charlie shrugged, ignoring this reference to Lourdes and watching Vicente in conversation with Jason. "He wants to modernize, go global. Has an MBA, I think."

"Is *that* why he needs protection," I muttered to Charlie.

"He's not getting any," Charlie pointed out. "None of us are."

"But Shaddaux told Alex—"

"Who are you seeing here," Charlie inquired pointedly, "for the first time?"

He was right. There was no one under the tent who didn't seem to belong there, no one I couldn't associate however vaguely with one of the horses.

"There's no protection," Charlie said, "because none of the Delgado clan is in danger."

"You think they *are* the danger?"

"I didn't say that."

Jason left Vicente and was making his way around the dancers. He was, in fact, coming in my direction. He stopped in front of me and was wearing an odd little smile. I stiffened because I had a hunch were I could find some bute, in liquid form.

"Mrs. Elledge?"

I was trying not to think about the bute. Vicente was watching us speculatively.

"Vicente would like to ask you to dance."

"Well, ah . . . I . . . Jason, this is lovely of you, but . . ."

Charlie's hand was on my back, pushing ever so gently. "Tink would love to."

With Vicente? Before I could squirm out of the arrangement, Jason had relayed the message, and Vicente was standing next to me, taking my hand. It was horrifying. I towered over him and danced like a scarecrow, my hand resting downhill on the shoulder of his sport jacket. It was good cloth, maybe cashmere. I was surprised that he didn't reek of aftershave and that he was a good dancer. The band seemed to be playing from a great distance, and the blood pounded in my ears because I was beside myself, confused and shaken. Vicente had a mission, and when he spoke, it was like he was talking to my neck. It was the first time he had spoken directly to me.

"We like Stephen very much," he said.

We? He and Lourdes? What was he trying to get at? A little lecture on family planning? My feet would not own up to being mine. I kept stepping on Vicente. He ignored this and said, "We would like you and Charlie to come to Mexico."

I was stammering again. "Oh, we would . . . love . . ."

Charlie was watching with amused detachment. Jason and Roger were trying not to look our way. I blundered on. I seemed to have agreed that after the stadium jumping the next day Vicente and Lourdes would make the arrangements with Charlie and me. I heard Vicente say "three weeks," and then the music stopped.

"*Gracias*," he said hastily about our time on the dance floor, and as he left me to rejoin Lourdes, the cry of "Limbo!" was going up around the dance floor. The band shifted into habanero. This was on account of Charlie. His dance trick was famous with the kids. Stephen was dispatched to the stables and returned with a long-handled rake. Charlie broke away, and I joined Paul and Win to watch. I was a little dazed and at odds with myself because, apparently, I had accepted an invitation to Mexico.

The beat drove on, the rake handle became a pole, and Charlie leaned back, marching forward so that his feet went under the pole before the rest of him. One of the young riders followed Charlie under the pole, and then another, and another. The pole was still too high to eliminate anyone. A few minutes later the beat grew louder, the kids dropped the pole a good bit, and a few of the dancers in the line behind Charlie, including Vicente, gave it up. It was remarkable how low Charlie could go. No one—except me, of course—would look at his long, pudgy torso and imagine how flexible it could be. Buried in his well-stuffed frame was a streak of athleticism. All it needed to fire up was a little music.

Vicente made his way to where I was standing with Paul and Win, apparently quite comfortable now in my presence. I was suffering. Was he really the polite and proper wannabe in-law? Or did he know what I knew about the marked bottles of Mighty Fit? Had he been the one to make sure they got to Patty and to Jason's place? I checked cautiously on Jason's whereabouts. He and Roger had taken seats at one of the tables. They didn't appear ready to leave.

Charlie sank back to a new low, and right behind him the tiny Lourdes bent under the pole. Her feet, now back in the little heels, and her back were very sure of the rhythm. I wished fervently that Lourdes would give up and Vicente would have to leave. It was time to make a move, and I didn't want him watching.

"This could go on quite a while," I said impatiently to excuse myself and left Vicente looking a little surprised and shy about having to make conversation with Paul and Win. To be sure none of them would ask any questions, I headed in the direction of the Porta Potties that stood at some distance from the tent. No questions were forthcoming. They seemed to assume what I wanted them to assume. I passed the plastic privies and kept walking. Charlie and I had left the Mercedes in the competitors' lot near the stables, and I found the flashlight Charlie kept under the seat.

I passed the night watch's trailer. The stables stood silently in the dark. Apparently I was the only one there. I went down the shed row, setting off the motion sensors and lights as if I were there to see about my horse. Exit Laughing was asleep. I panned the flashlight down the opposite shed row. Except for the horses, Jason Tomlinson's stalls were deserted. A quick check behind me, and I walked over to Jason's tack stall as if I had business there. If I had encountered someone, I would have to ask to borrow a martingale or a gag bit for the show jumping the next morning. But this gambit wasn't necessary.

There was no one in Jason's orderly equipment area. Bridles and halters and martingales hung from ceiling hooks. A number of saddles, clean and oiled, rested on their racks, and everything else was stowed in the gleaming maroon tack trunks that lined two walls. I had forgotten how many of these showpieces Jason traveled with, but six horses, six trunks. I started in on the first one. It yielded only protective boots for the horses and a couple of stable blankets. No liniment, no first-aid supplies. No supplements. I put everything back in the position in which I had found it. The second trunk was equally unrewarding. On a sudden hunch I went next door to the stall that housed hay and straw and feed bins, but finding no medical supplies, returned to the tack stall to open the third trunk. This was taking a long time, and as I progressed to the fourth trunk, I decided that if it didn't prove productive, I would have to come back later.

This trunk was outfitted with a top tray that held a collection of salves. The space under the tray was home to a plastic box partitioned to hold the steel calks that screwed into the horses' shoes and to a metal cabinet with deep drawers. I pulled out one of the drawers to reveal a few plastic vials with large tablets labeled as the usual kinds. Phenylbutazone tablets for pain and swelling—but I was looking for the liquid form, an open vial of it. Glucosamine powder for joint problems. Antibiotic, and a pill crusher. The drawer below this held jars of ointments with stained labels and salve caked around the lids, and the next below that held gauze pads and adhesive wraps.

I never saw what was in the last drawer or the start of stadium jumping. Never saw Exit Laughing enter the show jumping arena. I do not remember the blow. But I was not seeing black. I was not in darkness as so many people describe unconsciousness. Awareness and sensation were voided. I was reduced to absence.

7

Charlie lost the limbo contest, quite graciously, he thought, to Lourdes. She had stepped out of her matron's role long enough to have fun, and she was lit up from the dancing. Her dark hair had tumbled out of the twist on the back of her head, and she was even perspiring a little. No sooner had the dance beat stopped, he noticed, than Vicente appeared abruptly at her side. Tink wouldn't have tolerated him hovering like that for a second.

Charlie looked around for Tink and when he couldn't locate her right away loitered among the tables, preying on a lonely, untouched piece of lime pie. Stephen and Alex were the first of the kids to leave the party, walking slowly toward the stables, shoulder to shoulder but not actually holding hands. The girl had her dignity, and now that her dismay at discovering the role she had unwittingly played by delivering the supplement had made him certain she wasn't involved in her friend's disappearance, the sight of Stephen and her warmed his heart.

"Is that your *third*, Charlie?" Frankie ogled the pie. "My back is killing me. How can you do that dance?" She reached behind her to pat a plump hip.

The kids were still dancing, still lining up for wine. It made his head ache just to watch them—and truth to tell, his back was bothering him. The next morning would come too soon.

"Ready to call it a night—where's Tink?"

Charlie bobbed his head vaguely in the direction of the Porta Potties, and he and Frankie meandered toward them and waited at a respectful distance. But the only traffic to and from the plastic huts was from young people. After a few minutes, he said, "She's probably back at the stables getting in Alex's way."

"I don't think so," Frankie said when they arrived at Exit Laughing's dark stall. All the equipment was neatly put away and the tack stall closed. They could hear the gray horse's slow, deep breathing and the fluttering of his lips.

"What the hell!" Charlie was beginning to be annoyed.

"Uh-oh." Frankie shook her head.

"She is incorrigible," he fumed. "Absolutely incorrigible."

By the time they had looked through the stable area, he was furious, angrier with her, if possible, than he had been that afternoon, and a little scared. He punched Tink's number into his cell phone. It rang persistently until the voice mail switched on.

They rapped on the door of the night watch's trailer. "Sorry to disturb. We're looking for Tink."

"Thought I saw her coming back through here to check on her horse. Maybe an hour ago."

Charlie heaved a long, angry, anxious sigh. When he and Frankie found the Mercedes still in the competitors' lot, he didn't know whether to be reassured by the car's presence or not. Tink's cell phone lay in the cup holder on the console, where it had been ringing only a few minutes earlier. Then he felt around under the front seat.

"She's taken the flashlight."

"What does that mean? What are you thinking, Charlie?"

"I don't know. I really don't know what to think." He brought his fist down softly on the roof of the Mercedes. "And I don't know whether to stay here and wait for her or whether to go back to the hotel and hope she'll turn up there."

"She's on a mission," Frankie suggested.

"Some cockamamie mission," he agreed, truly despondent now.

"Should we call the cops or maybe just the lieutenant?"

"Not yet," he decided snappishly, further infuriated by the thought of the chaos this would unleash. "That would stir things up enough to disrupt the whole event—and maybe for nothing, nothing at all."

He glared at the dashboard at length and then said, "Let me take you back to the hotel. I've got to think."

At the front desk they checked for messages. There were none.

"You call me, Charlie," Frankie instructed as she took her leave. "You call me as soon as you know anything."

He nodded and watched the elevator door close behind Frankie. Then he rode it himself, up to their floor, where he found that Tink hadn't returned to the room. He left the hotel and drove out to look over the party crowd again. But the caterers were pulling the tablecloths and stacking the chairs. He stood in their midst mulling over his anger. He had been angry with Tink twice that day, and there had been only one other day in their marriage when he had lost his temper with her.

That episode had to do with his cat, Greenspan, whose marvelous aloof intelligence had drawn from Charlie for the first time in his life devotion to an animal. Greenspan was a kind of Cheshire cat, a tortoiseshell kitty so large and heavy that he flattened out to the shape of an enormous mushroom cap when he flopped down. His grin was enhanced by large jowls. All he lacked was the hookah. Charlie had suspected that Tink disliked Greenspan, although she never actually said this, and it was clear the cat had nothing but animosity for Tink. On a summer afternoon

Charlie was downstairs reading in his chair by the window. As Tink reported it, she was trying to remove the screen from the window directly above the one he sat next to. The cat was sunning itself in that window. When Tink tried to "very gently" nudge the cat out of the way, Greenspan bit her. Charlie looked up from that day's *Wall Street Journal* to see Greenspan passing upside down and straight-legged from the top of the window to the sill, his long dark fur fluttering up from his legs and belly, then out of sight. "That will do it!" he shouted furiously. Tink made it out the front door ahead of him. She couldn't find any sign of the cat. Thinking Greenspan had crawled into the shrubbery under the window to die, Charlie pawed morosely at the evergreen branches.

"This is terrible," she apologized, "but I couldn't help it. He bit me."

"Maybe he should have taken a bigger bite," he suggested savagely.

But Charlie wasn't angry now. He was alone.

He parked in the competitors' lot and walked past the night watch's trailer. The television was still live, but the silhouette of the watchman seated at the little drop-down table showed him with his head back, snoring. When Charlie arrived again at Exit Laughing's stall, the gray horse too was snoring, in long gentle tones like a French horn. He must have been lying on his side. Tink always said a horse had to be very relaxed and confident to lie down. This was because of predators, wolves and terrible big cats, she had explained. He stood staring for quite a while into the obscurity of the stall, the doorway a darker triangle than the dark side of the shed row.

It was nearly midnight when he returned to their hotel room, and he found he had a phone message. But it was only Frankie. Had he heard anything from Tink? He left the telephone idle and turned on the television. But before the picture formed completely, he turned it off and crossed back to the telephone.

"Yes," he confirmed. "Shaddaux." Then he said, "Lieutenant? Charlie Reidermann. My wife is missing."

At first Shaddaux didn't respond. Then he said carefully, "Missing."

"Missing."

"Or maybe just off on another independent excursion," Shaddaux suggested, still careful.

"I do not want this made public," Charlie instructed. "It will blow this event wide open and that will eliminate any opportunity to find her."

"I will want to put out an all-points."

"Please."

"Do you have a photo of her?"

He had never been so empty-handed. He glanced helplessly at their luggage and then remembered the poster in the secretary's office showing Tink on a flying brown horse.

"That won't help much," Shaddaux told him, but not because he remembered the image. "These people with all their gear and helmets are almost unrecognizable on a horse. But we'll get it first thing tomorrow morning. In the meantime, let's start with height, weight, identifying marks. You're at the hotel? Are you okay there?"

Only in a manner of speaking.

"Unless we get any news sooner, I'll plan to pick you up at the front door at five."

"I'd rather start right now."

"You mean driving around in the dark? Right now, there's nobody around except that guy in the trailer. And the squad cars will be on the lookout. Pick you up at five."

"That's not necessary. I can meet you—"

"Not," Shaddaux said softly, "a safe plan."

It had been years since Charlie had cried, since the desertion of his first wife, in fact. He didn't want to cry now. In fact, he wouldn't cry. It would be an admission that he had lost somebody else.

Frankie had no such reservations. She wailed into the phone when he related his conversation with Shaddaux. "It was precautionary," he put the lie quite firmly. "I'd like you to see it that way and go back to bed. I'll call you before I leave in the morning."

But ten minutes later he answered a knock at the door, and there was Frankie in her bathrobe. Dressed for bed, except for the green turban-thing she had slapped on, and the usually creamy skin of her face had a raw, scrubbed look. She had made no effort to stop the tears.

"Charlie," she said as she stepped into the room. "You look terrible! Put your pants on."

He had wandered about the room, trying to decide whether to get in the bed or go out again. At some point he had taken off his jeans to lie down in his boxers. He located them now and dutifully pulled them up. Frankie sat on the end of the bed, and he brought her a Kleenex.

"Oh, Charlie, what am I—" When she saw the grimness he had settled into she stopped needing sympathy. Then she burst out, "These fucking horse people with their wasteful, pointless fucking ambitions!"

He said, "Exactly."

Frankie straightened. "Okay, you're going with Shaddaux. What should I do?"

"Drive our car to the grounds. Take the videocam and stay through the show jumping. Tink will be fit to be tied if we don't at least get some video of the gray horse. If you get to the grounds before I do, tell Alex and Stephen that Tink and I are working with the police. Tell the Delgados the same thing. Tell them we'll try to make it back for Exit Laughing's round if we possibly can—and remember, the order of go works up from the bottom of the standings. I know our horse is at least in the top five, so he will start late in the afternoon. Stick to your story, and keep your cell phone on."

She looked at the door. "You don't want to be alone here all night, do you? I mean, I'm not going to sleep, and I don't want you to have to get through the night without someone to talk to."

She wasn't suggesting anything other than that, but he smiled a little and said, "Let's not add complications to anyone's story."

After she went back to her room, Charlie lay on the bed without undressing or pulling back the spread. He did not sleep, he rested and watched the edge of the curtain, where the lights from the parking lot seeped into the room. At one point he remembered the flask of scotch in his suitcase and poured a drink into one of the hotel's coffee cups. He thought of himself as very smart, and he knew that in one sense this was true. He was very adept at navigating the rational universe and seeing into its mathematical architecture. He used this and the rules of social behavior to negotiate successfully and provide reasoned counsel to corporate boards. So, yes, he was smart. But what he was not was astute, and now in his sleeplessness and helplessness, he fervently regretted this.

Tink was astute. She was instinctive in her dealings with people as well as animals, and she was curious about them. She often pointed out the fact that "a good horse has to be curious, Charlie. And he has to have the confidence to let his curiosity lead him." She let her curiosity lead her to the important questions about other people.

He wished he had let her ride Exit Laughing.

The light at the edge of the curtain washed pinker and lighter just before dawn. He rose, smoothed the wrinkles out of the bedspread, shaved, and brushed his teeth. Tink's canvas tote stood on the closet floor under the hems of her khakis. It held everything she had planned to take to the event that day—water bottle, sunscreen, hairbrush, lip balm, program, scarf, and gloves. Then he noticed something else in the closet that sent a small wave of shock through him. Her boots. She had brought her tall, black boots, and they were polished—in case, just in case, she might be called upon to ride a horse. What had she been thinking? Goddamnit, what the hell had she been thinking?

This prompted a little surge of optimism. Whatever she had been thinking, she would probably need a change of clothes. He emptied the canvas tote, tucked Tink's running shoes into it, pulled the khakis off their hanger, and folded them along with socks, a T-shirt, and a fleece into the bag. Then he picked up the hotel phone.

"Good morning, Paul. Charlie Reidermann here."

"Morning? For Christ's sake, Charlie, the cats aren't even up yet."

He was unapologetic. "I would have expected a veterinarian, particularly an officiating veterinarian, to be up and about by now."

"I was—in my dreams. What can I do for you, Charlie?"

"Tink and I are wondering about that analysis you arranged."

"Yeah, at this hour of the morning?" he groused. Then he said, "Right. The jar of Mighty Fit I sent to the mass spectrometry lab."

"What did that turn up?"

"What is this, Charlie? Have you been drinking? Or is this one of your wagers?"

"Something like that."

The Test of Agility

1

At some point I did become aware of blackness. It was complete darkness, and it persisted. I don't know how long it persisted before pain crept in. At first the pain in my head and neck was distant. But it loomed closer and more intense until it and the blackness formed my only thought. Then my knees and ankles introduced themselves with pain of their own kinds, twisting and crushing. For quite a while, this was who—or rather what—I was, a black, vacant mind, a head and neck seared with pain, knees and ankles tortured by their angles. I existed as sensation. I did not know I was someone.

Gradually this state expanded, and I became aware of my person. I did not know who I was or where I was. But I knew I was a person confined in total darkness, and this darkness was a bumpy, rattling place. It was difficult to breathe. My neck was curled and my head bent over, and the air was stuffy and thick.

I went bumping along, curled up in darkness with no sense of time passing until I was roused by a familiar odor. I knew the smell and finally it brought a gray horse to mind. I was jiggling around in darkness and pain with the image of a gray horse in my mind, and I began to remember myself. I had something to do with a horse. Gradually the picture filled. There were many horses, so I was getting older. I remembered some men. A little boy with tawny hair.

Jesus Christ, it was Stephen! Enveloped in darkness and pain I remembered him as he usually was now, in the midst of a tangle of wires and servers and keyboards and motherboards. Motherboards, for Christ's sake. He was my only real child. I knew exactly now who I was, and I remembered that there was nobody back at my farm. So where were they all?

I began to find out where I was. I opened my eyes, but this changed the view very little. I was still seeing black. The top of my head rested against something flat, like a wall. My foot, which seemed to be wearing a very light shoe, rested against its mate, and I found I could not separate them. They were tied together. Ditto for my hands. There was another wall at my back, and there was something—a jacket—bunched up in between. I couldn't straighten because two other walls pressed against my feet and shoulders. It was a box of some kind.

Abruptly the bumping and rattling stopped, and the sound of an engine registered. It was a big engine, a diesel. I was in a box being transported by a truck. More precisely—I was almost completely with it now—I was in a tack trunk on a horse van. The van moved forward again and after a while turned onto a gravel road. In a few minutes it came to a halt. The engine was cut.

The trunk was one of the expensive kind, wood with dovetailed corners. I tried not to panic and told myself that even a good trunk was sure as hell not airtight. But, as I said, it was pretty hard to breathe, and every limb whined to be released and allowed to uncurl. I couldn't scream because of the duct tape over my mouth. But a happy coincidence of being bent double was that I could stretch my head through the frills on my blouse to where my hands were, and my fingers could get at the duct tape that was gagging me. It was like ripping off the world's largest Band-Aid, and I was too squeamish to do it in one yank.

I was working away at it, head and elbows knocking into the walls of the trunk, when the side door of the van opened. I stopped moving and held my breath. I heard the ramp slide out from under the truck and drop. Someone dragged something heavy into the van and wedged it up against my trunk. The ramp rolled back under the van, and the side door slammed. The engine started, and the van rolled forward on the gravel again. I resumed pulling at the tape and considered the object next to my trunk. It was heavy. It could have been a bale of hay, but there hadn't been any scratchiness in the sound it made on the ramp. It had made a flat thud on the floor of the van, and I decided this meant the object shoved up next to my trunk was another trunk. Maybe I had company.

The tape had left the skin around my mouth raw, but I could catch a bigger stream of air now. My mind was on Charlie. I wondered if he had figured out I was gone. Then I had a thought about the other tack trunk. "Charlie?" I hoped my voice would carry over the tire and engine noise. "Charlie? Is that you over there?" and I quieted my breath so I could listen for an answer. But how could they, whoever they were, have got Charlie too? He was still at the party, still dancing when they put me in this box. "Is there anybody there? Charlie?" I was descending into panic. "Anybody? If there is anybody in this fucking van with me, why won't you fucking answer?"

The van rumbled on. After some time, it stopped, then jerked ahead on what had to be smoother road. Less rumble and jounce, more tire swoosh and sibilance of speed. I ducked forward again, and my teeth found the rope binding my hands together. With this motion, two things became apparent. A tiny but powerfully refreshing breeze sifted into my black box from the corner cradling my shoulder. My movements inside the trunk had caused some of the dovetails to spring loose. I would not suffocate in this situation, but someone had strangled me. Trying to chew the rope irritated a raw sore under my chin and put pressure against my jaw as if I were being throttled. There was something around my neck. My fingers discovered it was a towel, and they began to turn it slowly, rechafing my neck until they found the knot. After a minute of poking and pulling, it came loose, and my breathing was completely unrestricted.

Sooner or later, Charlie or Frankie or maybe Stephen would miss me. Surely one of them would miss me and send someone to come get me out of this box. Or maybe I would see my spot, break away, and get help. Either way, I would be rescued, I assured myself, and in the meantime, I decided, I could survive like this for a little while if I could fend off panic and further wear and tear on my body. I resolved not to cry and not to wet my pants, and I devised a strategy to soothe myself. Survivors of near-death experiences have often reported seeing their whole life flash through their minds, but I would have more time than they had. In fact, I might have quite a bit of time. I would slow my recall, so that it inched along frame by frame, and I would skip any frame that produced sadness, uneasiness, or regrets. I would dwell on the happy images, like Stephen choosing me, a blubbering mess, over Elledge, his father.

I had a store of good times to ease me through the darkness, to help me hold out until they found the trunk with me in it. I remembered Stephen at the science fair. The judges informed him that his photovoltaic cell was not eligible for a prize because it was clear that his father had built it. But that wasn't true. Stephen wanted that prize, and he knew it should have been his. "Excuse me," he said, and he was careful to be polite. "But my father doesn't live with Tink and me anymore."

I remembered Ready Humor making her victory lap at Radnor and bucking like a rodeo bull. . . .

I was having trouble concentrating on the past because the present was so damned uncomfortable. Who the hell put me here? And why? And what the fuck were they going to do with me?

The van came to a halt, and I heard the hinges of a gate. The van pulled ahead, halted again, and the gates closed. An airplane roared overhead, and the van toured through the noises of engines and rotors. The side door opened, the ramp came down, and I heard the voices of two men. I didn't recognize either voice. Their feet came down close to my trunk. They grunted as they picked up the other trunk or whatever it was, and five minutes later they came back, the toes of their shoes knocking the walls of my trunk. More grunting, and the trunk was lifted up and ferried aboveground for some distance. It slammed down, jarring every joint and every rib. Then it slid, colliding with some obstacle.

One of the men asked a question in Spanish. Vicente, I decided impetuously. I hadn't trusted him from the get-go. He seemed all too well acquainted with Jason, whose tack trunks I was rifling through when I was coldcocked. I tried to work through the facts to some kind of theory. Had Jason called the cops about the break-in of his tack room to throw them back to me and Alex and then to Win?

"A little harder. It has to go on—sure can't leave it here."

More ramming, more shifting. Then they let the trunk rest. Their pant legs swiped the wall of the trunk that confined me. After a bit of shuffling, their feet stopped.

Raising his voice over the rush of sounds from the airfield, another man said, "Get the door." The pant legs brushed the trunk again, and there was a sharp clunk as the door closed. Now the sounds of the airfield were faint. The two trunks—mine, as I had come to think of it, and the other one with whatever it carried—were on a plane, a plane just wide enough to hold the trunks.

"Locked?" The click of seat belts, and the plane started with the enormous vacuum cleaner din of jet engines and the rhythmic chop of propellers. The pilot began his call-and-response checklist of preparations, and although only scraps of it reached me through the harsh blow of the engines, I thought I knew the voice. The plane rolled ahead, turned through a little pirouette, gathered speed, and took off. Airborne, inside a box, I listened for the voice. But for quite a while, engine noise drowned out all else.

"So . . ." This was the voice I thought I knew. ". . . how?"

The response was a mouth sound, the ratcheted tongue winding used to simulate twisting. The towel. They thought I was dead.

"Bad judgment." This was criticism and possibly a threat delivered coolly. "She hadn't figured out anything."

It was Hugh Vaughn at the controls. I was sure of that now, shocked into certainty, but with scrambled thought. I tried to reorder my thinking to include Vicente and Jason in my theory. Wasn't this guy, the doctor, Jason's good client? Was one of those cartons of marked bottles in Jason's tack room intended for Hugh? And what did that mean about the clear liquid in the marked bottles?

I had no idea where the plane was going, but as it flew, the truth about the clear liquid presented itself in high definition: it was the drug Hugh was using, the one he gave to Frankie.

"*Aqui?*" This must be Vicente, I decided. He hadn't responded to Hugh's reprimand, but why should he? If I had things figured out right, Vicente was in effect one of Hugh's bosses. Managing the shipments of Mighty Fit to Alex, he was the one who controlled the flow of Hugh's miracle cancer drug to the other doctors, including Layton McLaren, involved in his so-called clinical trials.

"*En este punto*—okay?"

Which *punto*? Where the hell were we? And where the hell were we going?

"We'll wait," Hugh said imperiously. "We'll be out over the Gulf an hour after we leave Georgia." As far as the two of them knew, I was dead, and they were going to ditch the trunk with my body in it. So there would be no possibility of dying in dry pants or in fact of anyone finding me to observe the condition of my slacks. I realized, though, that at least my arms and legs wouldn't fly out and flail at the air on the way down. The trunk would spare me that. But it would be better if I fainted. I hoped that if it came to it, I would faint. That would be easiest. But I didn't just then.

I had to stay alive, and so I reminded myself about Charlie's cat, an expert at survival. Greenspan was almost too massive to be a real kitty. He liked to come to my feet and sit like Genghis Khan—long, silky hair, broad white bib, and glowing yellow eyes—refusing to budge and demanding to be stroked. He always required a pat, and even though I knew better, I always complied. Then when I took my hand away, he would bite, quick and hard. I tried to pretend a fond interest in him. But I never liked Greenspan. In fact, I could hardly look at him without animosity, and Charlie had always suspected this. But now the cat's brush with death brought inspiration. Greenspan had stayed alive. When the cat fell out the window whose screen I was changing, and I couldn't find his body, I hypothesized that the cat had crawled off somewhere to wait for his terrible injuries to kill him. I didn't see how he could have survived a fall from the second story, and when Charlie shouted at me, I knew he was justified. I was miserable with guilt. Long after dark that night, Charlie heard something at the back door and went to investigate. He returned with Greenspan on his shoulder, one long-haired paw curled presumptuously around Charlie's neck. Dropping upside down toward the shrubbery, Greenspan had clawed at the air. He managed to snap onto the gnarly head of an old ivy vine I had been trying to get rid of for years and he clung to that, righted himself, scaled down the vine to the ground, and skulked around the back of the house until he recovered his customary poise. "Just a correction in the market," Charlie said about Greenspan's prospects.

The sound of the engines changed, and the plane dropped down a little, as if it were going down a stair step.

The engines spoke louder, and the plane eased down again. After a few minutes without radio chat, Hugh made contact with a controller. "This is King Air N666MD—November 6-6-6 March Duck. . . ."

When Hugh's conversation with the controller ceased, the plane dropped. Packaged, even tightly as I was in the tack trunk, I felt myself a falling object. I had never had this sensation as a passenger upright in a purchased seat. But now when the plane fell, the wooden box and the object in it, my tortured body, fell with it. This is what it would be like in an hour or so when the plane was far enough out from the coast, except that the fall would take longer. Then it would hit the waves.

The plane jolted when it made contact with the runway. But my trunk did not slam down on the plane's floor, and the trunk beside it also rode out the landing without a bounce. So there was, in fact, something in that trunk. A cough, a little grunt, and feet moving, clothes brushing the seats then my trunk. The door alongside my trunk opened.

Then snapped shut. There were no sounds of anyone in the cockpit. Would this be Atlanta? The prospect of the city's big airport sent an electrifying lift of hope through my cramped legs and back, neck and arms. The two men had left me for dead. I had no idea when or whether they would be back. Someone might come near enough to the plane to hear me when I called out or to witness Hugh Vaughn when he discovered I was alive.

I was expecting jet engines, baggage dories, backup beeps. But there was very little sound from outside the plane. I couldn't be sure I heard even the wind. The place where the plane had come down was too quiet to be Atlanta, too goddamned still. My hope shriveled, and it occurred to me that possibly the plane had come to light on a private landing strip and would be left there away from the eyes of the rest of the world, which meant that in the end it might not be water. It might be slower, a lot slower, and more grueling.

One way or another . . . This certainty brought me to the painful facts that I would never see Charlie again, never see Stephen. No good-byes.

I had been fond of telling them there would be no nursing home for me, no sir. I would fall off, land on my head, and be done instantly. This was just vanity, denial because I was afraid of getting old and sick. But to be done with it in a tack trunk seemed like an outsize punishment for that bit of selfishness. I wouldn't be launched on my head because I wouldn't ride again.

And what about the horses? Talk about denial. The experts' columns in the horse magazines always advised, "Be sure your family knows what you want them to do with the horses." But I had made no arrangements for any of mine.

I was berating myself when there was the comforting sound of a truck engine. It came quite close to the plane before it was cut. Outside the plane, I heard Hugh, "Kerosene, right?" Then metal on metal, something knocking against the plane. Someone was fueling the plane. Probably not Hugh. I began shifting my weight violently, trying to make the trunk rock against the floor of the plane. But it must have been secured. It lifted only a hair's breadth from the floor. "Hey." I tried to call out, and this resulted in little more than a gasp. "I'm in here. I'm in here!" The effort nearly cost me my consciousness. One of the doors opened. I threw myself against the walls of the trunk. "I am in here." That made more noise, a blurry croak. Then plane door closed. I had not been noticed and was now defeated. It would be stupid to cry. I had to conserve my energy, my breath.

A few more knocking sounds of refueling. Then I heard the voice, a husky cigarettes-and-whiskey voice. "Yup. I'm it. Air traffic. Service. Maintenance—and cashier. Don't forget that last one. Cashier. Now just give me one minute here."

The plane door opened.

"See? I told you, you got a problem in that trunk."

I began working my shoulders and hips, making the trunk wiggle as much as I could. Someone was climbing into the plane. The new voice was quite near when it suggested, to no one in particular, just the situation itself, "Open 'er up."

There was some fiddling, a scrabbling against the lid, and something, whatever had secured the trunk, brushed the side of the trunk as it fell to the floor. Light blasted into the box. It stunned me, and the rush of air was overpowering. I turned my head.

"I'll be damned!" A face loomed in the brightness, huge and distorted and amazed. She, the owner of the new voice, had steel-gray hair. The gray was unusually uniform, and the hair was cut in jags around her face and neck, a pixie. She had bright blue eyes and thin, penciled brows, and in spite of the mechanic's coveralls she wore, she also wore lipstick. The label sewn on the breast pocket said IRIS. She was framed by a background of baby blue.

"Up," she said, "and out." When this didn't happen on command, she put her arms under my shoulders and lifted me upright. The pain of unfolding my arms and legs and back was accompanied by pins and needles all over. I was aglow with sensation. The pain in my head just behind my left eye was nothing new. It had been there for hours. I had no idea what time it was, what day it was, or how long I had been in the trunk. The towel dropped from my shoulders to the airplane floor, the letter L in LTS on the top fold.

The cockpit was baby blue. Baby blue upholstery, baby blue seats, baby blue curtains were strung in pleats above the oval windows. Heidi Vaughn's favorite color, I suspected. The cabin was fairly roomy, and in addition to the seats in the cockpit for the pilot and copilot, it was set up for four seats. Two of these seats had been removed and replaced by the two trunks. The trunk behind mine was still strapped down. The way we got out of the plane was half and half—half Iris hauling me out of the tack truck and half me crawling uncoordinated.

She stood under the plane's wing for a moment, supporting me. She was so small she fit right under my shoulder.

"Looks like you're on your way to someplace nice," she observed. But now my frilly blouse, the jacket, and the slacks looked exactly like they had been stuffed into a tack trunk for hours.

Hugh and—it was not Vicente, it was Ruben, the big Latino man who was Win Guthrie's new groom—had been left standing by the wing, just under the cockpit window. They gawked. Maybe I didn't have things figured out quite right, but neither did they. Hugh was evidently as stunned to see me standing there, alive, as I was to be there. He still wore the oilcloth drover's jacket he had worn out to the cross-country course. His arms hung at his side at the ready but unsure what they should do next. Even so, behind a mask of bafflement, Hugh was thinking about this. The big groom's square jaw hung. He was a study in abject misery.

The place was an airport, a blacktop runway and a Quonset building. Hugh's plane was just the level of posh I would have expected. It didn't shout money, but it spoke about it. Clean swept-back design, a glittering smooth paint job, and meticulously maintained. Even the turbo wells behind the propellers were as hygienically clean as stainless steel. The number on its side was the one he had given the controller, his call number. It ended with MD. Although there were three small propeller planes and a crop duster anchored to the asphalt near the Quonset, Hugh's plane brought the only activity this airport would see today. Surrounding us on all sides were flat fields of dark earth strewn with the pale dried sheaths of plants. Onions.

"I have to pee." I announced the urgency of this situation to all present. Iris poked me in the side and nodded at the Quonset. We started for it, me leaning on her, lurching like a cripple.

"I bet you do," Hugh mused menacingly. "I bet you do."

It was that easy. I was rescued. Iris opened the trunk, and I walked past the two men to freedom. We reached the Quonset, and Iris opened the blank metal door. "First plane in here in four days," she said, and locked the door behind us. We were in a small office partitioned off from the hangar that occupied the rest of the Quonset. She headed for a radio console on a table behind a prewar metal desk and pointed to a door down a narrow hall that led into the hangar. "Toi-dee."

The radio came on in a blast of static. Iris muttered, "Oh hell!" and shut it down. Something about it wouldn't work. I was having my own operational difficulties. Although I was regaining coordination and had managed to unzip my slacks, I could not organize myself to sit down. My limbs were disconnected from my intention. I approached the toilet head-on, then from the left, the right, and finally backed into it hard enough to remind my knees how to buckle. The relief was a kind of agony. But I had endured with my resolutions intact. I had not wet myself, and I had not cried. As soon as Iris could get that radio working and the police arrived, I wanted to talk to Charlie. I wanted to sit down with him over a glass of scotch and find out where Exit Laughing placed. I wanted to tell him all about the ins and outs of traveling in a tack trunk. I wanted to see Stephen and maybe even Alex.

Iris was waiting for me beside her desk. She was a pretty woman, I realized, and even in coveralls, quite feminine, like a female imp.

"You manage to make contact?"

She said "Yup," and stared meaningfully behind me.

The massive Ruben blocked the narrow hall and the door into the hangar. He held a gun. It had been somewhere in the plane.

"Goddamn." It was really more a question than a curse.

"Decided not to use the radio." Iris shrugged. "Thought they might have a gun in the plane—and if they had the plane radio on and heard me, they might panic and try to shoot their way in here."

"But how—"

"I sneaked out to use the pay phone in the hangar, and Poncho here bumped into me."

"Ah," I said, "Poncho." I used it as a taunt. I wasn't afraid of him or his gun. I was suddenly furious at my treatment, at the abrupt loss of my freedom. I said, "So Poncho. Now you've got two of us. And you need something more reliable than a tea towel, yes?"

He wiggled the nose of the gun at us to herd us toward the door to the runway. When neither of us moved, he pushed the gun ahead of him more forcefully. "*Vamos.*" Our feet were planted. He had to go through the wiggle-the-gun-*vamos* routine two more times and get close to Iris's ear with the gun's muzzle before our feet turned reluctantly toward the door. By now he was red in the face. Hugh was waiting for him beside the viperous little jet. "*Vamos! Vamos!*"

"Okay, Poncho," said Iris agreeably. But there was no way she could travel any slower and still be described as moving. "Who's cookin' dinner tonight anyway?"

Hugh Vaughn was opening the door to the cabin. I said, to none of my companions in particular but the airport in general, "I am not getting on that plane again."

The sun was low and shone a dull red on the runway and the tail of the plane. Had one day passed? Or only the last part of the afternoon? The cabin door was open.

"I am not getting on that plane again." Claustrophobia had its arms around my rib cage. The snout of the gun jabbed me from behind, just below my bra band, and I tripped forward a little faster. I repeated, "I am not getting on that plane again."

Wandering like sheep in front of a determined dog, we were conducted up to Hugh Vaughn. When we came to a halt, Iris said to him, "You know what you're doin', honey? How many hours you got?"

"Enough," he replied disdainfully, and our big shepherd wiggled the gun at the plane's open door.

Iris didn't move any farther. "How many?"

"Twenty-three hundred."

Iris shrugged and said, "Okay." She turned, stepped up into the cabin, and paused in the doorway.

I said it again. "I am not getting on this plane again. If you're going to kill me, shoot me right here."

As Hugh considered this request, his usually good-humored expression faded, and a look of distaste, as if he had put something disgusting in his mouth, remained. He said, "No."

"You may not have any choice," I informed him. "You may have to shoot me to get me on this plane."

I noticed his hand moving in the pocket of his drover's jacket. If it was a gun, it wouldn't do him any good. Shooting me wouldn't win this argument. I decided he was bluffing.

"Get in the plane, Tink."

"That your name? Tink?" This woman who had been forced into sudden intimacy with me did not even know my name.

The standoff lasted a number of minutes. I'm not sure how many. Finally, Iris took the role of mediator. She said, "Don't be such a dumb shit."

"Dead is dead," I insisted. I was more afraid of a free fall to the waves than I was of a bullet.

"It is not," she pointed out reasonably, "being alive. And Poncho and your other buddy don't want to leave two bodies on my runway."

"Only a matter of time—"

Ruben couldn't stand it anymore. He fired the gun into the onion field.

"Ruben!" Hugh exploded in a streak of vicious Spanish. The calm and humorous disdain that he usually wore on his face was twisted into a kind of anguish.

"You want to die here, not too far from home?" I kept it up. "I see you have a husband."

She glanced briefly at her ring. "That's just man-repellent. If that don't work, I get out the snuff."

"Or do you want to be killed up in the clouds and thrown out who knows where? And maybe they won't bother to shoot you first."

Iris smiled. If she had been happy and relaxed this would have been a delightful impish expression, but as it was, it was a mechanical upturning of the corners of her mouth. "Actually, Tink,

I like the idea of getting in the plane. I mean I really like it. We're worth more alive to them in the air."

"Exactly," Hugh agreed immediately.

"And I'm comfortable in a plane, Tink. Really comfortable."

"I'm not." But I wondered if she was trying to tell me something, and I could see that maybe she was right. If I persuaded them to shoot me here, it was an absolute certainty I wouldn't see Charlie again. Or Stephen. Or Frankie. Never throw a leg over a horse again, never present another horse to another fence. I followed her up into the baby blue cockpit, saying, "Not the trunk."

"Only room for one of you anyway," Hugh said cheerfully about the trunk.

Iris glanced at the other, unopened tack trunk. "What's in that?"

No one answered. Hugh gestured for Iris to take the copilot's seat behind the second set of controls and for me to take a baby blue seat almost back to back with it, except for a brief partition that jutted a foot or so between the seats to define the cockpit area. Evidently the seat that backed up to Hugh's seat was reserved for Ruben. But I suddenly knew. I knew what the other trunk held, and the realization struck like a blow to my body. Patty, Layton's delivery person, had been in Hugh's way. I crumpled in the seat, arms against knees, from the finality and hopelessness of what had happened.

Now that he was back in control, Hugh returned to his former good humor. I could see the force of his ego. It was tethered by his sense of being in control. When Iris and I had walked free an hour ago, he was lost, even to himself. Now that he had returned to the pilot's seat, the pleasant Hugh was back. He was the doctor, the gynecologist you could imagine managing your most intimate concerns.

"Ruben—their hands and feet."

The trunk where I had been trapped yielded only enough rope to bind one pair of hands behind a seat and one pair of ankles, mine. Ruben looked to the other trunk. "Lead ropes in there?"

Hugh shrugged and put on his headset. "Sure."

He started the engines and brought out his takeoff checklist. The groom untied the straps that were holding down the other trunk, flipped the latch, and raised the lid. The glint of bright red hair was too much for me. I looked away, up ahead past Iris, but couldn't erase the appalling sight or quell the outrage welling up. Patty's young dream had died with her. Iris stared at the dead girl curled in the trunk. Nothing else had intimidated her during our brief acquaintance, but this and the smell seeping into the cabin brought her up short. For the few moments it took for Ruben to rummage under Patty McLaren's body and come up with a couple of lead ropes, she seemed rattled, shrinking back into herself. The stench was powerful. I started to gag, choking on my own fury as much as the terrible air. In the front of the plane Iris and Hugh were coughing.

The trunk lid closed, and Iris and I were bound, hands behind our seats, feet in front of us. The plane lifted off into the dusk. Fastening our seat belts would have been redundant. Hugh was the only one who was afforded this safety measure. Ruben was having to sit sideways on his seat so that he had a direct shot at both of us. Maybe this meant they had only one gun between the two of them. He coughed on and off in spasms, and the gun in his hand bobbled, jumped up and down. Hugh joined in, choking, and even after we were cruising above the pink-iced clouds, he kept the air conditioner running on high. Jerking her head back toward the tack trunk next to Ruben, Iris said, "Why'd you wanna do that, honey?"

Although he had been addressed directly, Hugh did not answer.

"Too bad," she went on. "Now it gets to be just plain no goddamn fun. Don't it?"

All light leached from the sky, and the plane went on in darkness. Hugh didn't seem to have any rules against speaking, so I said. "Hugh, where are we going?"

"South southwest," he responded amiably enough.

"Mexico? Over the Gulf?"

"South southwest maybe," Iris commented. "But not very far south southwest."

"Mexico," he said firmly. This eventual destination meant that, although Ruben was his go-to guy, Vicente must be Hugh's partner.

"Honey, you ain't got the fuel to get to Mexico," Iris pointed out.

Hugh glanced quickly at the gauge.

"I never got a chance to finish what I was doin'," she said. "Like I told you, my airport is a one-woman show. If I got to get Tink here out of your luggage and into the toi-dee, I can't finish puttin' in the fuel."

2

A strong breeze caught the hotel door. The temperature had dropped. If the weekend had begun with an unexpectedly warm autumn day, with the anxieties and anticipation of autumn, it would close out in premature winter. The sky's early light showed dull gray clouds moving in on the biting air. A snowflake wouldn't have surprised him, but then, given the undercurrent of disorder that had carried the first two days, nothing much would. Charlie snapped up the brim of his outback hat to keep the wind from stealing it.

There was a dark green Monte Carlo in one of the spaces near the hotel entrance. Shaddaux didn't get out of the car or shake hands, but somewhere in the predawn he had found two cups of coffee. He nodded as Charlie settled himself.

"How'd you sleep?"

"Like a baby."

Shaddaux didn't look so bright-eyed himself. Unshaven, his jaw didn't seem to jut so much. He eyed the canvas tote at Charlie's feet.

"Change of clothes for her," Charlie explained. Shaddaux drew in a long breath, like a person trying to shush himself, and took the wheel.

They had already worked through the last-seen-last-said questions on the telephone, and now they drove in silence, Charlie waiting for direction and possibly even leadership from the lieutenant. But the detective wasn't forthcoming. Tink was right about the way the police hoarded information. They couldn't let trust interfere with objectivity, and maybe it was a kind of relief to hand Tink's fate over to a more worldly authority.

The road they were traveling was very familiar, but it was all wrong. He broke the silence.

"Where are we going?"

"Your place."

Charlie had expected the two of them would go directly to the event grounds. His instinct was to hurry back to the last place he had been with her, like one of Tink's terriers frantically digging at a hole that had produced a mouse. He wasn't prepared to go home, and he thought it was a waste of time. But he didn't protest.

Their tall federal house stood back from the road on a gentle incline. Every one of the long windows blazed with light. That sight was almost painful. There was a police van parked in the drive, and two uniformed cops had begun to search the house, one on each floor. Tink's two short-legged terriers ran up and down the stairs in high hilarity. That really did hurt. He didn't know what he would do with them if she didn't return.

He said, "The dog sitter will be here in an hour or two."

"We'll be out of here by then."

Charlie looked around the rooms as if seeing them for the first time. The parlor and his plump blue chair with the cushion hollowed out by his butt. The unruly stack of magazines beside it. The camelback sofa where Tink never sat but always stretched out, and her clogs left heel to heel under it. The card table in the little sitting room, a permanent fixture for Thursday evening poker games, which held a chip caddy, a litter of cards, a couple of pencils, and scrap paper.

"We're not housekeepers," he said but then was a little disgusted with himself for apologizing for the place where he had always been so comfortable. Upstairs, a cop went through her closet and then the drawers. Downstairs, the other cop had started on the table in the hall, where the phone and its notepad resided.

Observing this, Shaddaux began his own exploration. "Did your wife ever sell a horse to Win Guthrie?"

"Sure. Any number of them." The terrier Spit was wriggling between his ankles, and when he reached down automatically to stroke the dog, his brother Polish growled and pushed up under his hand.

"Buy any from him?"

"Not recently." Buy, sell. He couldn't remember. Horses usually came in only four colors—chestnut, bay, brown, and black. They walked into and backed out of horse trailers, and the only one he recognized on sight was Exit Laughing. Maybe this was because the horse was gray.

"Did she ever talk to you about Guthrie?"

"Yes," he said cautiously, wondering where this line of questioning was leading.

"Were there ever any hard feelings over one of the horses?" Were they friends? Still on good terms? Ever anything more than friends?

"Many years ago, long before I knew Tink, she had some kind of an affair with him."

"That over?"

Charlie didn't bother to answer. He was becoming impatient. "Lieutenant, I think you're barking up the wrong tree. I may not have all the information you have, but the direction you're leaning in seems truly implausible." He was confident that Tink had told him what there was to know about her side of the affair and that Win was nothing but what he represented himself to be—too busy to carry grudges. "You should probably scout the barn. That's where Tink's real business is."

The detective followed him to the kitchen door but didn't stop the two men working through the house. They walked to the barn in full daylight. At least an hour and a half had passed and, as far as Charlie could see, an hour and a half had been wasted. His anxiety doubled. The central aisle of the barn was splashed with sunshine. It was swept clean, and the halters and leads hanging on the stall fronts, the pitchforks and shovels in the equipment room, the saddles and bridles and bits and harness parts in the tack room were in strict order. Shaddaux passed in front of the small blackboard on the tack room wall beside the big rolltop desk. Written on the blackboard was WIN—THURSDAY.

"Do you know anything about that?"

He didn't, just then, and that rattled him. "What records there are would be right there and in old checking statements—left-hand drawer."

They entered the feed room, where the shelves above the grain bins offered an orderly row of ointments, poultices, medications, and a small clear plastic box that held disposable syringes. Charlie opened this to show the unused syringes with their guard caps still in place.

"Do you know, lieutenant, about the horse of Win's that collapsed in the vet box yesterday?"

Maybe this was news to Shaddaux because he said, "Guthrie's?"

"Yes. Tink had—" Why was he falling into this disheartening tendency to use the past tense? "—has a theory about that. And Paul Lamoreaux agrees. The horse could have been reacting to a painkiller they call bute—phenylbutazone."

"There was nothing on the patch," the detective objected.

"Right. She thinks the patch was there just to make sure the horse was blood-tested." Charlie tapped the lid of the plastic jar of bute on the shelf. "Usually bute is used as a pill that's mixed into the feed. Maybe it's ground up first. But it also comes as an injectable liquid. Works great, faster than the dry stuff if it's injected into the muscle. But it if goes into a vein, it causes convulsions, and it can kill a horse."

Shaddaux nodded. "Who did your wife share this theory with?"

"Paul and Win and me."

"She wanted to protect Guthrie?"

"*Lieutenant*," he was unable to hide his exasperation, "I tell you, you are barking up the wrong tree."

Shaddaux looked around mildly. "Anything else I should see down here?"

"Not unless you want to look the horses over. Where to?" Now that it seemed the detective had seen what he needed to at the farm, Charlie was in a hurry. He headed quickly toward the unmarked green car parked in the drive behind the police van.

His anxiety slackened minutes later when he saw they were on their way to the event grounds, but it would take another half hour to get there.

"Breakfast?" Shaddaux inquired unbelievably.

"Christ no!" His terrier instinct was taking over. He wanted to go to ground again in the original hole and start digging.

Even though the car was an unmarked green Chevrolet Monte Carlo, the detective declined to park it in the competitors' lot. He drove past that lot to the entrance of paid spectator parking a half mile down the road, and he pretended not to notice Charlie's impatience.

"This will be competition as usual," Shaddaux instructed. "Your wife will be along soon."

Charlie nodded. He too felt the necessity to cover up the news of his present emergency, keep things quiet. They had returned to the event to find out who else was still there—and who wasn't. No flap that might cause somebody with more information than he and Shaddaux had to flee the grounds.

"Anybody else know I'm here?" Shaddaux seemed to have a running account of all of them in his head. "Ms. Golden?"

"She knows that," he confirmed, "but she'll keep up a good front."

Shaddaux filed that away, then he reminded Charlie, "There is nothing out of the ordinary going on."

With the wind at their backs they walked along the side road that fronted the cross-country course and, farther away, the stables and trade fair. Taking the long way in seemed an unnecessary delay, but Charlie made use of it.

"Lieutenant, do you have the cases of supplement that were at Tomlinson's barn?"

"We're having stuff from each jar analyzed."

"Did you know that Paul Lamoreaux went into a case of the stuff that was hanging around Win's tack room and had it analyzed?"

"Analyzed how?"

"Mass spectrometry, he told Tink and me at the party. He and Win had a bet on."

Shaddaux smiled. "If you're a vet, I guess you don't fool around. What did they turn up?"

"Win won the bet. When I called Paul this morning, he said the compound in the Mighty Fit bottles had nothing to do with building muscle or aerobic fitness. It was apparently some kind of enzyme that's involved in reproduction."

"Reproduction?'

"Estrogen processing," he explained and hoped that might

clarify something for Shaddaux. All this information had done for Charlie was to put his thinking into dither mode. Ever since getting this report from Paul, he had been searching his memory for what he knew about estrogen and trying to link that to Tink, where she might be, and why. But the word that kept returning to him had nothing to do with Tink or with reproduction. *Cancer.* Cancer, because hadn't he read somewhere—where was it?—that estrogen and the way the female body processes it has something to do with women's cancer?

But Shaddaux didn't respond to the term *estrogen processing.* He sighed. "Our guys will probably take a few more days with the stuff we have."

Charlie couldn't be certain he had read it, but he had a strong memory of seeing *ESTROGEN PROCESSING*, black type against a white page.

A hundred yards before they came to the path into the stables and before they encountered anyone else, Shaddaux turned in the direction of the trade fair where the food vendors were just propping up their awnings. "I'll be at the secretary's office. You have my cell phone number?"

"Yup. Frankie does too."

They had come to the last test of the horses. At the stables the pace of chores was slower than it had been on cross-country day. Because there was less ground for each horse to cover, the show jumping would start later in the morning. The order of go would start with the horse standing last and work up to the top horse. This scheme is intended to draw out suspense and keep spectators sitting around the jumping ring in their lawn chairs for as long as possible. It works because even the top horses are tired from the speed and distance of cross-country day, and it doesn't take more than the tick of a hoof to bring down a fence rail. With even just a single rail down, the current leaders can tumble down in the standings, and a horse that has persisted in the middle of the field can rocket up to take the victory gallop. For the packers, the steady horses in the middle, the stadium jumping offers one last opportunity to prevail. For the horses enjoying the top positions, it offers the opportunity to lose everything.

People loved that, Charlie thought. But Tink always said Exit Laughing was very careful. He put off the inevitable face-to-face with Stephen by making his way first to the competitors' tent at the edge of the stabling area. The scores and time sheets were posted there for the riders.

THE FLYING TIGER: 32.8

SUDDEN SUNSET: 40.3

EXIT LAUGHING: 43.6

Not surprisingly, Barbara Beecher's buckskin—maybe homely, unprepossessing but a running and jumping machine—was standing second. Win's mare Ithinkican was a few places below Exit Laughing, and his bay, the other horse owned by Halefellow, was well down in the standings. Charlie patted the pocket of his parka and found he didn't have his program with its stats chart. He didn't care. He would have to face the kids and lie. Stephen wouldn't be fooled, but he wouldn't press him, which would only make the experience worse.

Charlie turned to the task and went on to the stables, where he found Stephen holding Exit Laughing and Alex working methodically at the gray mane, making the tiny, rolled braids the horses wore on show jumping day. Stephen looked at Charlie over the horse's ears. "Where's Ma?"

Charlie knew the necessary lie. He had rehearsed it, but for a moment couldn't find speech.

Stephen was looking directly at him now. "You and Ma still fighting?"

Charlie smiled. "I think I got that patched up."

"Charlie, you drink too much last night?" the kid asked with a large dose of disbelief.

"No, Stephen. Why?"

"You look like you tied one on."

"Sorry to hear that." Another smile.

"So where's Ma?"

Now Alex looked up from the braids.

"Chitchat with Shaddaux, and maybe a little field trip. But she's walked the jumps, and she'll be back in time for the horse's round. Anything I can do for you? Breakfast maybe?"

"No thanks, Charlie. But you better put something in your stomach."

Food was not what he wanted. He didn't know what he wanted. Maybe at this point it was only not to look as lost as he felt. He made his way past the trade fair and secretary's office to the hill just below the show jumping arena, where a number of grooms had brought their horses to graze. There was Tomlinson's young groom and Tomlinson, each with a horse in hand. Heidi Vaughn was with them. She gave him a twinkling little wave.

"Where's the better half?"

"Tink slept in."

"Of course, owner's prerogative, now that she's not riding. Hugh's had a call from the hospital—emergencies only happen on Saturday night. Fortunately, the plane makes that workable. He flew back up to the city, but he should get back here in time to watch our horse."

"Be a shame to miss the jumping, especially since your horse is in first place."

"Everything to lose," she said cheerfully as he moved past her and up the hill. He felt nauseated. He wondered what Shaddaux was up to, who he was telephoning.

At the top of the hill, the show jumping arena was set up in full dress, immaculately painted rails in bold colors guarded by big pots of yellow and bronze mums, and the coarse sand underfoot raked in shallow grooves all around the fences. A few riders wearing parkas over their breeches stalked purposefully among the jumps, pacing the distances, planning their rides, and hardier spectators had begun to gather along the edges of the arena and stake out their places with lawn chairs. He hadn't thought to bring the chairs. He didn't care. He hoped he wouldn't be standing around very long.

Frankie and Lourdes joined him, and Vicente came along behind, lugging chairs. Frankie wore a very natural-looking smile, and as she reached him, she said quietly, "No need to lie. I've already done that."

He smiled at Lourdes and at Vicente, a big, broad, fake-happy smile, and he wondered if the first horse would ever come to the in-gate. More spectators drifted up to the arena. He noticed a few of the more resourceful among them brought wool horse coolers and when they took their seats in their folding chairs draped the blankets over themselves. Would this goddamn show ever start? And would it ever end?

Frankie looked out across the arena to the spot where Heidi Vaughn had settled, and said to Charlie with a little annoyance, "Why isn't Hugh here?"

"Emergency," he reported before he had time to wonder about her question. Then he realized that all through the event Frankie had been keeping her distance from Hugh.

"How come you're worried about Hugh?" he asked. "You never speak to him, even to say hello."

"Charlie"—as in *Come on, stupid*—"this drug trial is very hush-hush."

"Frankie. Why should a trial, a legitimate drug trial, be hush-hush?"

"Well, because it's not just about confidentiality, it's about anonymity and—"

Estrogen processing. Now he knew where he'd read that term—the funding proposal from the Mexican firm.

Charlie stood up so abruptly that the wind took his hat in spite of its folded brim. The hat blew down the hill, where the first horse making its way up to the arena saw it, shied, and tried to bolt. He leaned over Frankie's and Lourdes's chairs to speak to Vicente, and in that moment the image of the smiling, expansive Hugh on the moving walkway at O'Hare flickered up from his memory. Hugh, who must have been heading into Chicago for an appointment with Layton McLaren—Layton McLaren, another gynecologist, another partner in Hugh's so-called trials, was now dead—and Hugh was smiling, smiling confidently.

The marked Mighty Fit bottles in Jason's tack room. The clear liquid in them.

Charlie pulled back and, leaving the Mexican visitors baffled, ran down the hill to find Shaddaux. Frankie raised the videocam to follow this. "God only knows what he's after," she suggested, trying to sound careless. Vicente wasn't listening. He and Lourdes were locked into a tense, whispered conversation.

"Why don't we stay put until Tink's horse jumps." Frankie wasn't asking a question. She was giving an instruction.

3

Hugh Vaughn showed no signs of panic at the news about the fuel level. He said, "We can drop down and pick up some fuel," and engine noise took over for a good, long while. The view outside remained the same, the orbs of the plane's lights shining into the darkness. It almost didn't seem as if we were moving. But we were, and we were moving fast.

"Something to think about when you get ready to bring this airplane down, honey," Iris suggested. "With her"—nodding at the trunk nearest Ruben—"and a full tank of fuel, you're over capacity. Weight wise."

"Are you the pilot?" Hugh demanded rhetorically.

"No, sir. No siree. Not right now." Whatever that meant about her plans. "But I figured you might not have thought about being over the weight and not really needing me, for instance, or Tink here. And when you drop down, you could just leave the two of us on the ground."

Hugh didn't even consider this proposal. He said, "We are going to Mexico. We are *all* going to Mexico."

Iris sighed philosophically, and since there was nothing else she could do with her hands tied behind her, gazed out the windshield into the blackness we were passing through. I wondered what he would do about fuel. I doubted he would allow the plane to run out and be forced down in the dark, although somehow landing on water wasn't as frightening as dropping in free fall into it.

There was a wide black leather briefcase between the two front seats, something very similar to a salesman's sample case, and after several minutes Hugh reached down, opened the case, and brought out a chart compressed in a complicated fold. He took his hands off the yoke for a moment to unfold the chart and align it across Iris's lap.

"See if you can find a good place to land and get fuel," he instructed.

"This time of night, you'll have to use one that takes commercial flights," Iris warned, keeping in mind his desire for his plane and our flight to be inconspicuous.

"I know," he said regretfully, and he reached into the pocket of his jacket where I had suspected there was a gun. But when he withdrew his hand, his fingers were curled around something that he put in his mouth and swallowed. Drugs, it seemed, were Hugh's livelihood in more than one way.

Iris watched this and suggested, "Happy pills? You know it's illegal to fly if you're on those."

"I'm okay," he assured her softly, and with his own reassurance, his mood seemed to shift a little upward.

A strange form of companionship was developing in the cockpit. It came from the stasis of capturing and being captured. We—Ruben perched sideways in his seat, a dead girl in the box, Hugh commanding our flight, Iris searching the flight chart, and me, wondering if landing for fuel could offer any possibility of escape—assumed a certain level of civility. Occasionally we spoke, as when Iris said, "I think your best bet would be Pensacola—six commercial flights a day, and one of them lands at ten."

"They'll have the fuel crew on," Hugh agreed.

If this state of enforced intimacy continued until we lifted off from Pensacola, we would be flying over water and Hugh would offload a few hundred female pounds. So why not risk pissing him off? I asked the same question about Patty that Iris had asked. I said, "Hugh, you were doing so well. You were saving patients, getting a big reputation. Why did you want to take such a big chance and kill her? Kill Joe? Why Layton?"

He turned briefly from the controls, and he said, "They were destroying me, and you're right. I had a useful practice, a good practice. I saved hundreds of women. I spared their families terrible losses. But they were trying to destroy all that."

"Who?"

He didn't answer the question directly, but he seemed relieved to be talking.

"Layton—I knew him from medical school, so I knew he had his principles. Principles," he repeated, "and the trials in Europe were going to be legal. . . ." Hugh seemed to think he was vindicating himself.

"Your trials weren't legal?"

He gave a short laugh to answer my question. "The drug worked. It was working. But approval takes forever, and I had patients—not patience. Those European trials weren't necessary, just more delay. Layton was backpedaling, wanting to wait for the results in Europe. I had to use some pressure."

"The truck fire."

"Yeah. It went wrong, way wrong. It never occurred to me she would ride in the back with the horse."

This apparently was all that Joe Terrell's death and Patty's escape meant to him.

"So Layton just got a scare. Then he goes—you tell me why—then he goes to Patty. Why did he need to talk things over with Patty? He knew me. Why couldn't he just trust me?" His question was preposterous.

"But couldn't you have just stopped the treatments and explained to your patients that your source was no longer available?"

"Goddamnit, Tink. I have them to think about. My patients."

He was sincere. He believed he was working on behalf of Frankie and her counterparts. The crack in this man's mind was so deep, the fissure in his personality so clean, that he worked back and forth across it without noticing the gap. He believed the violence he had resorted to and would resort to again was justified.

"So I had to go the direct route," he said.

"Patty," I concluded. "And Layton."

"Layton's conscience was a little scary. I couldn't have him talking—a prison term could ruin things for my patients, for me—and I had to make sure the girl didn't talk either. Before that—I needed to be very careful—I had to eliminate every scrap of paper that could tie me to the Delgados." He seemed to be remembering something and smiled. "Of course, there was nothing in your desk, but how was I to know that you didn't believe in supplements? You never had any idea someone had paid a visit to your tack room, did you?"

The reptile. I was too repelled to respond to his taunt. Him. Pawing through my desk.

He couldn't tell right from wrong, up from down, and was past the point of no return. He wasn't capable of making a decision. He was only capable of seeing whether or not he was in control.

If he wasn't, everything would go out of control. Iris and I had to get free of the plane when it came down in Pensacola.

I contemplated the stars that hung over the little jet. Off and on Hugh made contact with the tower at Pensacola, and after a while, the back and forth on the radio was almost steady. At that point Iris announced, "We're in range."

"Starting down," he announced to any of us who might be interested. "Pensacola tower. This is King Air N666MD—" Tiny pinpoints of lights from the airport grew into larger, steadier beacons as the plane made one sweep over the airport. "Roger. 66MD understand clear to land runway."

The plane banked and turned and dropped down toward the tarmac. We were low enough to look into the warmly lit windows of the airport bar and grill. I longed miserably for the light of my own stable, and then the plane bounced on the runway. But any escape scenario forming in my mind fell away as Hugh abruptly goosed the plane up into the air and back into flight again. As we swept over one of the hangars, I caught a glimpse of two patrol cars parked in the shadow of the building.

"*Problema?*" Ruben was as startled as Iris and I.

"Sneaking bitch!" He spat the accusation at Iris. "Tipped them off."

"Who?"

"You saw the cops!" He challenged all of us, his eyes still with the plane's trajectory. "Gathered like flies to shit. And there was only one way they could find out," he shouted at his hog-tied copilot.

"You're not going to land?" Iris suggested calmly. He didn't hear her because he was raging, losing control.

"I wish I *had* tipped them off," she said. "But I didn't get no opportunity. And honey, either you're going to have to calm yourself right down or you're going to have to let me fly this plane."

People who are furious do not respond well to being told to calm down. It only makes them more furious. In our case, it caused the plane to tip from side to side at irregular intervals.

"Hugh, is it possible," I intervened, "that those cops were on another mission, that they had no interest in us? Why are we assuming this plane is the one they are waiting for?"

Hugh put his face to the windshield to scan the patch of airport we were leaving behind, and he drew a long breath. "Only two cars," he admitted after a few moments. "But there was something about it. Didn't smell right."

The lights of Pensacola still reflected off the bottoms of the clouds below us, but as we climbed in the dark, these dimmed and died out. The illumination of the instruments was the only light. Hugh flew as if he knew where he was going, and I tried not to stare at the dial I had identified as the fuel gauge. I hoped Charlie would keep Exit Laughing, send the horse to Win's, and let Alex ride him as long as he could be competitive. Paul Lamoreaux could help Charlie place the young horses, if Charlie would only think to ask.

Hugh said something in a low voice, too soft to be heard over the drone of the engines, and Iris turned her face to him.

"I sure don't, honey. Pensacola's about as far as I know."

Hugh turned on the light above his head and reached back into the chart case. His jaws were clamped, and he flicked the chart impatiently until it opened over Iris's lap again. She ducked her head to consider possible landing sites. My shoulders ached from having my hands tied behind my seat. I stretched back to ease my shoulders, my wrists and hands passed briefly against each other, and I discovered something: a loop of rope and a free end of it flopping across my thumbs. I repeated the movement of hands and wrists, more slowly this time, to verify what I thought I had felt. Ruben had tied the knot that every groom uses to tie a horse's head, the quick-release knot. Win must have taught him that. The knot had an open loop, from which the end of the rope fell. This came in handy if a horse panicked and ran backward against the rope. Pull the dangling end and the knot fell apart to release the horse. Win must have also shown Ruben the trick that locks the knot. He had passed the end of the lead rope back through the open loop that could be jerked down to free the rope instantly.

"Okay, hon," Iris announced. "Biloxi. Maybe twenty minutes."

Apparently that was our itinerary. He turned off the light, and in the darkness I shifted my hands against each other to reassure myself that it was there, that simple thread through a simple loop. It was probably the only thing hampering the free use of my own hands.

4

Charlie's lungs were burning by the time he reached the secretary's office. Shaddaux was seated at the same folding table he had presided over the day before, the remains of breakfast on a paper plate in front of him. When Charlie rushed in hatless and red in the face, the lieutenant did a slow take.

"What's—"

"The airport," Charlie gasped.

"Philly?" Shaddaux looked confused.

"No, the little one. That's where Vaughn flies into."

"Vaughn."

"Estrogen processing—remember? That's the stuff Vaughn was smuggling in as supplement."

"For what?" Shaddaux snapped. He didn't like being in the dark.

"Cancer treatment. Let's go. I'll fill you in on the way. If you have doubts, you can ask Frankie Golden."

When Shaddaux stepped outside the little office building, he repeated this instruction into his cell phone. "Brandywine Airport. Can you get me the manager? And send a car out there."

Then he started walking out to the road, the cell phone held tightly to his head. Charlie hustled along beside him, gasping at a slower rate now. All of this demonstrated that it had, in fact, been a mistake to leave the car so far away. But in a moment, when Shaddaux said, "Right. What time was that?" he realized that the time and distance that separated them from the airport was no longer crucial. The plane had left.

"What about a flight plan?" the lieutenant inquired. He listened and then turned off the phone and tucked it into the little holster on his belt. Then, poking his key pad to open the doors of the Monte Carlo, he relayed the information to Charlie, "Hugh left about midnight, filed a flight plan for Boston."

"For what?" Charlie demanded. "He lives in New York. His wife told me he had to go back to deal with a medical emergency."

They headed for the Brandywine Airport, where a door on the side of the metal building opened on a room that was part waiting room, part coffee break room, part flight control center. They found the manager, a thin sandy-haired man with a reedy voice, behind a service desk along the back of the room. His neat blue shirt had RICH embroidered on the pocket. Rich looked carefully from the identification Shaddaux held out for him to the detective's face and acknowledged both with a nod. Then he repeated the message Shaddaux had recited: "Dr. Vaughn. Took off from here about midnight. Filed a flight plan for Boston."

From his place in front of the computer monitor Rich could easily reach back to the controls on the radio. "Let's see what happened after he got to Boston," he suggested and put out a call.

The voice that came out of the Boston airport paused and then came back with the news that no plane with Vaughn's 666MD call had come in during the last twenty-four hours. Rich rechecked the number he had entered on the computer. "Okay, it's not Logan. Maybe he changed his mind and headed out to one of the suburbs." He consulted a list on the computer screen and started putting out calls. Charlie waited restlessly through this process, and a half hour later the radio had returned only negative responses.

"She could be anywhere," Charlie murmured.

"Vaughn's plane could be anywhere," Shaddaux corrected him. "We don't know that she's with him."

"No. But she's missing. He's left. He has to know something."

By saying nothing, Shaddaux seemed to agree with that. His eyes rested on the wall map behind Rich's service counter. "Charlie, when you left the show jumping field," he ventured, "did you tell anybody where you were going, who you were going to see?"

"I didn't have time—you mean Heidi?"

Shaddaux nodded. "Yup. Maybe Delgado."

"They're all right there," Charlie objected confusedly. "How can they be involved when they're right there at the event—and they're not running?"

Shaddaux wasn't listening. He was punching his dispatcher's number into his phone. A moment later he said, "Go to the secretary's office and have them paged. We'll meet you—and them—downtown in forty minutes."

Back in the unmarked car and traveling again, Charlie noted the passage of those minutes grimly. At the troop's downtown headquarters, they waited in the small room that held the detective's improbably tidy desk, the only clean surface in an otherwise grubby space where the phone, the windows, and the filing cabinet had seemingly never been wiped clean. Too much time had gone by. His hopes were dropping. When Heidi Vaughn walked through the door with a uniformed officer just behind her, his hope failed altogether. Her blond bob and fresh lipstick spoke of careful attention on the ride downtown. But her cheeks were flaming, and her confusion was real. She knew nothing.

"Charlie! What in the world?" She came right over to him, oblivious of Shaddaux. "What are you *doing* here?"

"No idea," he said, and that was true. "What about you?"

"I told them, I told them Hugh had an emergency back in New York." Then she turned on Shaddaux. "What is the meaning of this?" She didn't wait for an answer. "This is completely illegal—a violation of our rights. You are damned well going to hear from our lawyer—and in the meantime, don't you lay a hand on either Charlie or me!" Her outrage brought a film of tears to her eyes.

The trooper who accompanied Heidi hadn't closed the door behind him, and now another trooper stepped through it with Vicente in tow. But Shaddaux motioned these two out of the room.

"Who *are* these people?" Heidi demanded, making no attempt to disguise her contempt of anyone who might better deserve the troopers' attention. No one responded, and the door closed.

"*Charlie*," she beseeched him, pulling at his arm. He stared at her numbly.

"Your husband flew out about midnight last night," Shaddaux advised her.

"I told you," she spat the words angrily, "he had an *emergency*."

"He filed a flight plan for Boston."

"For—?" She glared at Shaddaux. "That is a *lie*, and you are trying to trap me with it."

"His plane never went into Boston."

"Of course not!" Even in her fury, Heidi was a fluffy valentine of a person. "I told you, he was not going to Boston."

This was met with silence, and Heidi looked around uneasily.

"Your husband is flying around up there without an approved flight plan," the detective informed her, "and Tink Elledge is missing."

Heidi cocked her head, like a puppy trying to figure out what he wanted. She was squinting a little savagely. Then she stepped up to him, and although at that close distance she was speaking directly to his necktie, announced, "You are a lying little bastard, aren't you?"

Shaddaux was unfazed by her disrespect. Evidently he was familiar with this kind of hysteria. When she turned to flounce out of the room, he said mildly, "Just a few more minutes. We'll need a deposition."

"You don't need anything until I talk to my lawyer—" The trooper escorting her out of the room evidently wasn't intimidated by the sharp tips of her rose-pink nails or her threats. "—will cost you and everybody in this building!"

Then Shaddaux left Charlie in the cheerless office, went down the hall, and opened another door. Waiting seemed counterintuitive. Charlie wanted to be out of the police building, out of downtown Philly, driving around the paddocks of the Brandywine looking for Tink, doing something. Instead he sat.

He usually did what he was told. But his frustration with delay, with not being able to take action for himself, with his dependence on the cops, had reached the point of desperation—and about these, even, he could do nothing but note the passage of the minutes.

When Shaddaux returned more than a half hour later and said, "Want to take a ride back out to the airport?" Charlie sprang up and followed the detective outside. He was surprised to find Vicente sitting quietly in the backseat of Shaddaux's car. "He'll be joining us," Shaddaux said by way of explanation.

Charlie nodded at the face in the rearview mirror. Vicente nodded, his narrow handsome face set in resignation, and said nothing. The detective began a long call to the Brandywine Airport. They listened. Then Vicente tapped him on the shoulder.

"Charlie?"

Charlie turned to look in his strong, dark eyes.

"You remember when I came to make a presentation to your board about a year ago?"

Charlie said, "Halefellow" to be sure he was remembering the right meeting.

"Did you think that was my first business trip to the States?"

"No, your English was too good—and didn't you take the subway to get to the meeting? A newcomer wouldn't do that."

"Right. I've been coming here for the past six, seven years, since my brother and I decided we needed to diversify. The first time I came here was when Jason Tomlinson asked our company to sponsor him. Alex was now delivering Mighty Fit to him a little while, and he was asking every company who looked like they could maybe help him. We weren't going to do that without a personal meeting. Jason was keeping his horses then at an old and—*como se dice*, run-down?—place. Hugh stopped by, and when we talked, he told me about his interest in breast cancer. I mentioned we had this drug in early development—"

"And off it went," Charley said in subdued conclusion. "Your distribution system was already in place."

"We were not even then in clinical trials."

"You were trying to fund trials when you came to the board, but all the time you were getting money from Hugh and Layton McLaren—"

"My brother died," Vicente interrupted, apparently to explain who was behind the scheme with Hugh. "I could see the money from those doctors, in the long run that wasn't going to help us. Probably it would hurt. So I was looking for legitimate money."

"Which your brother wouldn't have done?"

"We were used to doing business in Mexico." Clearly Vicente

was trying to deflect criticism of his brother. "Paying bribes kept us in business, and we had bodyguards, guys like Ruben. They made it hard to kidnap us. So, if you are thinking this way, the money from Hugh and Layton didn't seem like such a sin, you know? For a while. But when he was gone and it was now up to me, I wanted to change that."

Shaddaux's end of the phone conversation ceased, and he poked at his phone. But Charlie wasn't done with his conversation, and even as the car turned onto the airport access road, he pressed ahead.

"The marked bottles?"

Vicente shook his head regretfully. "That's what was in them—highly concentrated."

In the pilots' lounge area, the same uniformed trooper who had escorted Heidi Vaughn was waiting for them and was setting out carryout sandwiches and sodas on the table near the microwave. Charlie avoided the food. At the service counter, Rich, the sandy-headed airport manager, wore the radio headset around his skinny neck. He was ready with a list on which a number of items had been checked off. Shaddaux pulled a chair around so that he sat beside the manager at the radio.

"Like you thought," Rich advised Shaddaux. "They're headed down toward the Gulf. The pilot called into Pensacola, and the plane started into a landing pattern. But then, all of a sudden, he veered off."

"Must have seen the patrol cars," the detective said.

"Why Pensacola?" Now Charlie was the one in the dark. "What's in Pensacola?"

"Fuel," Rich said.

"My guess," Shaddaux filled Charlie in, "is that Hugh is on his way back to Mexico."

"Back—" Then Charlie understood. Vicente had supplied some essential information. "Where the drug and the supplements came from."

Shaddaux nodded in the direction of Vicente. "He and Vicente may have other friends down there."

Rich donned the headset again so that he could listen. Charlie stared at a dot on the wall map that was labeled PENSACOLA. He had never been to the place, and so far as he knew Tink hadn't either. She would get a first look—if she was lucky. He glanced around at the available chairs. He was exhausted, but the chairs all had arms and didn't offer a place to stretch out.

"As soon as they get a response from the plane," Rich was listening even as he spoke, "I'll ask them to patch us in."

"And speak to him directly?" Charlie interrupted.

"Sure. As long as it's the lieutenant here asking the tower down there to do that."

The weight of Charlie's fatigue lifted somewhat. "I wonder what the chances are that you can talk him into turning the plane around."

"*We*," the detective corrected emphatically and motioned for Vicente to take his chair next to the radio. "And your guess is as good as mine."

With the headset clasping his ears primly, Vicente, evidently making good on a promise, faced the radio expectantly, and Charlie snatched up Tink's canvas tote with her change of clothes and headed out the door that led to the neighboring hangar.

5

The plane droned ahead. I noticed that Ruben had lost interest in the conversation between his boss and his captives. The monotony of the engine's wash and the difficulty of following our scattershot English had overwhelmed his need to understand what we were saying. He sat stolidly sideways, his shoulders following the tilt of the plane and the gun propped on his knee. He steadied it with both hands. It was aimed quite generally between my seat and Iris's, but that aim shifted when the angle of the plane changed.

I stretched to cover the movement of my fingers fumbling at my wrist. When the locking strand pulled down from the loop, I paused. In one more move, a yank of that free end of rope, my hands would be free. I waited for Ruben's attention to waver.

"Probably better try the Biloxi tower now," Iris said.

"I'll wait," Hugh snapped. The needle on the fuel gauge was settling low.

"We've been out of range of Pensacola long enough. Better keep your eyes peeled, honey. We ain't alone up here."

Hugh's hand went obediently to the controls.

"On your right," Iris said, and the plane banked. Ruben listed unsteadily, and I jerked the end of the rope. The quick-release knot earned its name. I left my wrists and hands together behind me, as if they were still bound. The light of another plane caught Hugh's attention. He gave his call number to the Biloxi controller. He listened for instructions, and the plane climbed.

"Holding pattern," Iris explained over her shoulder. "Commercial flight goes first."

"She doesn't need a short course in aeronautical etiquette." Hugh was trying to shut Iris up.

"No, but she may need a crash course, hon, if you don't get down to where they got some juice for this plane."

Without responding, Hugh sent the plane into the designated altitude, and it began to travel a slow arc in the night sky just beyond Biloxi. As it circled, I could see the ocean, the Gulf of Mexico, glimmering below. I kept my eye on Ruben. His shoulders and weight tilted toward the low side of the plane.

Hugh was engaged in call-and-response with the tower when suddenly his matter-of-fact conversation turned contentious.

"What's this all about?" he barked. I couldn't tell who he was talking to.

"Roger," he said resentfully. "Mrs. Elledge is with me."

He listened for a minute, his chin jerking up impatiently. "Neither of us has any information that would interest you," he said superciliously. Then ignoring the voice in the headphones, he spoke to me over his shoulder. "Tink, are you interested to hear that you and I are wanted for questioning in the disappearance of Patty McLaren?"

Did the cops somehow believe that I had run off with Hugh Vaughn? "Who *is* that?" I choked, furious that they could think I would have anything to do with this man at the controls. This lunatic who had ordered the strangling of Patty McLaren revolted me.

"Shut up!" he ordered because now he was trying to listen. Off air again, he said, "State police."

"Of all the screwball—"

"Shut up!" he demanded a little more desperately without turning off the mike.

"What kind of bullshit is this?"

"I told you. To. Shut. Up!" He raged slowly, at me, at the controller. Then I realized that bullshit was exactly what it was. The cops were misleading Hugh, steering him away from what they actually knew to lead Hugh to think he had more control over the situation than he had. This would buy more time, keep us safe a little longer.

Iris whispered, "You can't be in cahoots with him, can you, honey?"

"No, but they think so, or they're pretending to."

I saw Hugh's hands shaking. He was keeping the plane under control but not his rage. I was about to tell Iris that it didn't matter now what the police thought. Police custody would be a safe place to be while they sorted it out. I probably wouldn't need my hands free after all. But it would be stupid to give up that option.

Hugh was silent for a few minutes. I couldn't tell if he was listening to the radio or if he had anything to listen to. Had the tower cut off communication? This thought was frightening. I had been comforted by the radio presence of air traffic control.

At length Hugh said, "We have a hostage situation and a weapon. Are you aware of that?"

So there was only one gun after all.

Ruben woke up to the new volatility in the cabin, and he listened intently.

"Mrs. Elledge and I," Hugh made another astounding reversal back to his customary geniality, "have with us a hostage, an airport employee."

"I own it, honey!" Iris could not leave well enough alone. "I own the place."

"Okay, okay," he said off air. "So what is your name?"

"Iris Lanoir."

"I stand corrected," Hugh announced into the headset. "We have the owner of the airport, Iris Lanoir."

Pudgy bastard kept up the charade about my presence on the plane and deftly omitted any mention of our fourth, Ruben.

"We will need fuel." Hugh began to test his leverage with the cops.

There was a moment for the reply.

"Full tank." He was gaining confidence that he could get the upper hand. "We're going to Mexico. If Mrs. Elledge and I get guaranteed safe passage into Mexico, Iris walks free down there."

The thought of even another hour with the repellent Hugh filled my mouth with something rancid, something like hate. But evidently he was led to believe he would get what he asked for. I closed my eyes, kept my hands in position behind my seat, and said a little prayer that he was deceived.

"Bring the fuel tank to the east gate," ordered the imperial Hugh. Apparently he was now confident of his command over the situation. "No squad cars. No stowaways."

Hugh brought the plane down and taxied to the east gate. It seemed like a long wait. Then we could see the lights of the fuel truck. No cops jumped out of the cab, just a skinny black kid in new coveralls. It was depressing. The kid dragged the hose off its reel, glancing worriedly at the cockpit every few steps.

"Kerosene?" Hugh confirmed. We could hear the fuel door open and the nozzle rattle in. But nothing else for a few minutes. Then the kid was shouting.

"Hey! Hey, sir! I can't get this thing to pump!"

Hugh opened the window and considered the youth with a

kind of simmering frustration. "I wonder. Is there anyone in this fine establishment who knows how to pump fuel?"

"Yeah," the kid said fearfully. "I guess there is." He must have been sent out to the plane because he was the low man on the totem pole.

"Then walk back and send that person out here," Hugh instructed. "Walk. Don't drive. Tell the new guy that too."

Hugh shook his head. "Poor bastard." He was laughing softly. "Like big old Ruben here. The cops, everybody, were trying to chase down what happened to Patty. I needed to throw them off on another trail. And who's more obvious than Win? Very, very successful, and such a Boy Scout. Ruben was supposed to get the patch on and the bute in the mare—into the muscle. I told him the bute had to go into muscle. All we needed to do was get that bute in the muscle so that when the Ground Jury found the patch and ordered the test, the bute would show up. The muscle—pretty simple, hunh? But big old Ruben has trouble keeping track of all his toys—gets rattled with too many things in his pockets. He's got the syringe, bute, patch, the girl's cell phone. He's running to the vet box—her cell phone falls out. Maybe he realizes this, maybe he doesn't. He keeps running—he's got to get to the vet box before Win does, right? So he manages to get the patch on, but that one simple thing about the needle was just one dot too many to connect up. Forget the muscle, just get the needle in—and to top this off, he tries to put the bottle of bute *back*. What this gets him is a pounding from Jason's little boyfriend groom."

Hugh seemed to find this funny, and there was something worrisome about his laughter. He turned on Ruben. "This is what I get for rescuing you? Is it? Oh yeah, your lousy security job, which you were about to lose because Vicente worried so much about your little run-ins with the police. His brother Jorge was a little more patient with bail money—I think he knew how to account for that expense. But Vicente had had enough of you. So I help you. Thought maybe you could make yourself useful. So I say to Vicente, 'Oh, please don't fire him. He has a family, you know, and they all need him. It wouldn't be right to fire him. Just get him out of the country before he gets in any more trouble'—and I call Win to make sure you can immigrate." Hugh let out another unsettling laugh at this last word.

"Ruben here knew how to get things done. Knew people here and there in the States who could help," he explained to us as if he were leading into a joke. "He could do things to a car, told me he knew that little trick with the cell phone and using the brake pads for ignition—surefire." He made a noise like a giggle at this pun. "He just didn't know how to speak English."

So he hadn't planned on Patty jumping clear of the horse van. He hadn't planned for her to survive. He had programmed her cell phone, which she had left behind on the seat in the truck's cab—and after it worked, nothing else went as planned. Why was Hugh giving us this information? Because he wasn't planning for me to live long enough to pass it along? I tried to comfort myself with the thought that none of his plans thus far had been carried out as intended. But the plane was too far from the terminal, too far for the people inside to help. And only one of the men in service crew poised warily near the building in back would be needed to fuel the plane.

A man in coveralls appeared in the headlights of the fuel truck. He opened the door on the driver's side of the fuel truck and did something on the dashboard. The pump started, and he stood holding the hose for quite a while. Then he reeled it in.

The plane lifted up into the dark again. We hadn't had an instant of opportunity to alter the standoff in the cabin, and we were on our way to someplace in Mexico. The full fuel tank was no comfort. Ruben yawned noisily, and I wondered how many hours he had stayed awake. The noise of the engine shifted tone as the plane escalated, and then it settled into a low background yowl and whirr. As we listened to Hugh's side of the traffic control exchanges, a strange peace settled into the cabin. Secure in the knowledge he would confront no obstacles on his way to Mexico, Hugh collected himself in a kind of arrogant contemplation. Iris was silent. I guessed she was trying to figure out what I was thinking and if I really was an ally.

Then suddenly Hugh straightened and snapped, "Roger!"

Ruben started awake, and the gun flopped over on his lap.

"Shit," Hugh expressed dread softly. "Heidi." What was that all about? I tried to think back to the way they seemed together, husband and wife. They seemed contented enough. But Charlie had told me Hugh couldn't have supported the horses and the little jet on his doctor's income. Heidi must have been the source of this money.

After a few seconds without conversation, he said, "Yes, Vicente," and sounded relieved. He reverted to politeness. "To Mexico? Why are you pretending you don't know?"

Whatever Vicente was saying took a little time.

"Europe means nothing," Hugh challenged. "What are you saying, 'a few weeks'?" His hands were starting to shake again. "Don't talk to me about making it easy. It's not going to be so goddamned easy for the two of you either." He must have been including Lourdes for whatever piece of the company she owned.

Suddenly the light, humorous Hugh reappeared. "Turn around and go back to Biloxi? Not such a bad idea, Vicente. Everybody else who goes there is gambling," and he laughed at his own joke. He kept laughing, and Iris shot him a wary glance. She had no idea who any of us were or why any of this was happening, but it was clear that Hugh had slipped beyond the edge of self-control.

"You listen to me, you renegade bastard," Hugh spat into his headset. "If I change course now, it won't be to take me back to Biloxi.

"Vicente? You know where I will go? I will go to sea," he sang out the World War II ditty viciously. "Just like the Navy. Go to sea. And what will I see? I will see the sea." In full mania now, Hugh was giving up and furious at having to.

He nudged the yoke to drop the plane's nose and called behind him. "Ruben!" Ruben half stood to do whatever he would be called upon to do. "You want to see the sea?"

The hand with the gun in it waggled about a foot away from my cheek. I may not have been able to ride, but I could still see my spot. My hands were free, and he was less than a yard from me. In a dreamlike rage, I stood, my ankles still bound together, and swept the gun out of his hand. With both hands guiding it, I jammed the muzzle against his ribs. Then fired.

Hugh left off his crooning to the headset. Ruben tilted away from the shot, which had torn through his side, then tried to right himself with his flailing arms. He was clutching, trying to get to me. But the corner of the tack trunk stopped him. As he came facedown against the back of Iris's seat, he pinned one arm under him. I brought the pistol down hard on his temple, and he stopped struggling. I had thought a skull would be hard, and I was surprised at how soft this felt and how muffled the impact was. I was stunned by my violence and by the sight of his blood smeared on every baby blue thing he had touched on the way down.

Hugh was looking around wildly, trying to get out of his seat belt. He twisted the yoke, and the plane angled up sharply. It bucked, and then, amazingly, leveled and kept flying.

Operating in a kind of shock and physical overdrive, I fired another shot across the cabin. I wasn't particularly aiming for Hugh, but the bullet came close enough to cause him to try to duck under the control panel. The bullet left a small tear in the blue cushioned wall near the windshield. My free hand pulled the release on the knot that held Iris's wrists together. "Your hands are free. Get your feet. Then get mine."

To keep Hugh pinned against the controls I fired another shot. This went through the wall of the plane about a foot behind the first bullet.

"This plane," Hugh began complaining into the headset, "this plane is being hijacked." As if his rights were being transgressed. I plucked the headset from his head and clocked him the same way I had coldcocked Ruben, slamming the gun into his temple. Hugh's hands lifted involuntarily, and he struggled to keep his head up. I slammed him with the gun again, and he slumped into genuine collapse. Ruben started to look around, and I gave him the same treatment.

Mysteriously, the plane was still flying, and there was noise coming from the headset in my hand, a voice working for attention. Apparently the cops had brought in a hostage negotiator. Other than the voices coming over the radio, the cabin was calm. Iris appraised the situation, saw that Ruben was unconscious, and said, "Better tie him," nodding toward Hugh. "Better tie them both." Then she donned the headset to speak the airplane's identifications numbers clearly.

"Tink and me are fine, got the two of them hog-tied. The one's bad off, but I don't think he's dead. I need to file a flight plan."

I listened as her flight plan was read back to her and then showed her the holes in the cabin wall. "We're still in the air."

"Yeah, most planes are pretty leaky." She looked over the controls and the windshield and said, "Good thing you didn't hit nothin' vital."

6

Although it wasn't such a long shot, maybe forty or sixty out of a hundred or maybe a little better, it was a really expensive gamble. But as soon as Charlie laid his credit card down on the service counter in the hangar next door, he let go of the expense. The total on the line above his signature was just a number, nothing more. The pilot, a man named Shanley, showed him out to the charter jet. He was younger but only somewhat trimmer than Charlie, and he had shaved his head as a practical solution to going bald.

"Why don't you sit there?" Shanley indicated the copilot's seat and clapped on a headset. There were four other places Charlie could have sat, plump gray leather armchairs on swivels that allowed the chairs to face in various social arrangements. At the far end of the plane's sleek parlor was a refrigerator, also gray to match the seats.

"Get you something to drink?"

"Not yet. Thanks." Fatigue, fear, anxiety, and the giddy expense were all he thought he could handle. But the speed and the agility of the takeoff gave him a sudden undeniable rush. He could do what needed to be done, and that was to get to Pensacola or wherever the cops might be able to intercept Hugh, to be there on the ground if Tink were freed.

"This could make you feel pretty powerful," he suggested cautiously.

"You should try flying it," Shanley said, and Charlie fell asleep. He left his thoughts with the steady breath of the jet engines.

Almost an hour later, he woke to a scattershot radio exchange. Shanley was calling into flight control at Pensacola. "Biloxi," he repeated the destination change. "I'll file with them right away."

"They've gone as far as Biloxi?"

"Past it. They got fuel there and took off again. But now it sounds like they've turned around and are heading back."

Charlie rode watchfully, not talking, for more than an hour until Shanley said "Big Lake," and banked the plane so that Charlie could have a look for himself. The sky was full of strong sunshine and threw the plane's shadow on the surface of the nearly landlocked bay. They were over Biloxi. Looping back toward the airport, the plane swept low over the oceanfront, densely studded with hotels and casinos.

"Gambler's paradise. You ever do that?"

"Not in one of those establishments," Charlie said righteously. "The house take is too big, and the statistics on those places are too well known."

The wheels of the plane sent up only the slightest bump when they met the runway. Charlie brought out his cell phone to try to contact Shaddaux and the group back at the Brandywine Airport.

"Tink's on the plane," Shaddaux said right away, "and she's all right. Sounds like she and another woman are in control."

"Patty McLaren?"

"No." After a pause, Shaddaux said, "The other woman is flying the plane."

"What about Vaughn?"

"We don't know, Charlie. There's been some shooting." Then he said, "Go to the freight terminal and check in with the troopers there. They'll take care of Vaughn and the Mexican man who is with him. We'll need you and Tink back up here—downtown—as soon as you can make it. FBI."

"Okay," he said uncertainly. He hadn't even laid eyes on Tink yet.

"F-B-I. B as in Bureau, Charlie."

Charlie smiled.

Taking directions from the tower, Shanley taxied to a tall cinder block building at the opposite end of the runway from the passenger terminal and stopped a little distance from a squad car and ambulance parked behind the building. Charlie picked up the canvas tote and walked with Shanley to a featureless gray door in the building. They arrived in a small office. Uniforms and hats nearly filled the room. There were four Mississippi State Troopers there. Heading for the officer straddling the corner of a heavy metal desk, he said, "Charlie Reidermann. Mr. Shanley is a charter pilot. Lieutenant Shaddaux told me to see you."

"We're all waiting for the same plane," the trooper said and swept his hand back to open the room to them.

A half hour later an airplane taxied around the back corner of the freight terminal and came to a standstill behind the ambulance and squad car, a wing's length away from the plane Charlie had chartered. It was a jet, smaller than the one that Shanley piloted, with a streak of baby blue blazing along the side of its trim fuselage. The trooper rose from the desk. "Only be a few minutes," and the other troopers followed him out.

He and Shanley stood by the window to watch as the troopers approached the plane in pairs. I am too old, he thought, to have my heart knocking while I wait for a woman to show up. The door of the plane opened from the inside, and two of the troopers squeezed into the cockpit. After a moment the ambulance backed in and waited. Disappointingly, the first person to drop down from the cockpit was a small woman in coveralls, who began checking around the plane. But then Tink was on the ground beside her. Other than that she was a little crooked somehow, not quite sound, as she and the other woman walked toward the freight terminal behind a trooper, she looked okay—and just like that he had her back. Headstrong, passionate Tink, and probably she was thinking about the horse. Probably she had no clue about his anguish. Then he heard her say to her companion, "I hope to hell Charlie is here."

He didn't see the blood until she was inside the door. On her right side the frills on her blouse, the little jacket, and the pocket of her slacks were splotched with dense doses of it. But apparently she wasn't concerned about the blood, because when she saw him she rushed to grab him around the neck and press her full, blood-spattered length against him. Shanley backed politely out of the room.

"The plane flew itself, Charlie!" She started to cry. But how could he show the relief he felt?

"Only for a couple of minutes while I got myself settled." The woman behind Tink paid no attention to her gasps. "Charlie? I'm Iris."

She was a gamine, her delicate femininity armored by the coveralls and a little boy's haircut. There was a light sprinkling of blood on her coveralls.

"She flew it," Tink said.

"And she put the holes in it," the woman named Iris told him.

As the women made their way out into the hall to find the restroom, their chatter drifted back to soothe him. He sighed, aware again of the weight of fatigue, and returned to the window.

A stretcher filled the door of the plane, and he recognized Hugh's salt-and-pepper curls. The full face was no longer jovial. It was quite still. But the eyes were open, and Hugh's arm flopped up from his side to rest across his belly. He was alive.

"Probably just needs one of his happy pills," Iris said, coming up beside Charlie. Tink's arms went around him quite tightly. She seemed to be holding herself up that way. He stroked her hands.

Another stretcher was transferred out. It carried a much larger person, someone he didn't think he knew. Yet something about the dark head signaled a memory. "Is that—?"

"Yup, Win's new guy."

But evidently he wasn't actually Win's guy.

"Gonna take more than a happy pill for him," Iris observed. "He looked pretty pukey."

"He lost so much blood," Tink fretted, "and all I had was that towel." The monogrammed tea towel was what the bungee cord around his chest was securing.

The last stretcher carried a body bag.

"Patty."

But somehow he knew that.

"Awful." After a moment she added, "And pointless. Pointless. Maybe someday I'll be able to remember how she looked when she was alive. But right now—I mean I can't seem to stop seeing that."

He didn't ask for details because he was afraid she would fall apart.

"I was looking for the bute, Charlie. Honest to God, that's all I was trying to find."

Charlie shook his head. He wouldn't mention his frustration with her single-mindedness. There was no changing her.

After the rear doors of the ambulance closed, it idled for what seemed like a long time. The EMTs were in there working on Ruben and Hugh. One of the troopers had stationed himself inside with them, and one took the passenger's seat up front. The other pair of troopers turned back toward the freight terminal.

"You're going to get a lot of questions," Iris promised them.

"What about *you*?" Charlie said pointedly.

"Don't have much to tell. I only came into this thing in the last chapter, and I've got to get out of it pretty quick." She glanced up at the plain, bold face of the clock on the wall. It was a few minutes past nine in the morning.

Tink followed Iris's glance and said, "Show jumping just started."

"An hour ago," Charlie corrected her. "We're on Central Time here." He knew she was thinking wishfully about getting back to the event. And in fact, Shanley's plane might get them back to Brandywine before Exit Laughing jumped. But the airport wouldn't be the end of it. They would have to give their answers to all the authorities now involved in Patty's murder.

"Time and distance," Tink said wistfully. Then she said something he thought he'd never hear. "But show jumping isn't the most important thing, is it?"

Iris was fretting about time. She accosted the two troopers as soon as they reentered the office. "I got nobody covering for me at the airport. How long we gonna be here?"

"We'll just need a statement—for the moment." The trooper motioned for Charlie and Tink to go out into the hall. Tink released him from her bear hug and turned to Iris.

"How in hell are you going to get back to Georgia?"

"Walk over to the private terminal and wait until I can hitch a ride in that direction. It's a nice day, and free fuel ain't that easy to pass up."

The phrase "nice day" struck Charlie as quite odd, but it was only the weather, he realized, that she was talking about. As soon as she emerged from the office fifteen minutes later, Iris did exactly as she had proposed. She walked out of the freight terminal, crossed the tarmac, and disappeared into a flock of small planes tethered outside another hangar building.

Tink watched Iris's progress. "Can see her spot almost as soon as I can," she said appreciatively and went obediently to the troopers waiting in the office. Her question-and-answer took almost a half hour, and when he rejoined her at the office window, she said, "There's some more of the same waiting back home. I'm going to be officially 'deposed,'" she said. "Isn't that what they do to kings?"

"And queens, and dictators," he agreed and handed her the tote. "But if you're going to have to attend an occasion of state, you might want to think about some different clothes. Put the ones you have on in the bag. The troopers may want them."

Taking off the blood-spattered clothes couldn't change what had happened, but it put a presentable face on everything that had gone on—and putting her feet, which had been jammed in her flats against the trunk wall, into the running shoes was a luxury of softness. When she rejoined Charlie at the office window, she pointed at her feet. "So, so *nice*."

"Did you wonder how I got here?" For the first time, he drew her attention to himself, and through the window he showed her the chartered plane and Shanley doing a preflight walkabout. She wondered at this. "Charlie. I must be too tired. *You* rented this plane? And this pilot?"

Suddenly now that she was standing beside him, he was embarrassed about this, about the extravagance of it. "Well, I do have a credit card," he defended himself.

But of course Tink didn't care. She had always been able to treat privilege and expensive surroundings as if they were mundane matters of course, her everyday due. She stepped up into the plush cabin and strapped herself into one of the leather armchairs.

"Don't forget this," she told him. "You should keep Exit Laughing, for Stephen and Alex. Have Win supervise. And get Paul to help you find someone to sell the young horses."

"What?"

"When I'm gone."

"I didn't know you were leaving."

No sooner had the plane lifted off than she uncoupled the seat belt, slipped down to the cabin floor, and stretched out in true luxury on the thick silver carpet.

Charlie slept more sensibly upright.

7

I woke when the plane—which I will always refer to as "our private jet"—dropped to the runway. Charlie was giving the cell phone its exercise—Shaddaux, Vicente, Frankie, and a lawyer, maybe. He seemed to be giving Vicente advice. This worried me, and I wondered in a bleary way about Lourdes, more anxiously about Stephen and Frankie. And Alex. You might think it strange, or even contradictory that I didn't worry about my gray horse. But he knew how to take care of himself. I knew he knew because I had helped him get to that place.

In spite of my good nap in a fully stretched-out position, my neck was killing me. My shoulders brought pain when I tried to bring them into alignment, and even now in a running shoe, the toes of my right foot sent something like electricity up my spine if my foot shifted slightly. My eyes felt hot and too large to stay in my face. And, I had a bad, bad headache.

"Charlie?"

He pushed the HOLD button on his little phone. The pilot, someone Charlie introduced me to but whose name I couldn't pull up right away, was engaged in carrying out final instructions from whoever in the little airport was speaking through the radio.

"Why are you giving all that advice to Vicente?"

"He's working with the authorities," he explained quickly because Vicente was waiting for him at the other end of the connection. Vicente, it seemed, had had a fit of conscience. When Charlie, standing on the sidelines of the show jumping field tried to tell him something but then stopped with a stricken look and charged down the hill, Vicente realized he was in some deep, deep doo-doo. He wasn't sure what it was, but he went to the secretary's office and asked to speak to the troopers. Now Charlie was running interference for him.

"Too little, too late," I said, full of resentment. "If they had worked with the authorities in the first place, a talented young woman would still be taking good care of good horses."

In contrast to the four troopers who were waiting for us in Biloxi, only one met us at Brandywine. The trooper was waiting inside the terminal, away from the wind, which had tuned up. When he ferried us to headquarters downtown, though, there was a swarm of these uniformed people, along with some suits, male and female, and a few sport coats. Our escort led us down a hallway and then another one. A kind of claustrophobia was coming over me. I was hemmed in by all this authority and the pressure to make sense of what had happened. I took Charlie's hand, looking to him for a little help in this. What I saw did not reassure me.

"Charlie, you look like you tied one on."

He smiled, which in itself was reassuring. "That's what Stephen told me. And look what's happened to you, my fashion idol."

"My face," I worried. "Do I look like I shot somebody?"

"Or something," he said in a low voice. I didn't take my eyes away from his. I couldn't understand how the woman who had fired the gun, the woman who brought it down on the heads of those two men, who was surprised at how soft the first head had felt, could have been me. It now seemed reasonable to me that a murderer could pass a lie detector test. It wasn't me who started this flow of blood, it was a stranger. I could almost erase my history.

Ruben had not regained consciousness by the time Iris set the plane down in Biloxi. I had managed to stop his wound with the tea towel that had followed me from the event grounds and secured it by a bungee cord from the pocket on the back of one of the seats. But he didn't look good. He had lost quite a bit of blood while I was organizing this fix, and his golden face had gone pallid, the skin waxy. Hugh had stirred once, moaning something about his head, and then sunk back into unconsciousness. These two pathetic men, bloodied and stunned, had produced our saddest freight, the horrifying contents of the first tack trunk. For months, revulsion, and anger at its senselessness, would come back to me in sudden rushes, followed by waves of relief that I hadn't actually killed either one of the men.

We followed the trooper around one last corner and then through a door to a waiting room. There was a large window that let in light from a fenced yard behind the building, but the window too was fenced off, covered with a grate. Vicente was sitting in the room, and Lourdes sat beside him. An officer in shirtsleeves presided from a desk across the room from them. Charlie and I took chairs near theirs and waited to tell our stories.

"Who's in there now?" I asked. The desk officer didn't respond.

For a moment, something like panic set in. I wanted these new acquaintances out of the room, away from us. I wanted to be alone with Charlie. They were eyeing me curiously.

"How many times am I going to have to tell this story, Charlie?"

"We hope not more than once," Vicente answered for Charlie. He looked at me levelly. "When my brother died, I was done with this," he told me. "The pretense was wrong. It was no help in the States, and now we are just crooks."

Lourdes said nothing.

"I was trying to get it stopped," Vicente continued. "At first it didn't seem so wrong sending the drug into the U.S. undercover. It was something we had to do to stay in business. But when Layton McLaren insisted—he said with the trials in Europe, we didn't need to do this anymore—it was very hard to stop, because, of course, we were afraid."

"Of Hugh," Charlie suggested.

"He is an important American doctor." Vicente shrugged. "Our word against his word—but we are ruined, anyway."

"Maybe, maybe not," Charlie advised. "Depends on how you handle damage control. It looks like an effective drug."

Charlie put Vicente in touch with a lawyer. It turned out Charlie knew quite a few lawyers. Because reception inside the building was poor, Vicente went outside into the wind to pace the yard in front of the window, his head angled with the cell phone toward his shoulder.

It was just past one thirty. Charlie went to the desk officer to ask if it would be possible to order in food. Not really, he was told, but we would only be there another forty-five minutes to an hour. The officer might be able to offer us some sodas.

"Wonderful," Charlie said and seemed to mean it. "Haven't eaten since whenever."

"Since lobster," I suggested when he returned to the chair beside mine.

"Key lime pie."

The desk officer brought sodas. Mine tasted wonderful. I told him so and then asked him, "Do you really think we could be out of here in an hour?"

Show jumping would go on for at least another two.

"Don't get your hopes up," Charlie advised me. But I did anyway.

Lourdes sat silently as Vicente came and went. She was enduring this experience the way she would have endured a funeral. The family had lost something and stood to lose a lot more.

Pretty blond Heidi Vaughn wasn't this stoic. As we waited, we began to hear something, the sound of something part human, part animal, in a room not far away. Soon it became clear that this was the voice of a woman, dropping to low, threatening tones, then rising shrilly to something like a shriek. I heard my name.

"Heidi Vaughn," I suggested. The desk officer smiled. The harangue went on until Heidi throttled up to a full scream. She knew lawyers, big-time lawyers who would make these dime-store cops pay for this harassment. She would just have Hugh make a telephone call, just one call. But of course the troopers wouldn't let her anywhere near the good doctor.

"Maybe they should handcuff her," I suggested to the bewilderment of everybody except Charlie. "Keep those soft little paws to herself."

Vicente was the first of us to be called. He followed an officer out of the waiting room, and a man with a stenographer's pad trailed after them. When he returned twenty minutes later, his face betrayed nothing, and he resumed his seat next to Lourdes. He spoke in Spanish to Lourdes and then said to Charlie, "I have told them everything, and I will make sure they see all of our records."

Lourdes asked something, and Vicente shrugged. "We will do what we need to do. I have lost the most important opportunity." It was pretty clear that last referred to something with Lourdes, but her impassivity revealed nothing about her thoughts of him.

He escorted Lourdes to the door of the interview room to explain that her English was limited but she would do her best.

When it was my turn, I expected I would find Shaddaux there with the two other officers. But he was absent. I didn't have time to wonder about this before I was asked to take a seat.

Before the officer facing me could ask me anything, I told him, "I was looking for the bute in the stables. I thought it had come from the supplies in Jason Tomlinson's tack stall—see, I thought Jason was involved, that he had framed Win. It turned out the bute did come from Jason's supplies, but it was Hugh and Ruben who were trying to set Win up, get him suspended and maybe investigated for doping."

I told him I was the one who shot Ruben. I said I hadn't been able to hold the gun straight on and that I thought I remembered the shot went shallow through his side. I told him I had used the gun as a bludgeon on Hugh. "What I don't remember is what I did with the gun after that."

"You left it under the copilot's seat," he said.

My account of the events of the past day went much more quickly than I had expected. "You get the last word," I told Charlie. "Shaddaux isn't in there. What's happened to him?"

"Nothing. They just don't want him present. They want to be able to see if all the stories match up."

"Make yours quick, Charlie. Okay?"

It was now a few minutes before two. We might have as much as an hour and a half to see Exit Laughing compete.

"Do my best," he said, and he did.

Fifty minutes later, the four of us, Charlie and me and the Delgados were hurrying up the rise to the show jumping arena, which was whipped by a stiff wind. Exit Laughing was walking out of the arena, head down and relaxed. He had just finished jumping, and the whistle blew for the next horse to enter. Alex was hugging my horse around the neck, so I figured he must not have made many mistakes. The sight of him with Stephen at his head took away my soreness, all my aches. Lourdes marched up to the horse and turned her face up to Alex. I didn't want to interfere, but Stephen saw me.

"Ma! Did you see it?" he called. I shook my head.

"No rails." He lifted his hands happily. At that moment, the horse just ahead of my gray horse in the standings, Barbara Beecher's gold horse, started over the fences, his bouncing canter showing off his black leg markings.

"Time?" Charlie asked when we were close enough to Stephen to be heard. He wanted to add the time penalties to his calculation.

"Nope. None." Stephen gave me a jubilant hug. "Where you been, Ma? I think Charlie was worried about you."

"Like *I* wasn't?" Frankie came up behind me angrily. "Where the hell *have* you been? You and Charlie? You both take off on me and leave me with this goddamned camera. And pretty soon that's all I've got. Lourdes and her brother-in-law—whatever he is—disappear on me, and I'm stuck up here on top of this hill in the wind from hell. I don't know what you are trying to do, where you are, or even *if* you are. Don't know if I'll ever see either of you again. That's a hell of a way, a shocking hell of a way, to treat a friend."

"You're right," Charlie tried to pacify her.

To seek forgiveness I said, "I was only looking for that bute. That's all it was and—"

"You thought you saw your spot," she mocked me furiously. "Of all the fucking—" She turned away from me to watch Barbara's horse finish the course without a single penalty. It meant Exit Laughing would finish behind the buckskin. "You deserve that," she said, and she put the videocam up to her face again.

The whistle blew, and The Flying Tiger presented himself, the first in the standings, the last in the order of go. Jason circled him into a canter, and the big chestnut was athletic perfection over the first seven fences, spring action with his front then his hind legs. When he began to turn the horse into the last line of fences, Jason looked to the bright airy panels and saw us standing beside them. He told me later this rattled him. He told me he was suspicious that morning, not when Heidi turned up alone, but when Charlie did. Someone had rummaged through his barn one night and when I failed to turn up the next morning, he abruptly connected the dots. In any case, in that instant of bewilderment, he let his horse down. The Flying Tiger took down the top rail of the next obstacle, a triple-fence combination, and this rattled the horse. He didn't like messing up, and this caused him to run straight into the last fence, a big wide jungle gym thing dense with rails. The rails came down easily, scattering harmlessly ahead of the horse. He was finished.

"Probably not even fifth," Charlie calculated sympathetically.

No one connected to the Delgado business showed any interest in The Flying Tiger or the wreckage he created. They were celebrating. Just beyond the in-gate Lourdes and Vicente swooped down on the horse and the girl and, eventually, on Stephen. But Charlie and I knew how things stood, and after I had walked back to the stables with my arm around Frankie, who fumed all the way, she knew too.

"The bastard!" She spent the rest of her wrath on Hugh. "The egomaniac bastard—or maybe," she considered her own improvement at his hands, "just an insecure egomaniac."

I agreed. "He wanted to be the keeper of the magic."

Besieged by family, Alex was still holding my horse, although Stephen stood by, ready to take over that task. I took the reins from her and said, "Thank you. I mean for the ride."

Stephen and I took care of the horse then, while Alex and her family crowded around for a turn at Frankie's video. I pulled the bridle off over the horse's ears and let him spit out the bit. I replaced the bridle with a halter, and Stephen held Exit Laughing while I applied a poultice to each of his wonderful legs. As usual, I noticed what a beautiful piece of work the bone, ligament, and muscle made. I took the gray horse out to the rise below the show jumping arena and let him graze. When I returned him to his stall, everyone in the gathering in the little yard—Frankie, Stephen, and Charlie, and the three Delgados—was still talking. I removed my horse's halter and stood calf-deep in straw beside him. When he lowered his head to take a mouthful of hay, I made my move. I didn't think of it as seeing my spot, I just moved. I did what I had done all through my childhood when I wanted to mount bareback. Exit Laughing's head stayed down while he worked at the hay. I flopped across his neck, half of me on each side of him, and when he reacted, lifting his head, he threw me backward to land belly-down across his back. From that position I clambered up. It wasn't pretty, but after a brief, clumsy struggle, I was upright, mounted. He put his head down again because he was tired. He only wanted to chew. I only wanted to ride. I didn't care that the few strides he took were the incremental steps between the pile of hay and his water bucket. I sank forward and embraced his neck.

Frankie roused me by squeezing my knee. "You asleep? Listen, sweetie, Lourdes needs to have a talk with you, privately."

In this case, privately included Frankie. She beckoned Lourdes into the stall, and I bent down to the little woman beside my horse.

"I am aware of what you and Charlie think of my family," she began stiffly.

"I think no such thing," I said to deny categorically that we thought the Delgados were criminals or sleazy or underhanded in any way. But she continued speaking, and Frankie tried to pretend she wasn't listening.

"And what Stephen thinks, in spite of Alejandra."

"No," I contradicted, "he does not."

"He told me Vicente is charged."

"He hasn't been yet, but Charlie thinks he will be."

"Jail?" Lourdes didn't sound as timid as her question, and she was looking me straight in the eye.

Jail would foul up a lot of her family's plans. Charlie had learned from Vicente that before he bought up his brother's—Lourdes's husband's—shares from her, her husband had bought up the little pharmaceutical compounding operation Vicente had owned. Only one of the compounds it produced had been developed there, the estrogen processing inhibitor, but the two brothers had seen this patent as their company's passport into the international markets.

"It's too early to say," I said carefully. "It will take months to figure that out."

Lourdes stopped speaking. When she resumed, it was with a careful, surprising confession.

"I am responsible too, Tink. I am a director of the company."

"Did you know?"

"I should have. I read the spreadsheets. I am very clever with spreadsheets—and so, I review them before they go to the auditors."

I wanted to dismiss this because I didn't know what she should have done. "You couldn't have figured out a scam like this from a spreadsheet."

But she wouldn't accept this excuse. "I should have ask questions. My husband was a good man. He was more playful than I am—he could really limbo. This was good for me because I am so serious, and what he was serious about was keeping us safe. I knew there were people he had to pay, but I never asked where this money shows on the spreadsheet. I knew there was a plan for 'introducing' the drug into the United States, and I saw the expenses for that. But I didn't ask the questions. I looked at the spreadsheet and the numbers for the States, and I thought, 'Fine, that is all I need to know. I am a woman, and it's enough that I can proofread the spreadsheets. Let the men worry about how to push into the market.' "

I tried to respond candidly to her. "You're probably right. You probably should have asked more questions. But you had no reason to be suspicious, and you were hardly participating in a crime."

"Do you think I need a lawyer?" Lourdes asked, and Frankie answered this pronto—"*Sí! Sí, sí, sí, sí, sí!*"

"A different lawyer than Vicente's," I put in. "No matter what your relation to him is."

Lourdes shook her head and smiled ruefully. We weren't going to get any details on the two of them.

My view of her role seemed to relieve her, but she said, "There is still your family and our family." This caused Frankie to send me an excited glance. "There are questions I need to ask."

Alex appeared in the stall door, but Lourdes shooed her away with a quick, hard, imperious glance.

"You don't need to worry about Charlie or me," I assured her. "We are friends, and you can count on us."

She squeezed my hand. "Other questions. Of other people."

Frankie was positively alight.

"Stephen?" I guessed.

"Yes, and Alejandra."

"You're braver than I am."

"They are sleeping together," she explained as if she hoped I could handle this information. "So I have to ask the questions. I have to ask the two of them. Here, at least, I am sure of my duty."

Frankie breathed, "Uhh-ohh."

But I nodded appreciatively. Three days earlier this prospect would have been a little scary. But now I knew Alex and even Stephen better. They could endure a few close questions, and they were mature enough to steer Lourdes around the shotgun wedding she seemed to have in mind. Furthermore, I was grateful for Stephen's sake she wasn't threatening to take Alex with her when she was allowed to return to Mexico.

When Frankie and Lourdes had left, Alex appeared again in the stall door. I was damned if I was going to get down from my horse, but she was not concerned about this. She thought the cops, all of us for that matter, had overlooked something important.

"Jason was right there all the time. The shipments were coming in and going out."

"So were we," I pointed out.

"The money was pouring in all over him. How could he not know?"

"Focus," I explained. "As long as there's enough money to keep a couple of top horses under him, he probably doesn't pay any more attention to cash flow than I do."

"Or I do," Alex confessed. Being a child of privilege and sheltered from any awareness of wealth had only put her and her similarly cosseted mother in jeopardy. "Stephen says my checkbook is scary. He closes his eyes when I open it up."

I was amazed to learn that Stephen would offer her even the

mildest criticism. Was this in preparation for setting up housekeeping? He could probably take care of himself with her after all. But I didn't say this. I said, quite generously, "You can change. You have lots of time to change," because I myself had no intention of doing that.

She and I loaded Exit Laughing for the trip home, and Frankie drove Charlie and me back to the hotel. We were all too tired to check out and go home, so we ordered in pizza and washed it down with Charlie's scotch. As soon as a suggestion of night tinged the sky, Charlie said, "I need to call it a day. I have—hate to bring this up—a meeting in the city tomorrow."

"Which city?" I asked boldly.

"New York."

"We'll drop you at the train," Frankie said by way of good night.

Charlie was going to a meeting—when I showered and slid into bed next to Charlie, I thought sleep would grab me before my head could reach the pillow. Not so. Suddenly I wasn't sleepy. Thought kept lighting up my brain—a meeting. A holding company, a venture capital firm. I remembered something about the bank where I ran into him shortly after we met. He had been upstairs at a meeting. Was he a trustee or something?

"All these meetings you go to, Charlie—boards and whatever. Do these people pay you for that?"

"Of course, Tink. They ask you to be on their board, they expect to pay you."

"Nobody ever asked me to be on a board for anything except the hunt and the land trust."

"Well, now you know." He turned out the light, kissed me, and said, "By the way, congratulations. On your horse."

In my excitement, I barely acknowledged this. I forgot I wasn't able to ride and began planning a trip to Europe for lessons, a jaunt to California to check out some young Thoroughbreds. A new manure spreader. Charlie rolled over so his back was to me. I patted his side gently.

"Charlie!" I whispered. "Are we rich?"

A long sigh issued from the other pillow.

Acknowledgments

This book would not have come into being without the abundant talents and patient contributions of my agent, Ethan Bassoff, and my editor, Anne Bennson, and I am happily indebted to both of them. Early on, my adventuresome neighbor Jeanne Sullivan and my intrepid companions Caroline Cox and Gerard Cox came forward with candid comments about Tink and Charlie, and I thank them for making their observations easy enough to choke down but strong enough to goad me into further work. For a different sort of help, I owe a great deal of thanks to my friends Robert Thomas, professional pilot, who set me straight on technical aspects of small aircraft and private flight, and Lisa K. Bloom, doctor of chiropractic neurology, who advised me on the details of what can happen to the body of a person who falls off a horse.